SOME FUN

Stories and a Novella

Antonya Nelson

SCRIBNER

NEW YORK   LONDON   TORONTO   SYDNEY

SCRIBNER
1230 Avenue of the Americas
New York, NY 10020

SCRIBNER and design are trademarks of
Macmillan Library Reference USA, Inc., used under license
by Simon & Schuster, the publisher of this work.

For information about special discounts for bulk purchases,
please contact Simon & Schuster Special Sales:
1-800-456-6798 or business@simonandschuster.com.

Designed by Kyoko Watanabe
Text set in Minion

Manufactured in the United States of America

1   3   5   7   9   10   8   6   4   2

Library of Congress Control Number: 2005054424

ISBN-13:   978-1-4391-9092-0

Publication credits:
"Dick," "Eminent Domain," and "Only a Thing": *The New Yorker;*
"Strike Anywhere": *failbetter* (online) and *The Story Behind the Story* (Norton, 2004);
"Flesh Tone": *Epoch;* "Heart Shaped Rock": *The Cincinnati Review;*
"Rear View": *Ploughshares.*

For my big brothers, James and Billy

"She would of been a good woman," The Misfit said, "if it had been somebody there to shoot her every minute of her life."

"Some fun!" Bobby Lee said.

"Shut up, Bobby Lee," The Misfit said. "It's no real pleasure in life."

Flannery O'Connor,
"A Good Man Is Hard to Find"

And you may see me tonight with an illegal smile,
it don't cost very much, but it lasts a long while.
Won't you please tell the man I didn't kill anyone,
no I'm just tryin to have me some fun. . . .

John Prine,
"Illegal Smile"

Contents

SOME
FUN

⇐ Dick

THE EVENING SUN was a giant peach in the rearview mirror, apocalyptic and gaseous as it burned toward the horizon behind Ann Ponders. The daily L.A. paradox: toxic beauty. She was grateful for a polluted day on which to move; it capped an argument she had been making for months. For clean air, she told herself, they were leaving the only home her children had ever known. Her husband and son had taken the first car early in the morning. But then the cat had escaped, moments before Ann was to drive the family's second car away, and she and her daughter had spent the day in the empty, hot house, waiting for the fickle creature to return.

"You know," said Ann to her eighteen-year-old, trying not to sound as furious and exasperated as she felt, "I can't get used to the new reliable you. The girl who left keys hanging in the door and burners burning. The girl who forgot her brother at Von's."

"You told me to cancel the utilities, I canceled the utilities." Lizzie's voice said she was innocent; over from her apartment in Westwood to

help, she had left no margin for error. All day they'd sat on the tiled floor
in the vacant dining room, or on the countertops in the kitchen, air-
conditioning disabled, refrigerator door hanging open, fan inoperable.
"And I told Cole he had to meet me at the checkout or, guess what? I'd
leave him." Lizzie removed a pack of cigarettes from her waistband, free,
in her father's absence, to be a person with bad habits. Ann had sworn
not to tell him, but she wouldn't have, anyway.

Ann hauled herself up from her slump on the floor, ready to make
another useless perimeter sweep. "Kitty kitty kitty?" one or the other
of them had been calling for hours, circling the yard, culvert, street.
Neither cared for the cat—it peed on pillows, sharpened its claws on
pants legs, licked itself neurotically—but the boy, the eleven-year-old
who'd ridden away with his father at dawn, needed Winky. Taking
Winky fifteen hundred miles east to their new home, their hideout in
the mountains, was non-negotiable.

"Hate that fucking cat," murmured Ann; the image saving the animal was of it curled in the armpit of her sleeping son. She hated a few
other things, such as the way she looked in shorts and a sleeveless shirt,
especially when compared with her daughter, who looked beautiful in
whatever she wore. What consolation did age provide? Ann wondered.
Bragging rights for having arrived at forty-five or sixty or ninety-nine?
You didn't come through intact, that much was clear. Moreover, the
interesting things happened early, a piece of information Ann was con-
sciously, uncharitably, withholding from her daughter. Packing away
their belongings, she'd found crayoned pictures addressed to her from
Lizzie, pledging exclamatory, boundless love, filled with hearts and
a round-headed tribe of people grinning their drunken smiley faces.
The toddler who'd given herself to those drawings was gone, her features turned angular, her smile caustic, her thoughts sour and secret.
Easy to love little children, harder to love grown-ups. Ann had been
shocked to discover that, at fourteen, her daughter had shaved her
pubic hair. When she was fifteen, Lizzie's notebook had been full of
stick figures having scary sex, not to mention the sickening song lyrics
pulsing from her bedroom stereo, or the *Fuck Me* and *Cunt* she'd mark-

ered onto her own shoes. Now, unbidden and often, Ann would be visited by one or the other of these images, a slide show starring her sunny child who had become an alarming adult.

The only help was to picture her boy, Cole, coming toward her with, say, a cookie in each hand, one for himself, one for her.

Lizzie's cell phone tweetered in her hip pocket. She studied its pink faceplate nonchalantly. "Grandma," she told Ann. When she raised her eyebrows and held out the ringing phone, Ann shook her head and stepped back, as if her mother could reach through the line for her. "I'm not here."

Lizzie had put on her listening expression as she engaged the line. "Neither is Grandma," she said. "It called accidentally. *Grandma*," she yelled into the phone. "*Pick up, Grandma.* It's the cafeteria," she told Ann. "I can hear silverware. Old people muttering." Even if Ann's mother had called on purpose, she wouldn't remember who or why. Alzheimer's had been stealing her for years now. Eleven months ago, when she learned about the airplanes deliberately aimed at the World Trade Center, it was as if their collapse took what was left of her with them. "You know, I once lived in New York," she'd repeated that day, those words and no others, a refrain to accompany the repeating footage on television, a refrain that was perhaps her last coherent response to the world.

"Or maybe it's bingo," Lizzie was saying, tuned to the tabletop or the linty interior of her grandmother's handbag. Shock had unglued her mother, Ann supposed, the perfectly understandable desire to stop knowing any more things. A defense mechanism of the mind, a pressure valve in the heart. She'd had to be moved from one part of her assisted-living facility to another, demoted to the wing where the rooms were more like cells and the assistants more like wardens. The pill brigade, the nightly tuck-in, the sniffing hygiene police—wardens or stagehands or ventriloquists whose patients were wooden dolls it was their charge to animate. And Ann's mother, who lived this sentence, this shapeless ongoing performance, occasionally making her random accidental calls, a fleet piece of will or inadvertency exerting itself. Ann could leave L.A. because her mother would never know she was gone.

Lizzie said, "Grandma is telling Mrs. Carlyle to stop scaring her. 'You're scaring me, Mrs. Carlyle, you're scaring me.'"

"Mrs. Carlyle is dead," Ann said. "Your grandmother always thinks someone is scaring her. It used to be me."

"How?"

"By being myself."

"Same way I scare you," Lizzie said cheerfully.

"I guess." The secret life, the naughty self. Packing, Ann had uncovered an old cache of drug paraphernalia—stale pot, brass pipe, razor, and rolled dollar bill—duct-taped inside her own bathroom towel cupboard. Her clever, duplicitous daughter, who knew that her parents would never think to look right under their own noses, this girl who also was prone to losing or forgetting things. "About your grandm—"

"Jesus! I'm going to visit. Whose speed dial did she just hit, anyway? You have reminded me eight million times. Why do you have to endlessly repeat things, like I'm an idiot?" Lizzie reached around to scratch her back with her cell phone antenna, the pretty knob of her shoulder thrust forward, her halter riding up over the hollow stretch of her belly, the whole smooth suit of skin she wore without thinking. She clapped the cell shut like a castanet. "Goodbye, Grandma. Can we go sit in McDonald's?"

"I don't want to miss Winky." But really, Ann didn't want to be in public showing so much of her own flesh. She'd imagined herself hidden in the car all day, the car that was old and stuffed full of heavy breakables, likely to overheat, a yowling cat in a box who would dictate drive-through food and quick pit stops, a series of factors that had led her to her skimpy and regrettable outfit. Wife-beater, her shirt was called; fringed cutoffs.

"Can *I* go sit in McDonald's?" She wasn't rude, Ann reminded herself; she was just asking a question. If her son had asked, she'd let him go. Why always this flare of anger with her daughter?

"Go ahead," she said, pretending Lizzie was her son. Her son, who would have returned bearing an order of fries or clown cookies for his mother. Lizzie walked away swinging her hips, the lovely thinness she had accomplished with starvation and speed, more evidence of that plaguing paradox. The McDonald's yellow sign could be seen from the Ponders' stoop, Toys R Us behind it, Mobil, Exxon, Wendy's, competing like waving hands in a class of eager but dumb children. In Ann's future home, in Colorado, there would be no plastic signs within sight. Never again from her front yard would she hear the muzzled sound of a genderless voice at a drive-through intoning, "Please pull forward."

Water still sputtered from the bathtub spigot, although only the cold, which was tepid and chlorine-scented and already vaguely rusty. Ann sat on the rim dousing her legs. When the knock came—the doorbell was electric, she reminded herself—she had an absurd apprehension that her mother, in record-shattering time, had somehow finagled a way over here from the center, some cabbie or unwitting do-gooder who'd found her in bedclothes on the street, waving her bingo card. How did she continue to remember Ann's address when she couldn't often remember Ann herself? And say she did remember—the truth of her situation dawning however briefly upon her—then Ann suffered her mother's fury as if a colossal conspiracy had been cooked up behind her back. So it had, Ann thought. Soon her mother forgot—an expression like bliss, like the uptake of a painkiller—and returned contentedly to playing the coy dingbat, the innocent coquette from cocktail parties of Ann's youth, her flirting, drunken mother. The knock sounded again. More likely it was Lizzie at the door, returning for cash. Ann vowed not to get mad at her forgetful girl, this girl who, staying at UCLA, would be charged with visiting her difficult, declining grandmother . . . On the stoop she found her son's friend Dick.

"Dick!"

"Ma'am." He wouldn't look at her face, but in a blinking circle around her, as if following the flying course of a gnat. His odd-shaped head showed the track lines of a recent buzz cut, a monthly ritual his father executed in the family's front yard. "I came to say goodbye to Cole," he said diffidently. Dick never showed much life around adults, as though the effort would be a wasted one, or maybe he was afraid, the native dread a smaller creature has of a larger one. Alone with Ann's son, however, he'd been silly and affectionate. She had eavesdropped on them, touched by how they loved to laugh, how politely deferential they were with each other, butts wedged into a single captain's chair in front of the computer, drawing cartoons with their heads tipped together, building forts that featured not weapons but foodstuff and flashlights. "*Watson*," they addressed each other in hissing British accents, partners in mystery and adventure.

"Oh, Dick, I'm so sorry, Cole is gone!" Ann flushed—guilty. She'd engineered this separation of best friends. Subtly but relentlessly, slowly undermining connections to L.A. this last muddled and frightening year, nudging her family off its foundation and onto the road, away.

"Gone?" Dick said, his face falling.

"I'm so so sorry, Dick."

"Gone?" he repeated. Had Cole forgotten to say goodbye? Dick lived down the street. The two boys had come home from the hospital only a week apart; as toddlers, they'd pedaled their Big Wheels back and forth on the sidewalk, then braved kindergarten together with matching backpacks and lunch boxes. For years they'd gone around with their arms slung over each other's neck. "We're not gay," they had informed Ann sincerely one day. "We're like brothers." When Dick called on the phone, he would always announce himself: *Hello, this is Dick.* That name like a punch line, a throwback from the 1940s: Dick and his sidekick Jane, their dog, Spot. It wasn't until the boys had been friends for a few years that Ann realized her own husband shared Dick's full proper name. Her husband, Richard, however, had never let anyone call him Dick. What had Dick's parents been thinking eleven years ago?

But *Cole* probably seemed like a strange name to Dick's parents. Their bedraggled ranch house was surrounded by chain link, inside of which roamed two Rottweilers—"the living moat," Dick's father boasted. These dogs would leap and froth when anyone approached the yard, eventually turning their ecstatic fury on each other, one chomping into the other's throat until there was a whimpering retreat.

In the house proper, Dick's family bred Rottweilers; a litter was nearly always on the way or occupying a kids' plastic play pool in the living room. The home smelled intensely, nauseatingly, of dog—Dick carried the potent, gamy odor with him, on his clothes and in his hair. You could smell it on the pillow after he'd spent the night. His father, who insisted that all children call him sir, believed in discipline and respect, rules and belts. On the rare occasion that it was he instead of one of Dick's brothers who came to retrieve Dick, he stood rocking on his heels at the Ponders' front stoop, refusing in his clipped manner— "No, ma'am"—the invitation to step inside, as if Ann had greeted him naked, holding a highball.

The boys would come tearing breathless from Cole's room, laughing and shouting, brought up short by the sight of Dick's father in profile just outside the door.

Then the sober palm would be clamped onto Dick's shoulder, the command to thank Ann for her hospitality, and the forced march home.

Today she stared at the boy, aware that she would probably never see him again. "Do you want to come in, Dick?" But what for? She had no treats to offer, no games to play, not even a chair to sit on.

"No," he said. "Thanks," he added, pawing at her stoop with his foot. "Can I go up in the treehouse?" he finally asked, rolling his gaze painfully to her face.

"Of course!"

Rather than come in the house, he squeezed along the side yard, beating through the unruly oleander. Ann followed from inside, watching at the kitchen window as he climbed the ladder. His hands were like Cole's, slender and dextrous.

The boys had been born during the Gulf War. That was the safe topic Ann could fall back on with Dick's mother. Their politics did not agree—they knew to keep their husbands separated and not to mention the bumper stickers regarding guns on their respective vehicles—but biology had made them good enough friends. Even as Ann gave birth, she had thought about some poor woman in Iraq having a baby. Bad enough to be in Los Angeles, ignored as the entire maternity ward gathered around the television to watch the eerie green light of deployed Scud missiles. What if you were over there, hearing—*feeling*—them detonate?

Moreover, she and Dick's mother liked the other's little boy. Dick's mother had four sons, Dick her youngest. The oldest had joined the army recently; Dick was supremely proud of the fact. His other two brothers, the twins, fell between, bullies, brats. But Dick was neither a bully nor a brat; like Ann's own son, he was rangy, unathletic. They were children who deferred by instinct, not peacemakers but peacekeepers, knobby-kneed guys who had to be prompted to eat and encouraged to defend themselves against the other boys. Ann liked to think that Dick might find her home a respite, her family a good influence. And now he'd missed his chance to say goodbye.

She could have apologized for hours. Dick sat dejected in the treehouse, not even swinging his legs. Finally he climbed down, squeezed through the oleander, and was heading down the flagstones to the curb when Ann opened the front door. "Goodbye, Dick," she called.

He turned without stopping, his shoulders utterly slumped, scuffing his feet in baggy pants far too big for him. This gang-inspired fashion statement was another on the List of Reasons to Leave L.A. "Your cat is dead," he called back. The words, delivered in his typically uninflected way, took a moment to register. It was as if he were reporting that Ann had mail.

"Dick," she cajoled. He understood that she questioned the truth of what he'd said. He had a history of outrageous lies—this habit he shared with Cole of make-believe and stories.

"Really," he said flatly. "Look in your swimming pool."

The air was blaringly, blindingly clear in Colorado; if you didn't want to weep, you had to wear sunglasses to step into it. Behind the Ponders' new house, the foothills began, meadowlarks calling out their exhaustive song, that insistent, badgering goodwill. Everywhere you wanted to go, you could walk or ride a bike. The dogs were variously sized but all golden, with tails like happy flags. This was the other, better West, its flagrant seasons—first the red and orange and yellow leaves, which fell, it seemed, all in a single mad afternoon, a flurry of confetti, and then the snow, days and days, layer upon layer, the little city become a smooth, hibernating drift punctuated by chimneys and their nostalgic puffs of smoke. The lack of man-made racket was sometimes eerie, as if the landscape were waiting for something to happen. Even on the worst days in L.A., Ann had been able to sit on her front stoop and wrest a certain nostalgia from the atmosphere: the hum of an innocuous engine, either lawnmower or small plane, minor benign clouds filled with neither rain nor pollution, the shouting voices of children whose play could be fancied wholly innocent. The feverish unease of the city stalled for the moment.

"Did we do the right thing?" Richard would ask, putting his hands tentatively on Ann's shoulders.

She would resist the impulse to shake them off, restrain the flash of impatience: wasn't it obvious, this beauty just outside their door? A tangible beauty, like hard candy, something you could snatch at, bite. She wanted to ignore his real question, which was about the intangible, the baffling way his wife, without his permission or precise knowledge, had changed in recent years. He must have sensed that Ann's love for him had left; he was a man hoping to wait it out, or to lure it home, or, best of all, to wake one morning with the discovery that it had been merely a bad dream. "Of course we did the right thing," she would answer, if she answered.

At Thanksgiving, Ann went by herself to the airport to meet the Los Angeles flight. She'd forgotten that you couldn't greet at the gates anymore, that you had to lurk in the baggage claim area. She had pictured herself standing with open arms as her mother emerged panicked from the Jetway tunnel. Before Alzheimer's, her mother had had a wide-eyed, receptive relationship with the world, an anticipatory smile like that of a child excited for the jack-in-the-box to spring out.

Lizzie arrived by herself.

"Where's Grandma?" Ann asked, eyes casting over her daughter's shoulder in the sudden crowd. She was looking amid the Thanksgiving throng of visiting mothers for that small lost one who was hers. Lizzie, hair bent at strange angles around her face, wore a peeved, defensive expression; she knew she was going to be blamed for something that wasn't her fault. The plan, the careful set of directives Ann had supplied to a dozen different people in L.A., was supposed to result in her mother arriving in Colorado for Thanksgiving.

"She bailed."

"What?"

"I know, I know." Lizzie gave her attention to the baggage conveyer belt, now honking, now blinking, now disgorging suitcases. "We're at LAX, our bags are checked, we have a vodka for her nerves, then another for mine, then we're in line at security—all this time she keeps calling me her abductor, but not like a paranoid whack job, like a joke, you know how she gets after vodka—then one look at the guy putting his hand in people's shoes, and voilà, she freaks." Lizzie had herded Ann to the belt as she talked, all the time watching for her suitcase. She pushed past Ann now to retrieve a large boxy floral bag Ann recalled from her own childhood. Her mother's suitcase, indisputable—big enough to contain its owner. Tapestry, worn to threads at the corners, a part of a set that had gone with her parents many times abroad, on ships and trains, in Turkish cabs, South American buses, in a former gadabout life. Broken yellowed tag strings hung from this one's handle, testament to its worldliness, also its antiquity.

"Why is your grandmother's suitcase here?"

"It was already checked. In my name. You carry it, it weighs hardly anything. God knows what she packed. She had Equal packets stuffed in all her pockets."

"Where is she now?"

"At the center. I got her a cab. Before my plane even took off, she was back safe in her room. I called to make sure. Why do you always assume I'm a complete idiot?"

"I just don't understand—"

"Security is such a fucking hassle nowadays, and she was really pissing me off."

"Please don't talk about your grandmother that way."

"I notice you're not there to deal with her."

"I can't believe you left her—"

"Hey, Mom, you know what? No matter what I did, you would be mad right now. Think about it: If I come, you're mad 'cause I left her. If I don't come, you're mad because, hey, it's Thanksgiving, where's the family?" Lizzie waited for argument, her eyes wide and belligerent. And the words *left her* recalled for Ann that it was she, not her daughter, who had more fully done this to her mother. She let the subject drop. Lizzie turned to heave her own bag off the belt and began dragging it ahead of Ann, as if she knew where the car was parked. The tapestry piece—her mother had referred to it as her "grip"—felt as if there were nothing in it. Not quite nothing; one thing, maybe.

"Dude!" Lizzie greeted her brother an hour and a half later in Fort Collins. Unprompted, he threw his arms around her for a long hug. "What's with the outfit?" she said.

"It's a uniform?" he said, looking doubtfully at his shirt.

"I let you out of my sight for three months, you go geek." He submitted happily as she untucked his shirttails and frowsed his hair. They had their own intimacy, Ann saw with a tender pang, one completely removed from her or their father. Richard was trying to catch her eye, to let her know that he saw it, too, but she wouldn't look at him. She was training herself to scorn his collusion. But why?

The children shared amused glances over the Thanksgiving table, cracking obscure jokes that seemed to be at their parents' expense. Ann envisioned them as grown-up siblings. This, maybe, was the consolation she had been looking for, the knowledge that her children would remain loyal and fond, phone each other from their dorm rooms and apartments and houses, keep track and reminisce. Someday, she thought, they would be comparing notes about their parents, lodging their complaints, agreeing mostly but perhaps not entirely. Their father, Cole would speculate, had always had a soft spot for the daughter, and Lizzie would laugh—she and Cole would be drinking beer in a bar, or whispering in the kitchen of one of their homes while their children and spouses slept—reminding him that their mother had obviously preferred him.

This would be after Ann and Richard were old or maybe even dead, Ann thought. Neither age nor death seemed quite as formidable, put in this light. She flushed when she remembered the secret she had kept for years now, her escape clause and safeguard: she had given herself permission to divorce her husband when Cole graduated from high school. If she felt like divorcing him then, she would do it. But if she left their father, her children would be having a different conversation in that kitchen or bar she'd dreamed up. There'd be no disagreement about whose fault a divorce was.

"Doesn't Lizzie look awfully thin?" Richard asked in a whisper, in bed. "Did *you* smell cigarettes on her?"

His worries seemed so pale to Ann, so little, and so late in coming. Their daughter was no longer theirs; the world had had its way with her. Ann's anxiety had to do with Cole. What was Lizzie saying to him when their parents weren't around? It wasn't cigarette smoke that wafted worrisomely here, but that whiff of L.A., that musk of volatile adolescence, that had been let into the house.

"Can I call Dick?" Cole asked Ann on the Sunday evening after Thanksgiving. They were the only ones at home; Richard was driving Lizzie back to the airport. While Ann graded papers—*Change is a thing most everyone experiences,* they invariably began—Cole stared out the kitchen window into the dusk, looking lost. The looming fact of Monday morning inspired it. His sister's departure no doubt contributed; all weekend she'd played her loud music and monopolized the second bathroom and shown him interesting Internet sites, then abruptly she had packed up her cosmetics and clothes and noise and disappeared, leaving the house vibrantly still, the only sound the wet chugging of the dishwasher.

"Why Dick?" Ann asked.

"Never mind."

"No, it's okay. Call Dick." Back in L.A., even though they'd lived within shouting distance, they'd had lengthy aimless phone conversations, Cole pacing around the house, laughing and gesturing. Ann imagined him pacing through this new house, filling Dick in on all that was strange: home, school, weather. She had assured Cole before they moved that his real friends were ones he would keep all his life, no matter where he lived, friends who were more like family. "Years from now," she told him, "you'll be calling Dick in the middle of the night just to chat. It doesn't matter where you live."

She had told him this, although she believed he would outgrow Dick. Dick would adopt the politics and values of his family, would follow in his oldest brother's footsteps first and enlist in the military, then later move into the blue-collar world of his father, who installed heaters and coolers in addition to breeding dogs. Meanwhile, Cole would go to college and graduate school; he cared too much about injustice for politics not to matter, so Dick's conservative mind-set would bother him. They would have grown apart in time, anyway. Moving had allowed the break to seem like nobody's fault, sad yet unavoidable.

Not unavoidable, Ann scolded herself. She had insisted, she had cried, she'd shamelessly exploited the national disaster of two Septembers ago to aid her cause, to substantiate her fear, her conviction, that they needed to retreat to higher ground, and her husband had finally acquiesced. "The important things," Ann had assured Cole in L.A., "are coming with us."

"Not Lizzie," he'd responded. "Not Grandma."

Like Cole, she still thought of L.A. as home. They all referred to it that way, even though their house was sold and their belongings were here. They held the configuration of that place in their minds, as if they could return to it, sleep in its beds, or boil water at the stove overlooking the window to the backyard. As if the cat would jump into that window, the way she often had, and press her dusty nose against the glass, leaving another in a long pattern of smudges.

Ann passed her son the phone and noted how his fingers flew over the keypad, Dick's number still a reflex of his hand.

"This is Cole," he said, "is Dick there?" He paused, his eyebrows pinched. "Dick? It is? I don't know, it didn't sound like you. I guess." He paused again. "Okay. Bye."

"That was the shortest call to Dick I ever heard. What happened?"

"I don't know." Cole set the phone back in its cradle. "I don't think that was Dick."

"Maybe one of the twins was pretending to be Dick?"

"Probably." Cole gave his mother a trembling look. "If it was Dick, he sounded weird."

"Weird how?"

"Depressed. Really depressed. It didn't sound like him at all."

"His voice could be changing."

"Yeah," he said, unconvinced. Her daughter would have marveled about such a phone call for a long time, turning it over with her mother, then phoning up other friends to analyze it ad nauseam, but Cole just wandered away, troubled and scowling. He had a stoic's reserve, the sort that bred ulcers, migraines. Later, Ann would mention the call again, maybe when she was tucking him into bed, on her knees with her cheek next to his on the pillow. She would tell him to try calling Dick again in a week or so, that either he was having a bad day or one of his brothers was playing a joke. Either way, Cole could make another call.

She hadn't told him that Winky had died. Returning from McDonald's, Lizzie had found Ann depositing the cat's bloated body in the Dumpster out front.

"Oh God! Well, you said you hated that f-ing cat," her daughter said, sucking the last of her soda noisily up through a straw.

Ann whirled on her. "You think that meant I wanted it dead?"

"I'm just commenting."

"I don't like your comment." Ann wanted to slap warmth into her daughter's face, make her have some feeling for the animal. The cat had been spinning in one place in the pool, held there by the action of the filter. There was something scarily beautiful about the sight, the fluttering smoothness of the fur, the animal's perfect weightless suspension and revolution, the impression that it could continue, unchanged, indefinitely. Remarkable that neither Ann nor Lizzie had noticed it before. Dick's treetop view had been better than their ground-level one.

When they finally said their goodbyes, they had agreed that it would be best to spare Cole the death of his pet. They'd say that the cat simply had not wanted to move, that she had chosen to stay in the neighborhood, that Lizzie would drive over and fill a food bowl every few days and keep them posted in Colorado. If Dick ever mentioned the dead cat, Ann would deny it, reminding Cole what a liar Dick was known to be.

"Hi, Ann, it's Nancy," the woman on the phone said. Her voice was weary, familiar, and Ann exclaimed, generically sociable, making small talk as she tried to figure out which Nancy it was. She knew three or four. Why would this Nancy assume she was the only one? The longer they exchanged pleasantries—was Ann settled after the move? Did she miss L.A.? And the kids?—the stranger the conversation seemed. At what point would Ann confess that she had no idea who she was talking to? Finally Nancy said, sighing, "I'm really calling to find out if Dick has tried to reach you." The voice instantly assumed a body and a location—overweight, redheaded Nancy, Ann's former neighbor with her brood of boys and dogs.

"Dick?"

"He's run away."

"Oh my Lord, Nancy. When?"

"Three days ago. I thought maybe Cole would know something."

Ann took the phone with her to the window in the kitchen; she needed to find her boy. The yard at first seemed empty, nothing but snow and the things it covered, a slight wind lifting faint, glittering waves of it. And then there he was, the sight of him allowing Ann to breathe once more: pulling a sled, hauling logs from one end of the yard to the other, big rubber snow boots weighing him to the ground. Until this year, he'd never seen snow. He was speaking to himself, she saw, telling a story, lost inside it. This was the kind of thing he and Dick had done together. Their alternate universe, ready-made and waiting. Ann's eyes filled with tears; she could not bring up words. "Nancy," she said. "I'm so sorry." Sorry, and shamefully grateful, with her boy penned there in the yard.

"He's called us a couple of times, so we know he's alive. We're praying that he's just blowing off steam." Nancy sighed. "It's been such a hard year for him, you know?" she went on thoughtfully. "He started sixth grade at the middle school, and everything was different. You wouldn't have recognized him, Ann. I mean, you know he's always been kind of shy, but he just turned plain sullen. He put on some weight, got pimples, the usual stuff, and he wouldn't joke around anymore . . ."

"Poor guy," Ann said softly.

"And his critters started dying. The rats, the iguana, the lovebirds. I thought it was coincidence, but now I'm not so sure. I even found him pulling the legs off the lizards in the yard, like he thought they might grow back the way the tails do. But he knew better . . ." Nancy continued talking, citing this evidence with surprise and exhaustion in her voice, argument, even—as if she were making a case built on contradictions. It began with his separating himself from others, missing school in order to hang out at the Circle K, not speaking at home, painting his windows black—black! not a shred of light allowed in— refusing to care for or about his pets, hiding from his family in the overgrown culvert behind their house, that harsh place full of thistle and weed and trash, nothing like the snow-covered hills Ann now overlooked. Apparently the news of Dick's decline was something Nancy had reported so many times that she had stepped beyond its initial impact. It was a story, one she would probably be telling herself for the rest of her life, refashioning it as its end came. He had disappeared. He had been disappearing all year. She should have known, she would say, he was so quiet after he went to middle school. He'd started an awkward and unattractive puberty. He had a hard time making new friends. He didn't have any friends.

He didn't have any friends. "I don't know how I'll tell Cole," Ann murmured, thinking aloud, watching her son arrange the wood at the other end of the yard in the shape of a cabin. He was unaware of being watched, pushing his hat off his eyes with his cold red hand, talking as if to another boy. He would abandon this habit, become self-conscious, probably within the next few months. It took a great deal of restraint not to throw down the phone and run out and hold him against her—as if Dick might find him first and claim him.

"I'm so glad Cole didn't answer the phone," said Nancy. "I would have had to hang up on him, I just couldn't have talked to that sweet child." She paused. "But maybe you could make sure he hasn't heard from Dick?"

When the boys were little, Cole had returned home one day from Dick's to tell Ann, "Dick's mom says we didn't come from apes." Before Ann could decry, Cole went on, "Dick's mom says we come from angels."

"I'm so scared," Nancy said now, her voice wobbling. While Cole stomped through the snow, Nancy berated herself, saying she should have known how upset Dick was, that last day, by the way he'd walked through the puddles on the way to school, "letting all of that L.A. street . . . *shit* . . . get on him." Ann was shocked. Not by the puddles—boys, puddles, what could be more predictable?—but by Nancy's resorting to profanity. "He's hiding somewhere, I know, and he's afraid to come back." His father's wrath, Ann thought, his mother's fear—the glory of his having inspired it, the awesomeness of its combined force. Nancy said, "I mean, he became obsessed with negative things, black windows and all those dead pets, when did he get so fascinated with . . . *badness*?"

And this made Ann recall Winky the cat, her black body twirling in a current in a corner of the pool. The net extraordinarily heavy with its saturated load. "Your cat is dead."

Richard, listening later about Dick, was stunned. He had a hard time assimilating information that he didn't want to believe. It was as if his loyal heart had thrown up a shield around him, making the penetration of a dark impulse extra difficult; he had a kind of belief in angels, too, Ann thought. She had not done what she'd told Nancy she would, ask Cole if he'd heard from his friend. She waited until her son was asleep, until she and Richard were in bed. Then, when he had begun stroking her breasts, preamble to sex, she had stopped him with the news. His hand froze, moved back to his own chest, Richard immobilized, speechless. "Those poor people," he finally said. "Those poor, poor people." He disagreed with her plan to withhold the news from Cole: he might know something crucial. What if the situation were reversed, wouldn't Ann want Nancy to ask Dick? "But Cole would never run away," Ann insisted. "And I can tell by looking at him that he hasn't heard from Dick. He'd tell me." They lay in bed, talking quietly. Aside from issues relating to the children, they didn't spend much time, anymore, talking. "You know what else, Rich? I think maybe our moving played some part in Dick's changing. I mean, the cat was the first dead-animal incident. It was Dick who told me."

"What cat?"

Ann closed her mouth, realizing for the first time that the kind lie she'd told Cole last summer had not been corrected for her husband. Even Lizzie had heard a truer version of events than Rich. "Winky," she said. "On moving day." Now she filled him in, complicating background that made him angry with her, surprisingly angry. He rose up on an elbow and looked down on her. Why would she treat him like a child? he asked. Why would she not tell him this? "I don't know," she said, miserable. He wasn't part of her inner life; it was as if she'd already started leaving him, packing herself up in preparation, one secret at a time.

Rich lay awake thinking beside her. Then he suddenly rolled from bed, and Ann heard him go into Cole's room down the hall. When she got there, he was gently but insistently rousing their boy. "Son?" he said.

"Don't!" Ann said. "He needs his sleep."

But Richard would not be dissuaded. When Cole finally woke, he told them he hadn't spoken with Dick since that last weird phone call.

"Weird phone call?" Richard demanded, as if Ann had withheld that from him, too.

Her son sat sleepily awestruck, a frown gathering on his forehead. "Where's Dick?" he asked.

It became a nightly query. Where was Dick? Now, as bedtime approached, Ann felt the terror growing. In the dark, her son imagined the worst had happened to his friend. He imagined his worst, Dick's mother imagined her worst, everyone suffering a private fictional nightmare. At night Ann crawled in beside Cole in the bottom bunk, lying there until he fell asleep, assuring him that Dick was merely hiding at a friend's house, that he would be located and brought home.

"But whose house would he hide in?" Cole pointed out. "What friend?"

Christmas came tainted; when asked what he wanted, Cole requested going home and meant L.A. He wanted nothing else. Lizzie flew in from California once more without her grandmother. This time the woman had turned tail when she saw the cab at the curb of the nursing home.

"If you want to see her," Lizzie told her mother nonchalantly as she reached to switch on the car radio, "you're going to have to get your ass back to L.A."

Why wouldn't that place leave her alone? Christmas Eve, Ann dreamed it was Dick she found dead in the swimming pool, swirling there like a difficult pet. When she woke and the dream had evaporated into the cool air of her bedroom, the deep breathing of her husband beside her, she had an unkind, inexorable thought: she would be forced to take her son back there if Dick were dead; they would have no choice but to return for a funeral.

"What's wrong?" Richard asked, half asleep, his kind, blind hand out of habit groping to reassure her.

"Nothing," she said, sliding away from his touch.

*   *   *

Cole's twelfth birthday fell on a bitter January Saturday. Under duress, he'd invited three boys, somewhat randomly; they were in his same grade, they lived nearby. The doorbell rang at noon, although the party wasn't scheduled until four—the cake was still baking, the decorations unhung . . . Ann opened the door to find Dick's parents on her doorstep.

They were so out of place that she couldn't at first find their names. Their winter coats—the father's a hunter's camouflage jacket—further confused. And then why was Nancy holding a puppy?

"We couldn't just sit there doing nothing," Nancy explained as Ann invited them inside. The dog wore a bow. Her husband came in reluctantly, having never entered Ann's home before. But both the weather and the situation were too raw for him to stand outside. They looked haunted, as if drained of a shared vital fluid. It occurred to Ann that they couldn't be completely sane at this moment. "We're looking for Dick," Nancy said. "We thought he might have come to Colorado. Gary saw it in a dream, the KOA campground in Fort Collins."

Gary blushed deeply inside the hood of his leafy-patterned jacket. He was not a man accustomed to sharing his dreams, to having them made public. Nancy touched his sleeve with her free hand. This was how they stayed together, Ann saw, by giving permission, comfort; by being so much the other's missing half.

"Sit down," Ann said, indicating the couch before the hearth, where she'd just lit a fire. "Richard and Cole are out buying hot dogs. It's Cole's birthday." The baking chocolate cake was in the air, balloons drifting under the dining room table.

"And we brought him a present," Nancy said. "They're such lovers, these puppies. There's nothing like a Rottie, you'll see." She held up the animal by its armpits toward Ann, its little lump of a penis damp on its tight pink stomach. Ann took the dog awkwardly. He smelled like his family's home in L.A., like Dick.

"What about the other boys?" Ann asked, breathing through her mouth, blinking away tears. The puppy nuzzled into the crook of her arm, a baby creature in search of heat.

"We didn't clip his tail," Nancy said of the dog. "We thought you wouldn't want him clipped."

"The other boys are with Gary Junior," said Dick's father. "He was fixing to be called up for active duty, but we made this a priority. We're taking a proactive, uh . . ." he said, waving his hand as memory failed him.

"Stance," supplied Nancy.

"Stance." He wouldn't meet Ann's eyes. Just like his boy Dick that way. She guessed that he resented his youngest son's preventing his eldest from serving his country in this, its time of need. Twelve years ago, she and Nancy had given birth during another war, the same war.

In the room's lull, Ann thought to offer beverages, soda, tea, water, but what Dick's father requested was wine. And she liked him briefly. A little sympathetic tendril went out—she would have wine, too— then recoiled as she set the puppy on the kitchen floor. Seeing him precarious on the linoleum, legs braced and quivering, she had a chilly intuition slip upon her: this visit was not only to deliver a dog. They hadn't believed her when she said her family hadn't heard from Dick. They had come to see for themselves. She had to restrain herself from storming back into the living room, leading them on a glorious search of the premises, flinging open closets and thrusting their faces into the empty space beneath the beds. As if she would keep that kind of secret.

"Listen," Gary said after tossing back his wine like a dose of something medicinal, "we want to question your boy."

Nancy reached a hand in either direction, spreading herself between Ann and her husband as if to ward off blows. "Just talk to him," she said. "Honey, we don't want to scare him, I would never scare that sweet, sweet boy."

"It's his birthday," Ann said helplessly, hearing the familiar *punk, punk* of the car doors slam outside. Cole burst through the foyer, having recognized his friend's vehicle in their driveway, the California plates. Every adult in the room watched his face fill with the knowledge that Dick had not made a miraculous journey to join him on his birthday. They'd always celebrated their birthdays together.

"The KOA is closed," Nancy had been saying. Ann now watched her take in Cole—his new height, the very faint hint of soft mustache on his upper lip—Nancy's emotions so close to the surface, the sincere and fraught affection she had for the boy. Nancy would never not know him, Ann realized. None of them would ever not know the rest. The dog, still sleeping in her arms—if they accepted this gift—would live with her for years to come.

Cole went directly to Nancy to be held, laying his head on her chest and squeezing shut his eyes.

Richard did not want the puppy. Good deeds would heal Dick's family's hurt, Ann insisted, but she wondered if her openness had more to do with opposing Richard than the inherent wisdom of adopting the dog. She won, whatever the reason. She almost always won when she and Richard disagreed. He loved her too much.

"What will you name it?" they asked Cole of his new pet.

"Dick," he said without hesitating.

Dick the dog cried in the dark night. It was as if he were being tortured, as if solitude alone were killing him. Only human contact comforted him. Richard, who was the lightest sleeper, performed this role. Ann found him one predawn morning, sitting in the kitchen in the dim light of the open oven door, cradling the puppy like a baby, stroking it mindlessly. Her husband looked languorous and fatigued in that parental fugue state of too little sleep, too much tenderness. Not every man would do this, Ann told herself. The dog slept as if dead against Rich's chest, fat paws limp and folded at his chin. It was a scene to make her heart relent. Perhaps they should have had another child, a youngster to keep them young themselves, to distract them from the leakage of playfulness from the house, to preserve innocence. To surround them with it like a prevailing vapor.

When he glanced up and saw her watching him, Rich's face clouded, as if he were ashamed of, or perhaps only irritated by, having been caught. She had done this, turned him uneasy with his love.

Cole continued to ask after Dick. He'd promised Dick's parents he would tell them anything he could think of about his friend. One night Ann listened from the dark hallway as Rich comforted their boy. "Sometimes people grow so unhappy," Rich said, "that they think running away is the only solution." He went on to describe the hills and valleys of a lifetime, the fact that some people couldn't recognize a hard time as a temporary circumstance. He was positing a landscape, wide and full, elevations and declivities, a map meant to reassure himself, Ann thought, charting something that would allay his own fears about his wife, his daughter, his life. Cole said nothing, though Ann could perceive his listening, her husband's care in choosing his words and Cole's receiving them. Even as she was grateful to Rich for his gentle intelligence and his faith in its healing properties, she found herself arguing against it. Surely there was some instance in which running away was the answer?

In the hallway, Richard passed without meeting her eyes, not exactly cold, but wary.

His steps faded downstairs. The light in Cole's room was off, and Ann listened for crying. The silence of their new home often impressed her—no close neighbors, no talking signs, no freeway roar, no alarms. Simply the sound of snow falling through space onto tree branches. A vacuum of hush. She waited to hear Cole call for her, and when he didn't, she put her face to the crack in his open door. "Do you want me to lie down with you?" she asked into the dark.

"That's okay," he said, declining. She entered the room anyway and knelt by the bed, like a child saying prayers.

"What are you thinking?" she whispered. His hair smelled sour; he still needed reminding to bathe.

After a long silence, he turned to face her. "About Dick."

"What about Dick?"

"Me and him were going to live on a ranch," Cole said. Growing accustomed to the dark, Ann could now see his hands folded under his cheek, the shine of his eyes. "We were going to have three dogs each, and horses." He blinked thoughtfully, as if visiting that place. "And a barn cat," he added.

"Baby," she said, stroking his hair. In Ann's mind, his ranch sprang to life; she put it in the backyard of their new home, under the foothills of the Rockies, though it had its creative origins in frenetic Los Angeles, beneath high-tension wires and endless airplanes and ozone alerts. "Where was this ranch?" she asked.

"Texas," he said without hesitation. A massive utopian landscape neither boy had seen, a giant star on a map, full of astronauts and cowboys. "Me and Dick dreamed about it all the time. We invented it in our sleep."

"Maybe that's where Dick went," Ann said. "Maybe that's where his parents should look."

"I told them that," Cole said. "They said they would, but it's a big place." She wondered how her son was picturing his friend, what he saw in his mind's eye when he imagined Dick—Dick no longer in L.A., no longer anywhere in particular but everywhere and nowhere at once. He was, for Ann, fear itself, rumored, possible, unknown. Better for Cole to summon the Texas ranch and their future livestock, pets.

"Mom, I think I know why Dick ran away."

"You do?" She feared he would name her own suspicion, that it was their departure that had set events in motion. That in some skewed way, she, Ann, was directly responsible for that boy's sorrow, for the reverberating despair of everyone surrounding him, including Cole himself, right here in his bed. She laid her head on his pillow, ready to be accused. "Why did he run away, sweetheart?" she asked.

"I think he didn't want to turn twelve," Cole said.

Ann waited, but Cole had finished. She said, "But it'll still be his birthday . . ."

"I know." Her son wasn't going to explain the contradiction; Ann would simply have to accept it, which she did. "It already *was* his birthday," he added. His birthday and Dick's were only a week apart. They'd thrown joint parties, in Cole's yard one year, in Dick's the next, hands clasped together around a knife over a single layered cake like a married couple. Had Cole arrived at his insight concerning Dick because he shared the opinion about turning twelve, because he didn't find life, anymore, all that worthwhile? Ann couldn't bear to think so; she squeezed her eyes shut and hoped—it seemed a weak thing, *hope*, and it was all she had—with all her heart not. But even if he did, even if it were true, could she beg him not to feel the way he felt?

No. No more than he could beg her.

Strike Anywhere

THIS WAS THE next time after what was supposed to be the last time. The father parked at the curb before the White Front, and the boy found himself making a prayer. It was Sunday, after all, and this was what his mother did when faced with his father's stubborn refusal to do what he said he'd do. Or not do what he said he'd not do. *Please, God,* and God knew the rest.

"Don't move a muscle, buddy, you hear?"

The boy nodded. Afraid to look at his father—his father could find accusation in any expression turned his direction—he sat small on the truck bench seat. His father had inclinations like a dog, like a bear: he pounced on motion, a little witlessly. Just as the truck door creaked open, the bar's sign flashed on. His father climbing out of the vehicle grunted as if answering the neon light. A vivid imprint of the beckoning white letters burned into the boy's mind.

"Not one inch," his father reminded him, face looming at the window before locking the truck door, slamming it, and crossing the sidewalk. He slapped the wallet in his back pocket, cinched his hat, drew breath to make himself tall, and disappeared through the dark entryway of the bar.

The boy's name was Ivan and he was eight years old. He had been sent on this errand to prevent just this sort of thing from happening. His father had quit drinking three months ago. Today they had gone to the Sunshine Station on the highway for lighter fluid and stick matches. His mother was home with the other three children, waiting to ignite the barbecue. It was five o'clock on a Sunday in May in Portersburg, Montana. The snow had melted and the grass had popped up, bright green and bent, as if it'd been blanketed all winter, waiting. The boy's mouth watered for venison; they'd thawed a few steaks to celebrate spring, to congratulate his father's sobriety. His mother had fixed cowboy beans, and his big sister had made marshmallow-whipped-cream-maraschino-cherry fruit salad. Soft white dinner rolls you could squeeze into doughy spheres the size of eyeballs and poke all at once between your lips. The meal shimmered like a mirage, like a hunger.

Main Street bustled in the welcome warmth of the day. Finally it was time to step out. People dawdled on the sidewalk rather than plowing against a frigid wind. They had removed their coats so that you could tell who was who, the men from the women, the strangers from the locals. At Ivan's house, his mother had pulled the plastic from the windows this morning, a ripping unzipping. Every winter the family grew accustomed to looking through the blurry insulating wrap. Then spring arrived, and the house, like the people, shed a layer, stood naked and clear.

They lived next door to the police station and jail. With the windows open, you could eavesdrop on the dispatch radio, the funny codes the police used to mean one sort of mishap or another. "Nine-one-one," Ivan's sister Leanne said whenever she spotted their father's truck rolling home late and slow. "That's a big ten-four, you can just call us at one-eight-hundred-asshole, twenty-four seven."

What, Ivan wondered, had made his father come to the White

Front today? He felt both responsible for his father's bad decision and completely irrelevant to it. A few years ago, the grocery had been located downtown, a mere three blocks from their house. If it hadn't moved to the highway—wider aisles, more parking, bakery, and ATM—then Leanne would have been sent on foot for the forgotten supplies. Perhaps Ivan himself. The whole town might be said to have conspired in his father's fall, guilty cause of this effect. Or not. The truck cab was neither too cold nor too hot; that simple fact could have been the one that had decided his father. Gentle spring weather. It would be safe to leave his son sitting in it for however long necessary.

Inside the bar, Dwight took his stool. He hadn't been to the White Front since February, but of course nothing had changed. No seasons here. There was payday, and happy hour, and closing time. There was the first sip, the free round, and the flung-back shot that was a flat-out mistake. On the wall, the Hall of Fame. Your picture, a gold star pressed reverently on the glass if you happened to be dead. No matter how long you abandoned this place, it was waiting when you returned. Welcome to Miller Time.

"Dwight," said the bartender.

"Frozene," said Dwight, admiring himself in the mirror under the stuffed jackalope, beside the landscape painted on a handsaw. The Coors waterfall fell. "Jack and a Bud back."

Frozene nodded, polishing with her damp cloth diaper the worn wood before her new customer. Frozene's adopted parents had owned the White Front; she'd lived here all her life. At the other end of the bar sat the young wife of the jeweler, Mrs. Donoglio the second. Her husband's shop of sapphires was just down the block. An old man with a dowager's hump, he looked through his eyepiece at you when you entered his store, a giant wet oyster of a glance, suspicious and unctuous at once. Along with setting stones, Mr. Donoglio fixed watches. Fine motor, his skills were. His first wife had died a few years ago, alone upstairs while downstairs he catered to the town's meager tourist population. This new wife had come from Missoula, a college girl, bored here, a religious drinker and smoker always with her nose in a book.

"Hey, Miss Merry Sunshine," Dwight called to her. She shared only one trait with his own wife: they both thought they were better than him. However, this one's sullenness cheered him, set him in heckling mode. She waited a second before looking up, holding her place on the page with a finger.

"Don't be telling me to turn that frown upside down," she warned.

"Sourpuss," Dwight said. She would habitually lay a twenty on the bar and drink gin and tonics until there were only a couple of damp bills left for a tip. She lived a twenty-dollar day; think what she might save, Dwight thought. After, she walked back to the jewelry store, where she made her home upstairs, in the same bed, Dwight supposed, where the first wife had died. This scrawny female, profane and sarcastic, wearing Wranglers like a man, hair cut by her own hand, ready to swear at you and your cowpoke ideas, she seemed to think she was the first educated drinker the bar had ever served. Oh, by the way, Dwight could say, there was such-and-such the famous writer here once, also from Missoula, who set his famous poem, a moment of it, anyway, in the jailhouse beside Dwight's very own home right up the hill. He could send that snooty girl, the sapphire king's young second wife, to the copy of the poem that hung in the back of the bar, typed up and yellow, signed by the poet himself. Now who's smart, Dwight could say, now who's God's gift.

"What?" she demanded.

Whoops. Drinking, he often found himself inside out, thoughts transformed into words, urges into action. "Can't a fellow be glad to see you?"

"Unlikely," she said. "Extremely."

"I'm an unlikely type," he allowed, magnanimous as could be. Alcohol, its proximity and promise, spread wings in his chest.

"You and that freak," she said, indicating the customer who'd just entered. This was the crazy man with his piggybacked pets, the dog, the cat, the mouse, each member of the food chain sitting smack on the back of his enemy. The mouse was never the same mouse for long. The freak was notorious from last summer, when the tourists had fawned over him. Nobody local—that is, nobody who had to deal with him day in, day out—made eye contact. His eyes were the intense heat-seeking ones of barely contained insanity. They wanted more than to see. Now he asked for and received a beer and a bowl.

"*Here* you go," he said, loud enough for others to listen in, dipping his fingers tenderly in his drink to let his creatures lick it off. "Who sits on Mr. Mouse, you might ask," he asked the air. "Fleas! I say!"

Dwight raised his eyebrows at the college snot, colluding gamely. It was good to know that the two of them, while drinking in the daylight hours in the afternoon of the Lord, had not stooped to animal tricks.

The jeweler's wife pushed herself ungracefully from her bar stool and headed for the women's room, where she'd sneer at the sign that told her *No more paper products? Wipe your ass with a spotted owl!* But then Dwight saw what had happened to her since February: she'd gotten big with child. When she returned, she scowled at his appraisal of her.

"That's right," she said. "So just spare me the lecture. You and that frigging pharmacist. 'Madam, I hope you realize that Valium and pre-natal vitamins are not a winning combination?' Oh, *really?* Go ahead, call the SPCA, you can report a twofer, me and the mouse-cat-dog sandwich over there."

The freak looked hurt, but the bartender, like all wise bartenders, was keeping strictly out of it. Between her and the customers was a def-inite barrier: the literal bar itself, and her authority to cut them off. The Confederate flags hanging everywhere like a promise of loaded weaponry and a willingness to use it. Plus her simple, relentless sobri-ety; Frozene, legend had it, had been traded as an infant for a bottle of beer. One beer for one baby, her new parents the bartenders making the exchange. Just cockeyed enough to be true. Besides Frozene and Dwight and the jeweler's wife and the freak show, three Mexican construction workers sat at a far table speaking Spanish, ignoring all the whites, nutty or not. There was no one to whom Dwight could voice an appeal.

"I didn't know you were in a family way," he said.

"Oh, the *family* way," said the jeweler's wife, slapping open her book and glaring into its pages.

Out in the truck, Ivan cracked the passenger window. The air smelled of mowed grass. His stomach rumbled. He rustled the grocery sack idly, lighter fluid and matches. If only they hadn't needed these. *Strike anywhere*, the box instructed. Ivan opened the package and was pleased to see the plenitude, the rows of patriotic little sticks, white, red, and a blue dot like a berry on each of a hundred tips. He removed one of the ranks and stuck it in his mouth, first exploring the bland square end between his teeth as it turned, then reversing the match.

He chewed thoughtlessly. The match tasted like something he'd only smelled before, a curious crossover sensation. He had a missing tooth—"canine incisor," his sister Leanne had informed him—and the matchstick slipped into the space in a soothing fashion, his gum tender yet pleasantly satisfied by the square plug of wood. Eventually he pulled the denuded stick from between his lips. He could not tell one end from the other now. His mouth felt oddly dry. He removed another match from the box and set to work. Time could pass this way, he thought. You needed a way to pass time. After his father had entered the bar, the man with the three pets had followed. Ivan liked this man, the way he would stop on the street and let you stroke his animals. They were tame. The kitty rode on the dog's back. The mouse sat atop the kitty. All the children were cheered by the way they got along. "The lion shall sleep with the sheep," the man claimed. "Heaven is liketh that, a peaceable kingdom." The man's eyes reminded Ivan of horse eyes, big and brown, lacking the common tiny pupil that most humans possessed. What would you see without those little black pinpoints?

"Ivan!" a pack of girls called, banging on the hood. His oldest sister's friends, they adored teasing him, rubbing his head, wiggling his ribs. They clustered around, wearing what his sister wore, belly buttons one and all on display, henna tattoos wandering their wrists, hair washed and stylishly wild just for a saunter down Main. They were seeking other boys, in other trucks.

"You hungry, Mr. I.?" one asked, grinning, showing her mouth of metal, tiny rubber bands blue and white, the high school colors.

"You want a cigarette to go with that match?"

"Maybe a bottle rocket?"

"You see that guy?" the girl named Kimmy inquired, hushed, watching the White Front door as if the man with his pets might pop right back out. "Well, my mom and me took one of his mice. We found it in the Trusty Donut Shop. We knew it was his 'cause it was so tame and all, like on downers. Now it lives in my mom's dollhouse, that one with the lights?"

"Your mom lets it go poo in her dollhouse?"

"Oh, hell no. She's got him in little mouse diapers. Diapers and a dress. But he won't wear the hat."

"Whatsup with this?" Margot leaned over to ask Ivan, bent at a severe right angle at the waist, swinging her rear and chewing a tiny piece of gum at his window. He smelled cinnamon, Big Red. She was the prettiest, the girl her friends had designated royalty. Ivan could see down her tank top, a mole, a pimple, her small pale breasts. "You get to come downtown but not Leanne?"

"Where's Leanne?" the others asked, a vague refrain to accompany their skittery glances. They were following the traffic, endlessly running their fingers through their hair, over their hips, touching the corners of their shiny, shiny lips. They studied their reflections in the rearview, in the store windows, in each other's eyes. They pulled their shirts down, then stretched their bare arms to make their navels wink into view. For belts, they wore slim silver chains.

Ivan smiled around his match. His sister's friends used his father's truck the way moths used a streetlight, just fluttering.

"You think that weirdo misses his mouse?" Margot asked Ivan before she sauntered away, snapping her gum. But Ivan wondered if the mouse missed his man.

* * *

Dwight, on his third set of drinks, genuinely curious, asked the bartender if it was legal to serve a pregnant woman.

"Is it legal to serve a sanctimonious hypocrite?" said the jeweler's wife, face still in her book. She might have fooled some people, but Dwight had noticed the pages weren't turning. "You and Mr. Science at the pharmacy, him in his lab coat and his bulletproof glass with the little speak-hole."

"Live and let live," said the wise Frozene.

"Then we agree," said Dwight. "But see, my problem is, she's not letting that wee thing live. I mean, you've heard tell of the deformed infants, you seen that shit on the Discovery Channel."

"Discover this," the girl said, blowing a fat raspberry. Dwight laughed. He loved the ones who sassed back. Why, he asked himself, why did he love them? His wife didn't sass; she wept. Pathetic. She prayed and wrote in her diary, and she used to talk to her sister on the phone, but nowadays she was talking to their oldest girl, Leanne. When Dwight found himself driven to strike his wife, she never struck back. From the beginning, he'd understood she was not ideal for someone like him. This one at the bar would have given him a run for his money. Resistance was sexy; maybe she and the jeweler had some knock-down drag-outs. The thought made Dwight reconsider the old guy with his monocle.

"Listen up," he said, "you've got your warnings on every bottle of liquor in here, just look at 'em." Dwight pointed at his own Bud and its pregnant-woman clause. "Warning!" he shouted down to the jeweler's wife.

"Fuck! Off!" she shouted right back, which raised Frozene's watchful brow. Briefly Dwight pictured the husband dashing around that old iron bed, revving for this hellcat, his one magnified eye swimming after her. Dwight laughed again. He loved liquor; the past three months without it had felt to him like a humiliation, a sentence he had served for bending to his wife's will. And now his reward was a barbecue. Ice cream and cake. Getting through those months had not made him proud. It had been one dreary day at a time, lined up behind him like empty boxes, a train of hollow testament to his wife's saintliness and his own pussy-whippedness. He closed his eyes to visit the full rosy bloom inside his head, the fiery flaring heat. You either quit drinking or you ended up in the Hall of Fame with Shreve and Helmar and Evert and Tiger and Tex and all the rest, each and every one raising a glass for the camera, their tiny gold stars applied later, when it was over. *Rehab Is for Quitters*, Dwight's favorite bumper sticker said.

The Mexicans took themselves to the Keno machines to make some hopeless wishes with their wrinkled dollar bills. On the huge television hanging ominously over the room played the country music station, complete with captions for the hearing-impaired. Through the bar's front door drifted three slaphappy schoolteachers, spouseless and silly. The jeweler's wife didn't look up, the freak bent to confide into his dog's ear, and when the new people had settled, called out their orders, and started talking among themselves, Dwight rose to say howdy.

"Easy," warned Frozene, and Dwight reassured her with an innocent hand.

"Let me just ask you all something, you mind?" he began. They looked up gamely. One of the women he recognized as Leanne's teacher, and she, he discerned, recognized him. Not necessarily favorably. "You see that young lady over yonder?" Now the woman's smile trembled. She sensed, before her companions, that they were being enticed into a drama where they did not belong. Dwight insisted, "You see her? That smart girl reading a book and sucking on a long, tall drink?" The jeweler's wife, Dwight realized, was closer to his daughter's age than his own, a fact that derailed him briefly. "Well," he went on, finishing what he'd started, "guess what?"

Because he obviously wasn't going anywhere until they guessed what, one of the schoolteachers cleared her throat, took a breath, and said, "What?"

"Pregnant!" Dwight declared. "That's what. Just as knocked up as she can be, drowning her little one in liquor. Now, just what in the hell you think of that?"

They stared, sighing, this threesome of educators who'd rendezvoused for a giddy margarita at the tail end of the semester, who came to the White Front maybe once or twice a year, escaping the monotonous industry of responsibility, who, frankly, couldn't count the jeweler's wife among their concerns, and who, finally, politely, fearfully, ventured the opinion that the bartender had: none of their business. Dwight looked shocked, though he wasn't. Teachers. They'd confirmed a certain suspicion of his.

"Hey, Hortense," Dwight said when he returned to his stool. "Isn't that your name?" It was the ugliest name he could think of. The jeweler's wife didn't even look up. Just transferred a burning cigarette to her left hand and raised the third finger of her right, nail-bitten, both hands utterly ringless despite her husband's profession.

Smiling, Dwight glanced languidly in the direction of the freak's table. He finally made out that the man was dangling the mouse by its tail before the cat's whiskers. Back and forth the gray thing swung, its front fingery paws twitching together as if steepled in prayer, the freak gazing on as if to hypnotize himself. But why, you had to wonder, didn't the cat snatch at the creature?

Ivan was making a house with matchsticks on the truck's dusty dashboard. The girls had moved on, glossy hair, languid hips, tottery platform shoes, rowdy voices, their bright shirts each bearing a message: *Hard Rock Café, Angel, Mischief.* The sun had fallen, but the evening was light, temperate. A woman pushing a baby carriage had just walked by. At first Ivan thought she was speaking to him, her mouth uttering sentences in his direction, catching him, he thought, as he ate his matches. But then he had realized as she passed that it was the baby she spoke to, in front of her in his stroller, waving his hands, crosseyed, trying in vain to catch his own waving bare feet.

The rule was that Ivan could only use the naked matches to shape his house. Their square stems were like tiny one-bys. If he bit down, they threatened to give, like crisp carrots. Once he softened the wood beneath the tip, the red and blue substance melted quickly in his mouth. The taste was neither good nor bad, the flavor one that Ivan had grown accustomed to. He was reminded of the Fourth of July, the sizzle of sparklers. His house needed twenty-nine matches; he had completed the walls and windows and roof and was working on the chimney when he noticed the man.

Beside the White Front, in the dark entryway of the defunct wedding-dress shop, a shadowy shape suddenly began moving. Inside the old shopwindows remained the damaged mannequins whose rusty satin gowns still hung on their amputated figures, handless, some, headless, others. Fake eyelashes clung like daddy longlegs on the remaining pink plastic cheeks. The shadow emerging from between the dress windows assumed a human form, pale face first and then animate body, shocking, like a broken-down groom stepping out of the ruined wedding party. The dolls smiled but not the man.

Ivan watched wide-eyed as the man came forward, lurching, wavering, like a marionette manipulated by a child, one moment upright, the next slumping limp on the sidewalk, where a high school couple had to veer around his flung, booted foot.

"Totally trashed," noted the boy in the couple, and the girl fanned the air before her nose.

Then Ivan recognized the loose-limbed figure as Kermit Boyer, one of a few drunk men who haunted Portersburg, the quiet one who slept in a horse stable just outside town. Kermit gathered himself delicately from the pavement, collapsed skeleton in his flexible rubble. Ivan was tempted to aid him, to fetch the white cards that had snowed from his pocket, which Kermit seemed not to have noticed. He gained his knees and then his feet, swaying there. He closed his eyes very slowly and then focused on Ivan through the windshield, lining up his gaze like a pair of floating compass needles. He aimed himself at the truck. The match in Ivan's mouth went wildly into and out of the empty socket. Kermit reached the truck's hood and melted onto it, sliding along the fender, grabbing on to the side mirror of the passenger door like a handle. His fingers were brown, crazy with scratches and scabs. His face was like a large rotten apple.

"Little boy," said Kermit Boyer, rapping with his free hand against the glass.

Ivan scooted to his father's side of the truck, beneath the steering wheel. His fingers trembled on the horn, ready to alert the people in the street, who would turn and rescue him from his nightmare, this desperate drunken figure. When his father came home drunk, his mother would hurry the children upstairs to their rooms. His father was not a bad man, she would explain. Only Leanne had the nerve to yell at him. "Drunk jerk!" she would shout from the top of the steps, and his father would yell right back up at her. "Hussy slut!"

Ivan, like his mother, suffered those words. *Please, God,* the two of them whispered.

"Please," his father often sneered.

In the locked truck, in the oncoming dark, Ivan's fear paralyzed him. Kermit's appearance, its suddenness, its ugly publicness, a person crawling like an animal on the sidewalk, draped like dirty laundry on his father's vehicle . . .

"Little boy," Kermit Boyer repeated, his fingertips now inside the passenger window, chapped lips at the crack. A missing tooth, Ivan noticed, a canine incisor like his own, whiskers, loose jowls, eyes loopy. "Little boy, don't do that," he said, his breath powerfully upon Ivan, a wave of sour ferment. "Don't eat the matches, boy," he said. "Good Lord, son, that's *poison!*"

The stick in Ivan's mouth stopped. And then Kermit abruptly disappeared, dropped like a felled deer, unstrung puppet, onto the cooling pavement beside the truck.

⤖ Flesh Tone

Evan's dead mother had missed two years of his life, yet Evan often felt she was still with him. He'd taken her places she'd never gone when she was alive. For instance, psychotherapy. The high school counselor's office wouldn't have alarmed her. Evan could imagine her impatient shifting hips on the other side of Mr. Henny's desk, her hand perhaps revolving in a get-on-with-it gesture down below Mr. Henny's sight line; his mother did not like to have her time wasted, and Mr. Henny was a time-waster of the highest order, with a verbal tic, this long *ahhh* that followed many of his phrases, an *ahhh* that disallowed his listener to comment, that prevented his sentences from ever truly ending. Evan's dead mother wouldn't have thought much of Mr. Henny, and even Mr. Henny had seemed to understand that he was in way over his head with Evan. *Hard case,* he might have written in his notes, wiping his sweaty brow as Evan departed. *Lost cause.*

Evan's symptoms were basic: he was losing weight and failing to sleep much. He looked nonchalantly upon railroad tracks and busy intersections, curious about his fate before the pill bottles in the medicine cabinet, the knives in the drawer, the car in the garage. In addition, he was seeing things that were not there and, further, couldn't concentrate on what everyone else agreed *was* there. The algebra problems on the board sometimes seemed to rise off the surface and square-dance in the air, fragile, chalky X and Y, symmetrical, dimensional, harmless as clock hands, limber as the legs of a praying mantis. Other times he cried and didn't care who saw. Two girls in Honors English had taken Evan down the hall and to the principal; he'd been inconsolable, his head a fountain, his limbs those of a rag doll between them. The principal with her drawn-on eyebrows, looking upon the heap at her feet, her staff of ladies as helpless as she. No, high school special services would have neither surprised nor impressed Evan's dead mother.

But the downtown high-rise where the psychiatrist practiced couldn't help but daunt. Evan felt his mother seize, bashful before the red-uniformed security guard who took Evan's name and checked it against a list, and she accompanied Evan into the gold-toned elevator timidly. Evan poked 16 with a confidence she had also rarely witnessed. It was her death that had inspired this acquaintance with the therapist, an irony she would have appreciated, modestly, as one accepts a compliment well earned. Evan attempted to keep his doctor's name from her. Franklin Horsehead. Yes, Horsehead. Well. His rates were astronomical, his talent was not to be disputed. The checks that were written, monthly, for his service, they equaled nearly a mortgage payment (or so Evan's father said). It was remarkable, the chain of events her death had set off. Evan's father had obviously had no choice, not after the bathroom episode, certainly not after the crash at the graveyard. Although, Evan knew, as would his mother, that the disposal of the cats wasn't the massive tragedy his father pretended it was.

"Who was going to look after them when I go away to college?" he asked Dr. Horsehead. Evan's father was allergic, and the cats didn't like him, besides. "And what good is a grave if you can't visit it?" Evan wanted to know. Who, he inquired, was that particular grave for, if not him? Surely not for his father, who'd gone out and found another wife. You could find another wife.

"'Visit'?" said Horsehead provocatively.

"And who did I hurt, anyway, locking myself in the bathroom?"

Horsehead murmured knowingly, but Evan was daydreaming. His mother had loved her daily bath; the pale green bathtub had been her favorite place in the house, there waiting when she returned from work, that place where she stood all day in heels, drinking coffee and suffering fools, gladly, to this place where she could lie down naked with her tired feet on the spout. A pink vodka drink on the tub rim, that and a fat, moist paperback for her to reenter every afternoon, all by herself. There Evan had lain all one day, after her death. *Murder Makes Three* was her book's title. Evan ran himself a hot bath and began reading, stopping at the very page where his mother had folded down the top corner; the detectives, blundering and blushing, had begun interrogating a house of prostitutes. This was as far as his mother had gotten. He dropped the book back where it belonged, pledging to read no further, either.

His father's voice, on the other side of the door, he had listened to dreamily and then more carefully, discerning a certain lack of passion, a distinct had-enough boredom in his inflection.

"Open up, Evan. If you *don't* open up, I'll have to knock this door down. I don't *want* to break the door down, Evan, I'm not even sure where the *drill* is, but, Evan, you're giving me no choice. Evan. Son." And so on. Down the door had come. While his father had gone to fetch the tools to remove the hinges, Evan dressed himself and emptied the tub. They faced each other in the humid little room over the hardware and fallen plaster.

"Was this really necessary?" his father asked.

When the cats disappeared, his father hadn't noticed for a few days. Then, all of a sudden, he was alarmed; where were the cats? What in God's name had Evan done with his mother's cats?

"What do you care?" Evan had screamed, sudden anger—even of the pretend variety—stunning his father into a frightened silence.

"Your anger at your father is perfectly understandable," Dr. Horsehead assured him. The cats' fate, still, troubled his therapist.

It was later, when Evan had taken his mother's car for a drive, this car that he'd inherited, somehow constructing in his mind an exchange, as he wheeled through the city streets, of the car for her life, a piece of what Horsehead called "magical thinking." Presto!: *pow* into a tree. The tree lived, and everyone else at the cemetery—did he have to point it out?— was already dead. "Killing yourself is not an option," his father said flatly. As did his doctor; he'd gone so far as to draw up a contract.

Evan's dead mother approved of binding documents, although Evan's signature, his horrific childish penmanship, frustrated her. He never made any effort to put his best foot forward! Every Friday of the following year, after Calculus, Evan drove back home from college to Kansas City to see Dr. Horsehead; some days it seemed he was merely exhibiting his continuing status as a member of the living. Other times he wept, exiting the office with a cleansed, cathartic calm, dotting at his dried-out eyes all the way back to Lawrence with a fingertip he repeatedly licked. But never did his dead mother leave his side. And never did he tell the doctor that she was in attendance. Wasn't it up to Horsehead to intuit this particular phenomenon? When he had asked if Evan heard voices, Evan had been honest in denying it; there was, after all, just the one.

The cemetery was where his mother had first spoken to him: in the stunning silence after the bang, after the frolicky fact of aiming himself and her vehicle toward the tree, after the crunch and the breathtaking blow to the chest, the searing heat imploding in his gut, his head shaken like a maraca, and the tinkling glass raining all around him, the crazy crows taking flight in their black riotous wave, and the high-frequency whistle, like a tiny teakettle shrilling in his head. Eventually the birds relighted, draping themselves in their customary black sentry positions above the graveyard, sage and somber; he could stay, they seemed to agree, as long as he remained quietly bleeding, waiting as life leaked easily away. They didn't care. The car had cooled. The tombstones stood in the coming dark, immovable as a forest, the army of the dead. And then she'd arrived, gliding lightly through the ruined windshield like a wafting scarf. *Monkey,* she said, the name she'd called him for years and years. Evan had sobbed to hear it once more. How could he regret his dumb wreck when doing it had brought his mother to him?

If not for the teenagers seeking a silent place to park and toke, if not for their cell phones and hazy heroism, Evan would have slid sweetly into oblivion. Instead, the ambulance arrived in a flurry of light and sound, and a troupe of EMTs promptly whipped him out of the dark, intoxicating car and into the cool, bright ambulance, consciousness hitting him like a metal door. He lay shocked and cold, as if being transported in a refrigerator, riding on a shelf, a muffled wail outside the vehicle, a continuing clatter inside it as they bounced from the gravel graveyard road down the curb to the pavement, straps across his chest and thighs, his arms bound, his head held in a cushioned vise. And then, once he'd inventoried the loud and the large, he sensed the rest, that soft force, new, closer to him than the wraps and bindings, as close as his own skin. He felt his mother's hand on his cheek, her lips at his ear, heard her voice murmuring the names of the streets the ambulance sailed through, carrying him with her voice all the way to the hospital. It was her. Whatever else he'd done this night, he'd also brought her back.

Anyway, now here was Evan's dead mother going with him to college, another expensive journey to uncharted territory, big wooden doors anchored to buildings made of limestone, gargoyles on the roof, bells bonging sonorously. His mother was clever, funnier than his father, quicker than he, but she'd never been to college. Her education had taken place on the job, behind cash registers and display counters, in the offices of managers and floorwalkers, at the service of customers. College looked like a country club to Evan's mother. Hills, fall leaves, pretty girls crossing vast lawns, fraternity houses like mansions, lecture halls, cordless mikes, cappuccinos and bottled water, more chalkboards and dancing images. Oh, Evan's dormitory and his dormitory *room* and his room*mate* and their shared bath—*co-ed*?

Who had sanctioned such a thing? Down the noisy stairs, past the front desk and the student they called "Deskie," and out the door went Evan's dead mother, and what did she see?

A bar—Rowdy's Town and Gown—not fifty feet from the dorm entrance. His mother supported the idea of bars; in her opinion, they were the only social gathering spots with no particular agenda other than leisure. She had taken Evan to them all the time; she'd let him sip her drinks and play pool. She'd taught him to drive a car when he was twelve—first automatic, then stick. She'd told him, when the time came for the Facts of Life, that heartbreak was part of the package, perhaps the most shocking part, something the teachers at school with their condoms and STDs and nocturnal emissions failed to mention. In the way that he would acquire underarm hair and a cracked voice, he would also get dumped and damaged, and probably do the same to somebody else. She was forever preparing him for his life, setting up the tenpins, swinging back the heavy ball. Still, she wasn't sure she wanted him sneaking into Rowdy's.

"Stumbling distance," Evan quoted her aloud, referring to the proximity to the bar, although he was, more and less, alone.

This living with another man was new, too. Not a boy but a full-fledged adult, a teacher of high school students, Evan's roommate came from Dominica. His name was Roosevelt Skerritt. He had the exotic glamour of a television personality, lovely large teeth, and a fascinating accent. He spoke English, his second language, more eloquently than anyone Evan had ever known, and it wasn't so much speaking as singing, it sometimes seemed. Contractions were apparently forbidden in Dominica, which, in combination with Roosevelt's extremely dark skin and big polite smile, made him most impressive to Evan's mother. His manners were impeccable. One thing upset her: upon leaving his island, Roosevelt had received gifts deemed necessary for dormitory life—iron and portable board, microwave, popcorn popper, tiny refrigerator, clock radio, miniature television, compact stereo, and Mr. Coffee. Not being a coffee drinker, Roosevelt used the maker for laundering his underpants. Evan's mother pretended not to notice the soap flakes in the filter basket, the damp, steaming Jockeys left dangling on the drawer pulls.

Hum-hum! she said brightly in Evan's ear, her way of willfully overlooking something. When he was a little boy and asking of her the impossible, the ridiculous, she responded with the honking nonsense of the cartoon adults in the Peanuts special: "Wonh *wonh,* wonh wonh."

That Roosevelt ironed every one of his garments mollified her, however.

"We will find ourselves some of the blond-haired women," Roosevelt predicted, beaming from his side of the room, reclining on his single bed. The padded headboards folded back to reveal a nook for nighttime necessities. Roosevelt had filled his nook with imported snack packages, fried red pealike things. "The blond-haired women," he repeated, showing his teeth, brilliantly collusive. In Dominica, you did not need the fake I.D., but Roosevelt could take care of this minor inconvenience for Evan. "I think of it like child's play," he said dismissively. "Oh, how they will love our polite manners, our handshakes for the fathers, and our flowers for the mothers. It is so simple to be a fine boyfriend." The two of them lay on their beds, the relief and expectation of Saturday night in the atmosphere. A kegger was raging in the dorm basement—the throbbing in the walls, the stench of beer in the air—and Evan was tempted to go down, down there with the coin-operated washers and dryers and Coke machines, yet one other place his dead mother had never set foot in, but Roosevelt sniffed at the invitation. There'd been others, these famous keggers, and after Roosevelt had determined that the blond-haired women chose not to attend them, he opted against as well. In Dominica, Roosevelt was married. This one year he would have his grand adventure, and then he would return to Dominica, settled and smarter, to teach the children and faithfully love his wife. He honestly saw no disharmony in his plan; it was as if, leaving his neckties on the island, he'd left his husbandhood as well. To stimulate his brain, he had screwed inversion boots to the doorway of the room's shared closet and spent at least an hour a day upside down with his arms crossed over his chest. "Fruit Bat," the hall had named him. Roosevelt cherished his nickname; America amazed him. Having no fixed expectations, he found absolutely nothing the matter with Evan, and that alone was enough to make Evan fond of him.

(Sometimes Evan studied Roosevelt's apparatus in the closet door frame, imagining how a noose might be lashed to the boots. Near the top, of course, to provide enough room to swing . . .)

Evan's mother wanted to know if he thought Roosevelt had an odd odor about him. And was this odor the product of his black skin or his foreign homeland or some combination?

"Don't be prejudice," Evan scolded her.

*Preju*diced, she corrected.

"Don't be it."

"I beg your pardon?" asked Roosevelt, turning from his bed with a hand cupped around his ear.

One weekend in November, Evan decided to stay in Kansas City after his session with Dr. Horsehead rather than drive back to Lawrence. His father and his father's new wife (he could not think, let alone use, the word *stepmother*) seemed glad yet vaguely burdened—it was in the eyebrows and the grimaces, if you cared to look—to see him. He felt like what he apparently was: a guest. The wife, Sondra, had been slowly rearranging Evan's childhood home. Now you did not wear shoes inside. You left them in the foyer and padded about in socks. There by the front door were all of the household shoes, his father's sad loafers, Sondra's sensibles. His dead mother could neither believe that her husband would consent to such a practice, nor what Sondra wore in public, moccasins and Birkenstocks and garden clogs. *Geez Louise.*

Sondra believed in stockpiling provisions and had turned the laundry room into a pantry full of malodorous health foods. Upstairs, the spare room, where Evan's mother paid bills and spent some nights when his father's snoring or her own private irritations had gotten the best of her, had been converted to a studio for Sondra's weaving. Her long gray hair suited her; she might have woven a sweater out of it, push coming to shove; she had shelves of unlikely fur products that she planned to spin into hats or mittens. Her clothing was the bland colors of cooked vegetables.

In the bathroom, the old unfinished murder mystery had disappeared, as had the floral curtains and hamper. The towels had changed color from pink to hemp. Sondra's toiletries consisted of a Water Pik, a pumice stone, a loofah, olive oil, and a chunk of salt-crystal deodorant to rub under her arms and on her feet. The soap in the dish resembled a nutty piece of oatmeal bread. Evan's dead mother looked upon these dull objects, alarmed. What had become of her Estée Lauder and Chanel No. 19, her magnifying makeup mirror and her collection of hairbrushes, the pretty decanters of bath gels, the slide trays of eye shadow? The bathroom had been her sanctuary, her shrine to her self-image. What did it mean, this hospital white and these herbal unguents? All the walls were white, one room after another, freshly spackled and mute. Only Evan's old bedroom remained as it had been, the pale blue his mother had decorated it with when he was eight. He'd restored to these walls the framed posters his mother had given him, Gauguin, van Gogh, Picasso, these bright, gaudy reproductions waiting for him in the living room one Christmas morning when he'd thought Santa might bestow on him a computer or television set. In the dark, hopeful space beside the pine tree, the pictures had looked, briefly, like a big box that might contain some sort of terrific appliance.

"I'm sorry," Evan murmured to his mother now. He thought to her, he whispered, he mouthed. His face, he knew, bore the expressions of his thoughts, pensive, argumentative, repentant, amused. On campus, people sometimes noticed. A pair of frat boys had pulled Evan away from a curb when he'd been just on the verge of walking off, deep in debate at a very busy intersection.

"*Dude*," they said in tandem, shaking their scrubbed, pitying faces at him.

Sondra was a psychologist, which meant that Evan avoided being alone with her and was forever second-guessing his sentences, replaying them in his mind for symbolic, diagnostic possibilities. His father seemed sedated. He practiced tai chi in the backyard now; Sondra kept a few Angora rabbits out there, and Evan had watched his father slowly semaphoring while the bunnies loped around nibbling grass. His volatile temper, often evident at dinner, seemed to have disappeared, leaving this peaceful person who often resorted to a chuckle when called upon to comment. Evan's mother mimicked him: *uh uh uh uh.* He'd quit drinking and was disappointed when Evan bravely requested a beer with dinner. Evan didn't even want a beer; his mother did, although not to drink. She wanted it in front of her son, fizzing there like a sparkler.

"Can I tell you about a study I read," Sondra said sincerely as she unscrewed the cap of the green bottle. "It was about alcohol and brain chemistry?"

"I sort of wish you wouldn't," Evan confessed. "I really feel pretty full up of studies right now. They really . . ." He motioned toward his forehead, rolling his eyes to indicate the dizzying amount of information his professors were steadily heaping in his direction. His mother snorted, though she, faithful drinker of a few evening highballs, had no more use for a depressing alcohol study than he.

". . . ethanol," Sondra was saying, watching the foam grow in his glass.

"Got a girlfriend?" his father asked out of nowhere.

"Honey," Sondra scolded. Her rabbits had been brought inside as dusk approached, and they now sniffed silently under the table, warm fur suddenly on Evan's bare ankle, softer than the cats' had been, skittish, accidental encounters. Sondra turned to Evan. "I used to so hate it when adults asked me such things, always assuming I ought to have a boyfriend. I mean, what if I'd wanted to have an edu*cation,* for starters, something really useful? And moreover, why assume I would fall in love with a boy, why not a girl? Why didn't they ever ask if I had met interesting people, any one of which I might have fallen in love with?" Sondra presented a sincere, imploring face to Evan.

He shrugged, wide-eyed to match her wide eyes. *Now she wants you to be a gaylord,* said his mother.

"Have *you* met interesting people?" Sondra asked Evan, broadening his father's question. She served herself from a steaming casserole dish. Its contents were not immediately clear to Evan.

"My roommate is from Dominica."

"How *inter*esting!" Now the casserole was in Evan's hands. "Eggplant Parmesan," Sondra clarified. "Without the Parmesan. Lactose intolerance." She nodded toward Evan's father. "Probably all his life, and he never realized it. I had him go in for the tests."

"Now I know why I was always sneezing," Evan's father said. "I thought it was those cats, but it turns out to be cow milk. Isn't that something?" He chuckled.

That's something, all right, said Evan's dead mother dryly. And now Evan missed the cats, their lazy satisfied selves, strutting and preening, bored, entitled, occasionally throwing themselves into a crazy whirl around this very table like the tigers in *Little Black Sambo.*

"I use a soy stand-in," Sondra explained. Evan's eggplant slid across his plate as he approached it with his fork. Also for dinner was a spinach salad and raisin flatbread. Another of his father's allergies, it turned out, was yeast.

"It's called a scratch test," his father said. "I tell you, my arms lit up like a pinball machine. Dairy, *bing,* yeast, *bing,* Bermuda grass, *ba-bing,* mulberry—"

"Which is your favorite class?" Sondra asked. "What do you think you might major in?"

Roosevelt Skerrit's major was education, and that was the first thing that occurred to Evan to report as his own. However, he sensed that his father would find education disappointing, as majors went, and Evan rejected premed as being too transparently ridiculous, so he said, "Sociology," hoping to strike a pleasant unsuspicious middle ground. He was taking no classes in the subject but had seen the building on his way to the student union and knew that it must be a discipline large enough to support a major.

"Sociology?" his father repeated, as Evan could have predicted he would.

World health, his mother prodded him. "World health," Evan said.

"World health," Sondra said, thrilled. And now she launched into her own college days, her studies in English and Psychology and Journalism and Art. These, too, were buildings, majors, topics upon which one could converse genially over slippery eggplant and tough flatbread, Sondra the expert, his father the willing, chuckling blue-collar naif, Evan the attendant son.

"So, seriously, you got a girlfriend?" his father asked once more when Sondra was away clearing plates.

"No," Evan answered, reddening. He and his father had never discussed girls, sex, anything, actually, aside from the checklist of routine maintenance between Breadwinner and Tax Write-off; his mother had been the messenger, arbiter, specialist, interpreter of each for the other. For a moment his father seemed to remember her and her role, those and the grief-stricken fog that had filled this house, the tiring shared atmosphere he and Evan had breathed in and out during those first months after her death. Over dreary frozen food at this same table. Evan ought not to visit; he apparently brought the fog with him, like Pigpen.

"My dorm is co-ed," Evan offered.

"Oh, good," his father answered blankly; he seemed to have forgotten what he'd asked. *There are no mirrors in the house,* Evan's mother noted. *He doesn't have any idea what he looks like anymore.*

"What happened to the mirrors?" Evan asked.

His father glanced to where the decorative one had hung in the dining room. "Sondra . . ." he said. Under the tablecloth, Evan felt a bunny pass his socked foot. A moment later, his father's face registered the animal's presence over there, which cheered rather than alarmed him, bringing him fully around to his new, better life. "Hey, did I tell you about the acupuncture Sondra's got me doing?" He pressed his thick fingers on his cheeks. "Your old man the pincushion."

After dinner, there was a British dramatic series on public television to view. And following that, there was the safety of Evan's bedroom with its closed door. On his dresser he found some guestlike niceties, tiny shampoo, lotion, toothpaste, sealed two-pack of Tylenol (Sondra would know to stock no more than two), and several books that he did not recognize, an anthology of gay fiction among them. This, too, would be Sondra's doing, presenting Evan with the option to reveal a homosexuality that would explain absolutely everything about the preceding two years. She would smooth the way for his finally unveiling his secret, she would ease his father into acceptance . . . Evan lay back, exhausted, on his old bed. Outside, the same tree that had always whipped before his window was doing it again tonight. His mother reminded him to brush and floss, but she didn't push, allowing him to drift off dressed.

Evan had a professor with a seeing problem. The notes from which Dr. Schweiner read were written in enormous typeface, and he turned pages frequently, a flutter at the front of the room. He was old; his necktie and jacket and pants, none of them went together and were all variously stained; his eyebrows needed tending. When he took roll, he looked up to see the person who'd shouted back to him, to give an indecisive smile wobbling with his scowl. It seemed a matter of manners, this time-consuming eye contact. And maybe it was Evan's imagination, but it seemed as if Dr. Schweiner's blurry gaze lingered slightly longer on Evan. "*Mis*ter Johnson," said Dr. Schweiner.

"Here," said Evan.

And then the lifted head, like that of a sleepy heavy-skulled animal, the furrowed frown, as if Evan were familiar to the professor, along the lines of a minor player in some nearly forgotten bad dream. His skin lacked what the Crayola people once had called *flesh tone*. His mouth trembled before he blinked back down to the list on his podium, the shaking pencil tip making its check beside the next name. "*Miss* Johnson."

He's near death, Evan's mother predicted in Evan's ear. *And for Lord's sake, who dresses him? He should have a barber work on his face.*

Maybe he figures, why bother? Evan thought.

True.

It's sad that he's going to die.

Everybody dies, Evan.

It's still sad.

Look at this roomful of people still taking notes on what he says, and he gets to flunk them if he likes. He's led a rich life. What more could he want?

"More of the same. More and more and more of the same."

The girl sitting beside Evan shifted away from him and his odd muttering and sniffling.

This happened. He and his mother might carry on a conversation as if commenting on a film or stage performance, as if Evan were in her world instead of his own. He could forget his real surroundings or at least lose consciousness of their containing him rather than going on for his contemplation. College accommodated such peculiarity, landscape of a thousand alternate universes, and in their midst—the preachers and mutterers, musicians and protesters—Evan blended, camouflaged.

"Why does the professor pause when he looks at me?" Evan whispered.

You know why, his mother informed him.

The good news was, Evan wasn't crying as often here at college. The novelty of a new place, its baffling proportions, the sheer work of putting on and taking off his coat and scarf as he entered and exited buildings, the constant rushing river of *strangers* (strange *and* strange) who simply did not see him, that liberating dearth of people who actually knew or cared about him.

"What is this word," Roosevelt asked, "this *palindrome*?"

"Same word or sentence, same letters, I mean, forward and back. Madam. Did. A man, a plan, a canal, Panama. Racecar." Evan had put his finger on the line he was reading in his own textbook. "Mom," he added. Back and forth it went, that word, brick solid. In the dorm hall lingered the scent of popcorn, which made Evan recall nights in front of the television, old movies with his mother, his father losing the TV vote and left grumbling behind his study door.

"I prefer the naughty rhymes, those limericks," Roosevelt was saying.

"I like those, too."

"There once lived a Roosevelt Skerrit," he began.

"Who lived in his room like a ferret," said Evan.

"His roommate was vile, his life a deep trial, and furthermore lacking all merit." They grinned at each other. Roosevelt slammed shut his book, ready for an adventure. He had a penchant for bending rules. Their room blew more fuses than others on the hall; maintenance had warned them that their quarters were not a kitchen. In the tiny freezer of the tiny refrigerator lay a lump of mountain-lion meat Roosevelt had won in a bet. In the evening, Roosevelt often invited Evan to go out and wreak havoc. The passport he'd found for Evan showed the face of a brown man age twenty-five, also from Dominica.

"This northern climate is terrible for your complexion, Ruben Morteband," Roosevelt said sadly as they sat in the bar closest to their dorm. Rowdy's was always their next-to-last stop, the one before sobering up at the hot-donut shop. "I do not like my beer served in clear bottles," Roosevelt said to the bartender. "They bear a resemblance to urine samples." Evan looked at the rows of Millers. Over the past few months, he had come to understand what his mother had liked about drinking. Under its liquid influence everything flowed more easily, perspective and good intentions and the future. Out into the freezing air Evan carried his sunny optimism, warm and unafraid.

"Hey," he said to Roosevelt later, in the hot-donut shop parking lot, eating hot donuts, bleary, jukebox-deaf, the thought for the first time occurring to him, "you don't really think I'm vile?"

"My friend," Roosevelt said, his mouth full, obviously disappointed in Evan's deductive abilities. Moreover, they were Evan's dead mother's deductions, not Evan's; his mother had been trying for years to teach Evan skepticism. Roosevelt swallowed rapidly, polishing off the small carton of milk he had shoplifted. "You are my roommate, and as a result, you are my good companion, my fine friend. We have our adventures together, the Two Roommates." He used his gloved hands to make a marquee.

And my mother, thought Evan. And you, Mom, he thought.

But some nights, when they'd returned to their room and said their pleasantries after preparing for bed, Evan lay wakeful, sobering up before passing out, donuts a lump in his gut, fear a vapor in his head. Roosevelt was a light sleeper. His easygoing island manners disappeared in the dark, and he grew impatient with Evan's insomnia. "Go to sleep, mon! No more squeaking back and forth on the bed there. We have classes early in the morning!" But Evan could not bear to lie awake in the dark. He shared this trait with his mother. There were mornings he'd woken, groggy with loathing of school, when he found his mother sitting at the kitchen table with her feet up, reading a book and drinking coffee. She'd been awake most of the night, she would tell him cheerfully. Sometimes she'd baked bread, scrubbed the sink, drawn a picture. You had to have a hobby if you were an insomniac.

Evan took a book with him at two in the morning as he descended in the dorm elevator, thinking of the lobby and its chairs with ottomans, the radiant heater under each chilly window. Outside the wind blew grandly, a howling disturbance that had been growing all evening. Nights like this, the windy January ones, made you want to curl up before something warm, a fireplace, a television. His anxiety seemed more manageable here on the ground floor, less likely to tumble down the walls. The giant TV played videos, and Merry Christmas, the graveyard-shift deskie, sat on the counter with her back to the set, swinging her legs, a notebook by her side. She was not happy to see Evan, but no less happy than she would have been to see anyone. "Don't mind me," Evan said as he took a seat.

"*Mind* you?" Merry repeated.

Evan smiled into his book, which he would not be able to read with

Merry in the room. She began writing in the notebook. A leftie, Evan noted. Like his mother.

After what seemed like a casual amount of time in which to grow curious, he asked what she was writing.

"A poem about the seasons," she said. "Not the seasons as you know them," she added, before Evan could say something inane.

"What seasons, then?"

"These are the college seasons. I've been here three years now, and I see a definite pattern developing, seasonwise. At this moment, for instance, we are deep in the heart of the Season of Dead Grandmothers."

"Now?"

"As we speak. You can't believe how many grandmothers die this time of year, just after Christmas. In this dorm alone, there've been six since semester."

"Wow." *Wow?* Another of Roosevelt's palindromes, *Mom*, upside down. "My grandmothers are both still alive." His mother had died out of season, he supposed, in August, at work, of an aneurysm. In his mind appeared the distended bulb of blood he always associated with the word, its explosion just behind his mother's eyes. He squeezed his own eyes shut, then asked Merry, "What other seasons?"

She appraised him; his pause had apparently piqued her interest. "Next: Girl Scout Cookie Season. They'll be coming here, there's a troop leader in the neighborhood, and she knows how the freshmen fatties love cookies. Followed by Everyone Wants to Be Blond Season, Even the Teachers, and then, thank God, not a moment too soon, Parole."

"Summer?"

"Will you watch the front?" she asked him suddenly, setting down her notebook and, rotating neatly on her rear, hopping off the counter on the public side. "Don't let anybody in. Don't answer the phone." Why, he wondered, did she need someone to sit here in her place doing nothing? She pushed through the swinging doors that led to the stairs. "I'll be right back. I'm going to the cafeteria."

The heavy fire doors closed behind her. Even if she ran down there and ran back up, Evan would still have time to take a quick look at what else she had written. Had she left it there as a test? An invitation? He opened the book, despite his mother's fervent disapproval. *Privacy,* she had repeatedly told him, *is a human cornerstone.* On the first page was an elaborate doodle of a fish in a frying pan, the paper smooth and heavy with ink. The next page yielded the title *Holiday on Eyes.* And after that came a sentence.

Whipped by currents larky and brazen, Disraeli abandoned his calvary. What?

Evan closed the notebook; he couldn't properly concentrate, with the threat of Merry's return. Plus, his mother impinged, correcting the spelling of *cavalry* close to his ear as well as chastising his snooping habit. Evan returned to his own book and settled back into the armchair. It had horsehair cushions, he heard from his mother. Imagine all the freshmen it had held, the dust mites and hair oil and history.

His mother had always meant to write a book. It was called *Things to Do When You're Drunk.* It wasn't a joke. Since Evan was small, she'd collected insights on her subject. Play LEGOs. Do sit-ups. Pluck eyebrows. Phone in-laws.

Merry returned with a yogurt, the rubbery off-brand the cafeteria served, and switched the television to country music videos. Although other deskies relinquished the remote control for the television, complacent with a democratic model, she wouldn't. You could put a TV in your room, but the dorm disallowed cable hookups.

She looks like a boy, Evan's mother noted. It wasn't a fashion statement, Evan had a feeling, it was a lack of care. Merry's hair was pushed back from her face, the straight kind of dirty-blond hair that boys had, unstyled, and she wore black-rimmed eyeglasses, slightly large, that rested on her evident cheekbones. Her ears were not pierced, she wore no makeup, her pants were baggy cords. On her feet, generic tennis shoes. She rounded her shoulders slightly as if to hide her breasts. He had always assumed she was a genius, her name a droll ironic touch. Rumor had it she was an orphan, on full scholarship.

"There's a cat down there in the cafeteria," Merry told Evan as she broke the tight pink surface of her yogurt with a spoon. "I heard it crying. Could you help me catch it?"

A cat!

"It's feral," Merry told him as down the dorm steps they went. In the kitchen, Evan approached the restaurant ovens with an apron over his hands. "They live all over campus," Merry went on softly. "Sometimes the great horned owls eat their kittens. Those owls live in the campanile, maybe you've seen them sitting up there? It's a regular food chain on this campus. Little kitty, come on, kitty, we're not going to hurt you. She crawled in through one of the dryer vents. I found her in a dryer two nights ago, just mewing and mewing, but I couldn't catch her. I thought she might have calmed down by now. Meow, meow, kitty, kitty," she called in the high falsetto cats responded to, maybe even feral ones.

Half of what she'd said didn't quite attach to Evan's consciousness. He had to listen also to his mother, who had mixed feelings about this endeavor, one part of her in love with all cats, one part of her worried over rabies. She herself had been treated once, *a series of shots in the stomach that, believe you me, were no picnic* . . . In the midst of her fretful debate, Evan proceeded toward the big metal oven behind which the cat hid, crying as if stuck. He hadn't been this close to a cat since he'd gotten rid of his mother's. When Merry jammed the broom underneath, Evan was to tackle the animal as it fled. His mother warned him that the apron was far too thin to shield him from scratches or bites, that he might better go about this with a can of open tuna fish and a live trap. Or maybe . . .

The cat flashed past like a rat, small and low to the floor. Evan had approached as if the creature would attack him, but it had no interest in such a thing. It hugged the wall, slithering out from behind the stove and along the base of the glinting refrigerated units like an electric wire, like currency, disappearing into the vast looming dark of the dining hall.

"Oh, kitten," cried Merry, clasping her nail-bitten hands. She turned a sad face toward Evan, lit red by the bright exit signs in the room. Her eyes were damp behind her glasses. Now she did not resemble a boy. Evan wanted more than anything to hug her. *Hug her,* his mother instructed. He suddenly did it, apron dangling from one of his hands that he reached around her back. Merry did not return his embrace, but she did not resist. Evan had not hugged anyone for a long time. She felt small yet solid, her torso warm, her hair cool on his cheek. He could feel the soft, secret parts of her chest. He was aware of their breathing together, the way their shoulders lifted in tandem. The gleaming kitchen appliances surrounded them, steadily whirring. There was no other sound, the wind upstairs utterly muffled down here in the basement, the cat silent. It felt profoundly safe to Evan, this synchronized breathing. He thought he might never want to let her go. A familiar stinging sensation rose to his nose, the one that meant he was in danger of bursting into tears.

They abruptly separated.

"Damn," Merry said, brushing her nose with her hand as if she, too, were on the verge of serious weeping. They studied the dark place where the cat had disappeared. It crossed Evan's mind to bring her a different cat, one from the pet store or some other tame litter, to show up bearing some fluffy pet in a basket tomorrow night during her shift at the desk. Was it his mother who let him know that the domesticated kitten would not interest Merry Christmas? Or was it Evan himself who understood that Merry needed to rescue the cat she would own?

He loved his insomnia, although Horsehead warned about a change in sleep patterns. Evan accomplished it honestly, without the aid of an alarm. Somehow his eyes flew open, *Merry Christmas!*, on the four nights a week she worked her shift at the desk. Rarely did anyone interrupt for long their strange hours together, Merry reading or writing behind the counter, Evan pretending to read in one of the armchairs, a yellow highlighter in hand, Evan's mother pleased with the nostalgic atmosphere of the lobby, the warmth and peachy lighting, the closed,

intimate innocent studiousness of Evan and Merry. She approved of
Merry, with her unattractive eyeglasses and her care of the wily cat in
the basement, uncaught as yet. When confronted with a buzz from the
foyer, Merry would jump, surprised, each and every time. Even though
this was her job, one of only a few duties she was assigned to perform,
she continued to startle—hand to her chest, little squeal of alarm—
whenever somebody came home late and rang the buzzer. They had to
produce their dorm I.D. cards and slap them up to the glass before she
would let them in. They were often drunk, often with people who could
not, by dorm rules, come in after midnight. On Merry's shift, it was
always after midnight. Frequently she had decisions to make over the
intercom. Evan marveled at her critical acuity. Those cold residents had
some pretty convincing stories to tell through the mouthpiece on the
other side of the glass vestibule door. Merry listened, weighed evidence,
made judgments. They would plead, hassle, swear, gesture, bribe. She
wrote down the names of the people who bothered her, whose stories
she wouldn't accept, and reported them to the resident associates, who
were simply other students, seniors, who lived on each floor. Many of
them were worse than the freshmen. They were the ones who routinely
held the keg parties.

The others, those whose situations tapped into her sympathy, she
buzzed in.

During their nights together, Evan had grown accustomed to Merry's
long silences. When he'd mentioned her to Roosevelt, his roommate
refused to believe in her. He had never seen her, day or night. "Go visit
your ghost," he would grumble as he went to sleep. "But do not waken
me." Evan realized he did not care if Merry was his secret; his mother
had taught him the beauty of a secret life, the one unmeasured by
others, and if unmeasured, then also unjudged, unknown in the most
fundamental way, something held close as a heartbeat, a phantom voice
near the ear, that most intimate of places.

Sometimes Merry joined him in the musty sitting area, resting on
the stuffed chair arm, leaning her head against his. She did not ask
about his tragedy, and he didn't ask about hers. Death was involved,

he knew they both knew this, an early exposure to it. They had not kissed, yet they often touched—arms, hands, heads. Evan relished the moments when he could feel the two of them breathing together, like that first night in the dim cafeteria kitchen. They'd embraced again behind the mailboxes in the small room on the other side of the counter. Together they had been investigating their fellow dormmates' packages and letters, guessing at contents. There were an inordinate number of Columbia House record club members living here. In that tight space, while Evan was reaching into yet another tiny cubicle, she had suddenly wrapped her arms around him from behind, leaning her head between his shoulder blades as if to hear his heartbeat from the back. *Orphan,* his mother said or he thought, holding still, inhaling deeply, as if at the doctor's, waiting to be told he was fine.

His first semester's grades had not been stellar, but his father had chosen, on Sondra's advice, to give Evan time to acclimate. Now, however, midterm second semester, Evan was failing every single class.

"Hey, pal, what's going on?" his father asked over the telephone. Evan heard Sondra murmuring in the background. She would be telling him to ease up. She would be encouraging him to allow Evan to come out of the closet, there at college, and worry about career moves later.

"I'm fine," Evan reported. "Really."

"Okay. But what's with the F's in everything?"

"College is hard." It was especially hard when you slept through your morning classes, when you remembered to attend lab but lost sight of where the lecture hall was. When your real interest lay in the predawn hours at your dorm with a girl named Merry Christmas. Moreover, he'd already heard a version of this lecture from Roosevelt.

"Horsehead says you missed your last session."

Whoops. He hadn't meant to forget Horsehead.

Now Sondra got on the line. "Evan? Go talk to your professors, honey. Ask them what you can do to salvage a passing grade this semester. You don't have to make A's; just pass. They'll understand." This time his father was the one murmuring in the background— psychiatrists, tuition, car repair, how much would it cost to get this boy back in the saddle? Evan's mother was oddly silent through the entire conversation, a silence that distracted him more than her comments generally did. Maybe it had been Sondra's *honey* that had momentarily flummoxed her. Or it could have been Sondra's superior knowledge of navigating college. But perhaps his mother was more concerned with matters other than paying bills and passing classes.

Roosevelt went with him to find his professors. Sondra had been right about all of them but the dying economics professor, whom Evan mostly disliked yet felt a certain kinship with, and so had signed up for another semester. Dr. Schweiner, yellower than ever, turned his large skeletal head and frightening wild eyebrows on Evan and told him, flat out, that he had already missed his chance to do anything but fail the course.

"That fellow is one hard-ass fellow," Roosevelt noted as they crossed the campus afterward. "And his office, it smells like a zoo."

"Yeah, it did." *Like death,* his mother noted. They sat, as they often did, in the union entryway, watching girls. Their clothing and hair tended to blow around as they came through the doors, an effect Roosevelt particularly enjoyed. Evan looked, but he thought of Merry and her unremarkable corduroy pants, the quick way she could launch herself up on the desk counter, the smooth, slightly oily hair she impatiently tucked behind her ears, the studious frown she employed when writing in her notebook, and the half-smile he'd learned to look for. She was already developing a little wrinkle on her left cheek where that smile had carved its niche.

"I think this university has a larger-than-average population of beautiful women," Roosevelt often said as they tracked the comings and goings of the school's female students. "It cannot be the normal percentage, do you think?"

Normal? Evan did not think he was qualified, or even interested enough, to say.

* * *

"I have to tell you something," he said to Merry one night. This was the night he planned to have sex for the first time. His mother seemed to be humming tunelessly. Evan needed to clear up just the one thing with Merry before he would feel comfortable having sex with her.

"You don't have AIDS," she said without doubt. "And there's no way you're married." She looked him over, turning shy. "And it's perfectly fine with me if you're a virgin. You still want to spend the night, don't you?" Stiffening as if realizing his *something* might be a change of heart.

"For sure," Evan answered, taking her hand, touching the Band-Aids on her overchewed fingertips. They sat on her bed. This was one of her nights off. She lived in a corner room on the top floor of the dormitory, and had no roommate. Her windows were curtainless, overlooking the hill behind the dorm and the campanile beyond. It was as if she lived in a turret, an effect she had emphasized by hanging no posters and using candles as light sources. *A romantic,* Evan's mother noted amid her humming.

"No, it's about my mother," Evan said. "Although I *am* a virgin."

"Oh."

"It's about her cats," Evan clarified. His mother stopped humming, curious, he felt. "When she died, I did some crazy things. One of those things, which by the way I think my mother would have approved of, was to get rid of her cats." (Think? He knew she approved!)

"Get rid of?"

"Yes." The chore had taken him all day. Retelling it, he feared, would take another.

"You *killed* them?" Now Merry withdrew her hand, her expression horrified, betrayed; it would have been less shocking, he thought, to tell her his dead mother was in the room with them. The cat in the basement had become their mutual project, the food they left for it, the bedding behind the clothes dryers.

"No! Not all of them, just the old one, and the wild one, and the

incontinent one. The other three I found homes." Close enough; he'd
left them in pleasant-looking yards.

"Your mother had *six* cats?" Merry said, sidetracked, impressed—
ready, Evan believed, to forgive whatever trespass those three deaths
might have suggested. "That is a lot of cats." She was nodding thoughtfully. He breathed a sigh of relief. He had not lied. He did not tell her
how he had killed the cats; that seemed unnecessary. Let her imagine
a veterinarian with a gentle needle. And now those deaths had begun
to nauseate him, as if someone else had performed them. He knew
that Horsehead and Sondra and even probably his father, though
grudgingly, would say that his grief had overtaken him, forced him to
do what he otherwise would not have done. That he had killed his
mother's cats because he could not bear doing nothing in response to
her death. At the time, the action had seemed merciful—fated by
virtue of the fact that Evan had felt like taking it. No one would love
the toothless twenty-year-old Ginger, nor the hissing, untouchable
Max, and certainly not dumb Denise, hit by a car at an early age and
left brain-injured, peeing on herself. He'd shot them, he thought,
because they were imperfect and helpless and unlovable. Sobbing furi-
ously, he held their warm bloody bodies to his chest, and then, wrung
out, wrapped them in his mother's embroidered floral pillowcases. He
dug the holes and then stood confused and apologetic as he poured
dirt on the bundles. He'd returned his father's handgun to its box in
the study. He'd let the blood dry on his clothes and hands, the count-
less cat hairs caught everywhere, of every color. The syllogism went
something like: *if* only his mother was capable of caring for the cats,
and *if* she were gone, *then* . . .

"My stepmother keeps rabbits," Evan said. In place of the cats, in all
their old haunts, quiet, guileless creatures, prey. *Stepmother,* he'd said.
"They make me nervous."

Merry guided Evan's hand beneath her flannel shirt and onto her
bare breast. There it rose and fell with her breathing, warm, precisely
the size of his cupped fingers and palm.

"I know what you mean," she said. "It's those damn red eyes and twitchy whiskers." Evan felt himself slipping around Merry, her undoing herself before him. His ability to see had fallen away; now she and he were pure sensation.

Had it been Merry or his mother who'd said that about the rabbits? He did not know.

Evan woke with what he believed was called a start. His heart was way ahead of him, hammering uselessly against absolute peace. Never had there been a more silent atmosphere. Merry's dorm room was enough like his own for him to momentarily mistake his surroundings. But where was Roosevelt, and his odor of Dominican detergent and coconut lotion and those bright fried seeds he ate? This place had no odor; instead, a coolness, like a crypt. Yet there came Merry's breathing. In fact, her arm was beneath Evan's neck, the backs of her fingers on his cheek, her calf on his calf, the air from her mouth at his ear, white noise, static. He remembered that she liked to sleep in a cold room; she'd opened the window and the heat flew out, a shimmering flow that poured like a waterfall over the windowsill in the reflected light from the street lamps far below. Before his mother could announce her thoughts on such a practice as leaving the window open, Evan did so himself, thinking the words she would have spoken, *Now we're heating the great outdoors?*

But once issued, these words died unheard, thudding uselessly inside his own head. Evan sat up abruptly, blinking rapidly. His dead mother was no longer here. Merry recoiled from his departure, curling into herself contentedly, fetal. But his mother was gone. It was clear in the chilly air, in the sour scent Merry continued to push forth from her half-parted lips. Evan studied her frantically. What had he traded when he'd stuck his penis inside of her? What had escaped in the exchange? He knew without really chasing the topic very far. His mother had finally left him, two and a half years after having abandoned the rest of the world.

I hope you're happy, he thought desperately, snottily, a big baby shaking his fist at a force of nature, puny mortal to voluminous dead. Lost, utterly lost. And then, like some strange echoing reverberation— as if Merry were briefly speaking in tongues, a voice in the cool noc- turnal wind—he heard his words alternately inflected, returned to him the same but different, unironic, tired, and very, very faint, as if from far away, *And I hope you're happy.*

Heart Shaped Rock

THEY WERE ON that same road again. "Do you see the foxes?" her father asked Jilly, his voice a reverent whisper, his hand straining to point.

"I can't see them from here, Dad." This at least was true. From the hospital window, the hillside was too far. She'd corrected him the first few times, telling him that the motion he saw was not foxes but vehicles on the freeway beneath the mountain, people coming and going on Highway 90, traveling between Butte and Missoula. The view was stunning, not unlike that of a windshield before a driver.

"Ahh! We passed that exit before," her father said dismissively. "You've gotten us lost." He'd never trusted her driving, and now he jerked his head in disgust. When the nurse entered and rounded the bed, he drew in his breath, tried to cover his eyes. It was as if she'd popped onto the dashboard, Jilly thought.

But his hands were bound to the bed rails.

"He doesn't like his meds, do you?" the nurse called out cheerfully.

She was the kind of woman he would have named Lard Ass in another, more virile time. He would have been quick to put her in her place, bland, fat girl, not an ounce of irony in her, gold cross dangling from her neck as she reached around his oxygen and I.V. tubes.

His desperate eyes found Jilly's. He might disparage her driving, but he believed that she was still on his side, complicit in his vision of the world.

"You're in the hospital, hon," shouted the nurse. She wasn't somebody Jilly would have befriended, either, but what she might have lacked in sensibility, she more than made up for in her willingness to lay on hands—at the mouth and genitals—and perform those tasks that the able person performs privately. Jilly didn't want to wipe her father's nose, adjust his bedding, or wrestle him into an intimate half-hug to guide him to the bathroom, let alone assist once he was in there. On the wall hung a box of disposable latex gloves that the nurses employed as casually as Kleenex. "It's Tuesday, and you're in intensive care."

"Tell me something I don't know," he grumbled. He had in his arsenal of rejoinders some all-purpose ones, aphoristic oddities that sounded, more or less, appropriate. *What's time to a hog? He who laughs last. Now is the summer of my discontent.* How long had he been letting them substitute for true responses?

"Okay, mister, spit." The nurse cupped her hand beneath his chin, and he sure enough discharged a wad of gum into it. Before he could fully close his lips, she slipped in three small pills, tipped a paper cup of water to his mouth, and then, while he completed the last stage of surprised swallowing, she poked the gum back in, wiping with her sheathed finger at the corners of his frown. He hadn't had time to resist. Then she snapped off the gloves, wrote a note or two in the nurses' notebook, and trundled away. "I'll catch you later, honey," she called.

Her father frowned at Jilly. "What was that bitch on about?"

Jilly shrugged.

*   *   *

She wouldn't be able to afford the hotel room for long, but she'd been kicked out of the St. Francis House, where the bereaved and waiting families usually stayed. First she'd brought liquor into the place, which she had agreed not to do, and then she'd lit the bed on fire. She'd been trying to locate her book in the middle of the night and had used her cigarette lighter to search. The underside of the box springs went up instantly. It was an old, old bed.

At least her hosts had not known about her overnight guest the night before. He hadn't been allowed, either.

At the Sleep Inn, you shut the door to your room and did whatever you wanted. Jilly uncorked her bottle of wine and called her ex-husband in Tucson. He hadn't heard about her dad yet, and he'd liked the old man. "No one found him for at least thirty-six hours," Jilly said. It hadn't been clear whether he was performing the morning or evening chores on his property. If the sheriff hadn't come over to reprimand him for violating the water restrictions, he might still be pinned between truck bumper and shed wall. "Now he's in and out of lucidity." Her ex snorted, as if to say that had always been the case. "He thinks we're on a car trip—he's got a great view from his room—but why he's letting me drive is a mystery."

"So he can drink," Pete guessed.

"Yeah." Jilly poured herself another glass of wine. "Although here in Montana, it's not illegal to drink and drive."

"That a fact?" He had a sexy voice. Sometimes it seemed mistaken to have left him. If only they could have kept being married over the telephone, in two homes, and only in the evening, after they'd each had a drink and softened up. But his desires had been of the conventional husbandly sort—shared meals, children, gentle familiar sex—and Jilly couldn't satisfy them. Wouldn't, anyway. Eventually he'd had to give up. He'd begun an affair, which had led to marriage counseling. Their therapist required them to make promises, one thing each would do for the other. "Leave her," Jilly said, not believing he would abandon his affair. She'd driven him to it, and he deserved to have it. Yet he wanted to be told to quit; he'd been waiting, it seemed. Jilly was like his mother, perhaps, catching him, punishing him, then forgiving him. But she wasn't his mother. He quit the affair and she punished without forgiving, punished by not caring enough to forgive.

His request of her had seemed simple: "Stop drinking?" That question mark was a piece of punctuation too flimsy to save a marriage. An exclamation mark might have made all the difference.

Exquisite torture, her father had named his marriage to Jilly's mother.

In the background at Pete's house in Arizona, Jilly heard a baby cry.

"You should go," she said.

"Your dad would call me pussy-whipped."

The warm wine, plus general languor, kept Jilly from telling Pete the much worse things her father had routinely called him. But really, what man would her father have wanted her to marry? She couldn't imagine.

Every day there was a new tube stuck in the old man. A new tube in him, and another restraining strap around him. He was dying, Jilly understood; he had internal bleeding that could not be stopped. But he would fight. Had he ever gone anywhere easily?

"You calm him down," the nurse flattered Jilly, touching her arm. "We've all noticed it." In the night, he'd given one of the aides a black eye. Security had been summoned; no one on the floor had slept well.

But he smiled placidly when Jilly sat beside his bed, in the driver's seat. "I love those pups," he said of the foxes on the distant hillside. No doubt there were foxes on the hill, though they wouldn't yet be ready to emerge from their dens. Come midsummer, they would be everywhere in Montana, with their sharp, sentient faces and swift grace. They rolled and pounced like familiar pets, like cats or dogs, and it was impossible not to find them comical. In her youth, Jilly had been taken evening after evening to locate them around the small town where she'd grown up, eighty miles south of here.

"Now, I did love to tie flies," her father confessed to her, as if she'd asked. He was whispering. His theatrics in the night had ravaged his vocal cords. His hands were clasped together at his chest, over the thin fabric of the hospital gown. This outfit embarrassed Jilly, polka-dotted, emasculating. The placement of his hands reminded him of other occupations. He demonstrated casting a fly line. This gesture led to another, throwing horseshoes. "You have to rock forward on your toes, then back on your heels."

"Yeah," she agreed. He studied his fingers before his face, not seeming to understand why he'd put them this way. He'd brutalized the aide by swinging the double fist into her temple. Now he picked at the elastic glove that was holding an I.V. tube in his wrist. He'd explained a number of times that he didn't feel a need for it, nor the pretzel of oxygen tubing at his nose.

"Jilly?" he whispered, closing his eyes.

"I'm here, Dad." She put her hand on his. Having lived with him, she didn't find it difficult to follow his thoughts. They circled around the family land, Jilly's uncle, Jilly herself, her mother—the acres he'd sold to a man who lied about his plans for it, his brother's objection to that same sale, his daughter's need for the money, and, long before, his wife's death, that abandonment. These things were related to one another. Every day Jilly felt as if she'd entered into another of his dreams with him, a surreal place where all the parts were understandable but completely mixed up, a confusion of time, character, and event. They were driving, they'd missed their turn; her inattention was to blame. His anger was momentary; before she knew it, he was enjoying the foxes again. People, and his obligations to them, confounded him; his mind sought out creatures for relief. When he located the animals, he seemed younger. Somebody shaved him every morning before she arrived, and he'd had various moles on his forehead and cheeks removed since the last time she'd seen him. Yet it wasn't these cosmetic alterations that had transformed him. It was the relieved, neutral face he wore in between waves of emotion. Rage, perplexity, nostalgia: three gears he more and more frequently idled among, lost, gone. Jilly never would have guessed she preferred anger to absence.

"Trees?" he said. The flush of plumbing next door had recalled for him his trees.

"They're fine," she answered. "Dan is watering them." Her uncle, who had phoned her in L.A., had waited like a sentry outside her father's hospital room door while she trekked across three states, then he'd disappeared when she arrived. "I've got to get to the watering, the feeding," he'd claimed, practically sprinting from the building. In addition to the flock of sheep they kept, the two men had planted a forest of aspens and spruce on their family's land. Sheep were notoriously foolish, and the trees required more water than the region's rainfall provided. Uncle Dan and her father shared not only their stubborn caretaking jobs at the property but a physical resemblance as well— rangy and rugged, temperamental, handsome in their uneasy social manners. They were men made queasy by illness, by weakness of any sort. When Dan's ranch dogs had displeased him, he'd shot them. "Good thing he hasn't got children" was her father's only comment.

They'd both dated Jilly's mother, if *dated* was the word. The brothers lived on eight hundred acres in the Bitterroot Valley, outside of Hamilton in the hills. They had been raised on this property, sent away by their father to serve in Korea, then to be properly educated, and later restored to the ranch. They hid their education from their neighbors, refused to discuss the war, voted in every election without fail and wouldn't tell anybody how. Spent their evenings reading books; open the door, you'd hear Mozart on the stereo. Jilly's mother had lived with them, a wild runaway girl who'd shown up in 1959 and stuck around for twenty years. The relationships had at first been casual— Jilly's mother shared herself with the men like a hooker or a housekeeper—until pregnancy complicated the arrangement.

Jilly's father was her father because he didn't object. He didn't relish the role, but he'd agreed. He was the elder brother, and therefore occasionally called upon to shoulder such burdens. When she wanted to scandalize a new acquaintance, Jilly would tell her life story, leading up to the punch line, which was that she didn't know for a fact that her father was her father, that it could just as easily be her uncle. She had spent her adult years using that information like currency, her odd life as both trump card and disclaimer.

Jilly had driven away from L.A. without a plan other than aiming herself at Missoula. Outside Reno, Nevada, her eyes burning from uninterrupted squinting at the road, she called her cousin. Rudy, the sole relation Jilly knew on her mother's side, lived there with his girlfriend and her children. Over the phone, he offered his couch, but by the time Jilly arrived at his house, the girlfriend had prevailed, and Rudy got a motel room for Jilly instead.

When they were young, Rudy had been sent to Montana to stave off his certain delinquency. Rudy's mother must have been desperate, Jilly later thought, trusting her runaway sister to look after the boy on the ranch. From the time they were little, the two cousins had kissed and groped and fondled, then later shared their first sexual shenanigans, telling themselves that as long as they didn't actually have intercourse, it wasn't disgusting. Summer after summer, they'd been each other's plaything. Apparently, in the time it had taken Jilly to cover the distance between the outskirts of Reno and his front door, Rudy had mistakenly confessed all of this to the girlfriend.

"What, does she think we're going to hook up tonight?"

Rudy laughed. "Maybe. She didn't like your looks, I guess."

"She didn't even see me."

"Well, she's pretty sixth-sensey." They were in a bar on the strip, drinking vodka tonics. They'd done this when they were teenagers, too, when he'd come for his annual visit, stealing bottles from Uncle Dan and climbing into the woods, drinking under the scrub trees, up in the mine ruins, letting the liquor and the privacy of the abandoned landscape lead them to their bodies. It had never seemed wrong.

In Reno they got drunk and ended up in Jilly's motel room, lying clothed on the bed, her face at his throat. "You're the best kisser," Jilly murmured to her cousin. She made a fist and he enclosed it with his rough hand, just the way he always had. They'd never had more than a seasonal engagement; this evening would do no harm. The objects in his pants pockets—knife, key ring, lighter—chafed against Jilly's hipbone, made her ache pleasantly for what they weren't going to do. Always it had been this way between them, intoxicated, unconsummated desire.

"Tell your dad hey," Rudy said, holding her at the door just before dawn. Only then did she notice the tattoo on his bicep, a yellow Tweety Bird. When she touched it, he confessed that Crystal had one just like it.

"What's she gonna think, you here all night with me?"

"I'll suffer," he said, sighing.

She met his red eyes with her own, bit his lower lip, hard enough to maybe leave a mark, give Crystal a scare. "Bye, Rudy." After watching his truck bounce out of the parking lot, Jilly decided she might as well get on the road. She wouldn't be able to sleep, anyway.

Some days her father thought he was in a kitchen, and that he was preparing mutton stew. His hands, then, held a knife. The sink was his at home, the scarred enamel basin, and Jilly was herself, learning how to make the best of an old, tough animal. When she sneezed, her father blamed it on the paprika. "What is going on?" he cried out when her sneezing wouldn't stop, impatient as ever with Jilly's inability to control herself. "I don't know," she squeezed out between explosions. Embarrassing. How had it happened that she—bathed, dressed, vertical—was the one in the room blushing?

"There's two kinds of paprika," he went on. "A handful of one is like a teaspoon of the other." Wine, he recommended, no need to buy the expensive stuff.

"He cooking again?" asked the nurse who came to change his I.V. line. "He cooks up a storm, but he won't eat a thing. You have to eat," she shouted at him. "We're gonna have to stick a tube in your tummy if you don't eat." Her father blinked in alarm. Who was this loud woman in his kitchen? The nurses might twitter gamely at his rambling, but Jilly wondered how long they'd laugh if they saw his home.

He had an indoor and an outdoor kitchen, outfitted for the slaughtering, draining, and dressing out of animals. The cooking was the penultimate step, then eating—no side dishes, just meat and bourbon. A set of knives lay ever ready on the table. The place resembled a torture chamber, dark, smelling of blood, and full of sharp implements that looked more like weapons than utensils. Cooking, in that kitchen, didn't seem such a harmless pursuit. He looked at the nurse as if he were taking her measure for the spit. He'd flayed creatures larger than she, plenty of times.

"He's giving me the hairy eyeball," she said playfully. He could kill you, Jilly thought. Would the woman be alarmed by the savage thoroughness of his fantasy? Should Jilly have been alarmed by her own ability to so confidently know the contents of her father's mind? The nurse winked as she left, so saucy and sure of herself.

"Mutton always made me gag," Jilly told her father. "All oily."

"You have to know how to prepare it," her father said. "Get me the big Dutch oven, that first." He motioned toward the television, which, if the sink were his sink, was where the black cast-iron Dutch oven would be hanging. If Jilly opened the window shade and positioned herself on the other side of the bed, they would be in the car again.

He had a marvelous view, and it wasn't exactly wasted on him. But he might have seen anything in it, so it seemed generous to wish that some more cognizant patient could have the full glory of the mountain, the highway, the train track and frequently passing boxcars, pretty as beads on a string, snaking along the river. Church steeples, chimneys, flash of lightning, flock of birds.

Later, another nurse came to walk him around, pull him out of bed and expose his naked ass. Shifting her glance to the nurse, Jilly hated her instinct to think like her father and uncle, the critical eye that saw an ugly, unsexual being—nothing more. Not a person, not a professional, not a woman with skills and tolerance beyond the reasonable call of duty, but an ugly female they'd label *dog* or *cow*.

"I don't think those are foxes," her father said feebly when he returned from the bathroom, when Jilly had opened the shades and put herself to his left side. "They might be rats, they're so furtive." The same traffic rolled steadily along the road, to and from. Behind his head, the bed's engine recovered with a whirring, adjusting beneath him to prevent bedsores or blood clots. This elusive noise made him pause and blink; he accounted for it differently, guessing at its source. Sometimes it was a train. Sometimes a storm approaching. Geese passing overhead.

"Dan," he said rustily. Jilly followed the association, the geese he thought he heard reminding him of his brother, who was a hunter. At the sound of birds, he would turn skyward, narrow his eye, and wish for his rifle.

He'd kill birds and field-dress deer, but her uncle wouldn't visit the hospital. When Jilly had first shown up, he was sitting in the waiting area beneath a poster showing a choking victim, tapping a rolled magazine on his knee. His physical resemblance to her father always threw her, as if the two were interchangeable, lean, ropy men with high foreheads and iron-gray hair, twitchy with impatience. They looked younger than they were because they had not let themselves submit to age, because they dressed tidily and did not appear in public in anything less than long pants and a button-down shirt. Once her father had been tied into a nightgown, her uncle wouldn't enter the room.

"I had to fight with him to get him to come here," Dan had said, showing her the purple gashes on his hand. "He just knew I was out to kill him. You don't want to hear what I had to do." He laughed. "Electric tape, you can't guess what all. It's good to see you, sweetheart." He hugged her hard and passed off the magazine like a baton, his sweating fingers having left a kind of twisted handle. Dan walked out of the building then and hadn't been back. She would not ask him to come, nor would her father request it. The code they shared said that they did not witness each other's diminishment.

Having to explain this to the curious nurses made Jilly aware of how complex the rules were. If her uncle visited, things would never be the same later, at home. Hard enough for their close brotherhood to have survived Jilly, the arrival of encumbrance and mess. A swing set and sandbox—wind socks, riding toys—littering the landscape; curtains and rugs—tampons, cosmetics—altering the home. The kittens Jilly had begged for, who were later killed by her uncle's mower. First Jilly's mother was taken from Dan by her pregnancy; then motherhood had claimed her, and finally cancer had fully removed her. Jilly could recall the tension between her mother and uncle, the way they disagreed about most everything, although never in any blatant way. Her mother probably had the same kind of make-believe arguments with Dan that Jilly did, arguments held exclusively in her head, her own voice and his, responding. *You haven't left Montana in forty years!* she might lob at him, or *How would you know, never having been married? Never having had a child?* Her father became the common fond fulcrum, the referee, arbiter, object. And Jilly? If she'd been her uncle's dog, she might have been shot a dozen times over. For wandering off as a toddler. For the same as a teenager. For bringing liberal college scorn to the house. For complaining about her family's drinking too much, then drinking too much herself. For becoming the kind of woman who spent hours at the bars, thereby ruining them for her uncle. But mostly, Jilly came to see, her biggest crime, the most outrageous trouble she was responsible for, was separating them. They'd shared a woman for many years, with the identical understanding of what it meant. The brothers had agreed in their youth not to have babies. They did not want to care for or about children. And once one of these men had become her father, he was no longer first and foremost a brother.

The stranger she'd met at the bar called Gentle Ben's had been older than she'd thought. He'd followed her to the St. Francis House, and she'd been too drunk to resist. It was her first night back in Montana, the first night since she'd left L.A. that she actually slept. She'd fallen asleep as he had his way with her, the limp nonresponse seeming perfectly acceptable to him. Drunk, he probably had to concentrate on his own performance. She'd made him sneak out before the other people in the house woke. A stringy couple whose daughter had been in a single-car accident, an old man whose wife had had a stroke, a stunned son whose father was on dialysis. In the kitchen, they all drank weak coffee and ate moist packaged muffins. You could speak, or not, and nobody would think you unfriendly. Jilly sat tentatively among them, grateful to discover that her guilt and hangover seemed to resemble grief and therefore required no explanation.

She would miss them when she was asked to leave.

"How's it going today?" the ubiquitous fat nurse inquired aggressively, entering the room without knocking. Her father had assigned them different names: Mud Slide. Hulga. Thunder Thighs. Were these girls used to his type, the rough-hewn Montana man with his crosshatched neck and sharp eyeteeth? Or weren't they from here? Were the other men on the hall just as difficult, or did her father stand out?

"We're just careening down the highway," he said gleefully to this one. "The sheriff's right behind us."

She snorted. "You better slow down, fella."

"She's got a lead foot," he said of Jilly. He held up his linked hands. "And here I am, hog-tied." Her father had never been arrested, that Jilly knew of, but she thought the restraints might remind him of handcuffs, which perhaps had led to the sheriff. Of course, you didn't have to be arrested to wear those.

"I'm getting your blood pressure, buddy," the nurse said, squatting onto a rolling stool and paddling with her feet around the bed. She had chin whiskers, tiny lensed glasses, a bun of hair on her head. "You gonna help me today? Be a happy camper?"

Why this patronizing prattle? Why the ridiculous smiley faces on the reports? Why the stuffed animals at the station or clipped to their stethoscopes? The candy they kept in a plastic pig? It wasn't just that they treated their patients like children, they indulged childishness in themselves and one another.

But over the days, from the I.C.U. to the neuro unit, Jilly's scorn toward the nurses—the scorn she'd grown up with, toward softness—

had transformed into a kind of awe. The nurses did not flinch when her father made outrageous comments. They did not avert their eyes or bristle, they steadily plowed forward, in comfortable clothes, sensible shoes, balancing a medical background against a flighty fixation on something silly. Either God or a cartoon creature, some icon adorning each and every one of them, gave away a lapse in purely rational thinking. What was it about? Jilly had put them in a lumpy category, but she was rethinking it now.

"He's a tough bird," this one said fondly. She wore teddy-bear scrubs, a Hello Kitty charm bracelet. The father Jilly had grown up with would have retorted skillfully, witheringly, reducing this ninny to tears. But he had been stripped not only of his clothes but of his physical freedom, of almost every bodily function, of most of his mind. In this, the kingdom of nurses, lesser beings might have tyrannized. Yet the worst these did was approach with brusqueness, plunge a cold hand here, jab a sharp needle there. Yell inanities into his face.

Her hair, she had confessed to Jilly, touching the bun on her head, reached the floor.

"Why?" Jilly asked.

The nurses believed his condition was improving, but Jilly knew better. He'd been more often himself the first day—enraged, unkind. Now he was growing docile. He'd slipped into and gotten stuck in nostalgia. He would have been ashamed of this maudlin self, these fat tears of self-pity. He wouldn't have tolerated himself for a second.

"But *all* of the rocks are heart-shaped," her father said now, plaintively, playing his part in a tender argument. "Your mother's rocks." He was gazing off toward the hillside again. "But they were all . . ."

"Yeah. She always thought she was being so particular." In the yard at home her mother had made a kind of cairn, a collection of stones she picked up on her walks or rides, of two basic shapes. One was the symmetrical valentine, the rocks that formed jagged approximate V's. The other shape was the hard fist of the actual human heart, atrial passage like a lifted thumb. Most rocks conformed to these, given squinting appreciation, which had been a joke with Jilly and her father: what rock *wasn't* heart-shaped? When her mother died, when her casket had been lowered into the ground in the family graveyard at the far northwest corner of the property, Jilly and her father brought the rocks there in the back of Dan's pickup. Unloading, the two of them gently tossed the collection to the damp black square of sod, leaving a strange tumbled shrine to the woman who was buried there.

Jilly went to the bar she'd frequented in college almost twenty years earlier. She'd come here a few nights ago with the fireman after the bed had burned. "Drinking *and* smoking," the brittle old nun who ran the St. Francis House had accused. "Both!" No point in explaining that Jilly had refrained from smoking inside. The evidence—empty bottles, smoldering mattress—said otherwise. Afterward, the fireman had taken her first to the bar, then to his house on Higgins, a house just across the street from an apartment building where Jilly had once had to fight off a potential rapist. There'd been a party and a fair amount of LSD. Maybe that guy from long ago hadn't been intending to rape her. Maybe she had agreed to have sex with him. Appraising the building from the fireman's front porch, Jilly felt its dark shadow subsiding, diluted by the questions time brought up for her. In her mind, the place had acquired a haunted status, but looking at it now, with its windows lit, harmless cars stubbed along its base, bats swinging from the eves into and out of the swarm of bugs, she couldn't feel menaced.

The fireman was too timid for her taste. He kept asking permission. "Can I kiss you?" he said. "Does that feel good? Do you want to move to the bedroom?" She held her tongue, wishing he'd do the same. Eventually she rolled irritably from his mattress and claimed concern about her father as the reason she couldn't go on. And of course the fireman totally understood. Could he give her a ride?

He wasn't in the bar tonight, but someone else she knew was. Would anybody in L.A. believe just how small this giant state of Montana was? Mr. Robins, father of her first boyfriend, Tony. She knew him, but he wouldn't remember her. His son Tony had been a wild teenager, someone Jilly had met at a party in the woods the summer she was fifteen and he was sixteen. There, on the edge of a bonfire, a face in the wavering flames that had focused on her and never shifted. He lived in Missoula but had friends in Hamilton, near Jilly's home. For the length of that summer, they'd been together every night. They got together to have sex, to let its surprise spring them open again and again. Off they drove in his truck, drinking that cheap beer Jilly'd seen nowhere else, the cans decorated with pictures of wildlife. They hardly spoke, simply smiled shyly, smoked cigarettes, then fell back into pure carnal happiness. She had loved him because her body loved his. It was the most mysterious of loves, she understood now, years into the future. It was the rarest to find, the saddest to miss.

When he had abruptly cut her off at the start of the school year, it was his father who'd taken her desperate phone calls. "Do not call here," he'd threatened. "I don't know who you think you are or what you think you're doing, but Tony is done with you. Done!"

She was as physically devastated as she had been enthralled, as if she'd been cut off from the source of an addiction, one that left her humiliated, body and soul. She lay on her bed, feeling as if she would spin out of control, disappear, die. Losing him was more painful an experience than losing her mother, which had happened two years earlier, and recognizing that fact further derailed Jilly. What kind of girl missed a boy—a boy she'd known for only one summer, and with whom she'd exchanged no more than a hundred total words—more than her mother?

For years she replayed that summer with Tony, trying to pinpoint the mistake she'd made with him, the reason he'd so suddenly and thoroughly found her unworthy. She blamed his father, since he had been the last person who'd said anything to her about Tony. When she moved to Missoula to attend school, she made a point of seeking out the family, Tony and his parents. She saw them occasionally around town. His father was a wealthy man who'd taken early retirement to move to Missoula from New York. He could be found at the bars ogling the college girls, or at the library or university swimming pool, doing the same. Over the years, Jilly had kept up with Tony via rumors or newspaper articles. He'd joined the navy, he'd been dismissed from the navy, he'd gotten married and then his wife had left him, he'd opened a restaurant and then declared bankruptcy, his parents had divorced and then his mother had died, he'd moved to Alaska then back. A pattern of attempts—to grow up, to move on—and subsequent failures. And just last year, out of the blue, he'd killed himself. Age thirty-nine, living alone in Missoula, arrested one too many times for DUI, he'd been dropped off at his trailer by the officer who'd ticketed him, and there he'd used a gun to blow himself away.

At suicide he'd been successful.

If she drank too much, Jilly might sidle up to Tony's father at the bar and tell him what she thought, that he'd doomed his son long ago in insisting that he break up with her. Was that even remotely feasibly the truth? That Jilly could have made any difference whatsoever in Tony's life? And was it only that phone call, that long-ago heartbreaking conversation, that made her think it was the father who'd determined what happened next?

Mr. Robins stared at the television hanging in the corner of the bar. A sports channel cutting from one event to another without sound. Of course, as usual with people, his punishment outweighed his crime. What possible point would there be in making it worse?

"Hey, Mr. Robins," Jilly said on her way out an hour later. He looked up, startled, taking her in without recognition. "I was a friend of Tony's. I just wanted to say I was really sorry to hear what happened."

He smiled weakly. Like her own father, he'd lost his ability to frighten her. He didn't know who she was, didn't know what he'd done to her, didn't deserve to be reminded.

The next day the nurses were discussing a woman in the news. They switched on the set in each of the rooms they visited, wanting to keep up with the details. "Have you been following this?" they would ask, giddy. A woman in Philadelphia had recovered her daughter six years after having been told the girl had disappeared in a fire. The fire had suspicious origins, and there'd been no body, but the firemen had informed the mother that her baby had burned up. Then, six years later, the woman had discovered her girl at a birthday party in the neighborhood. Today she was being awarded custody of that child. Each and every nurse who came into Jilly's father's room was eager to see how the saga had been resolved.

"Clever cunt," her father said as the one he called Mud Slide waved from the door.

"You mean the nurse or the woman on TV?"

He indicated the set, where the mother and her daughter were flashing an identical broad smile. Jilly had a flinching sensation in her chest, then investigated the reflex. *Clever cunt.* Why would he say this, and why would it hurt her? Because that woman had wanted her child back so badly? Because her father never would have gone to such lengths? Seek his girl out at a birthday party, stick gum in her hair, and then yank it free in order to take the stickiness to the lab, where science would substantiate his claim in no uncertain terms? How handy it would have been, thirty-eight years ago, for someone desperate to have come through the open window of infant Jilly's bedroom and spirit her away, lighting a fire in the room to explain the loss. The thief wouldn't even have had to leave a fire.

The mother on television *had* been clever. When her daughter had disappeared, she hadn't spoken enough English to take on the authorities, to demand an explanation of there being no body. Yet, six years later, she'd become savvy enough to prove her case, not only speaking English but speaking biological technology. Today, as the child was restored to the woman, Jilly heard her say what she felt: "Thank *God* for DNA!"

Maybe that was how to understand the nurses here at St. Francis's, nurses wearing crosses, nurses who passed under the guiding visage of Saint Francis each morning when they entered the building. Thank God, they said, for the miracles of man and science.

* * *

Her father's last doctor was a woman. He was moved out of the neuro unit one Saturday night and back to intensive care. This change of venue mimicked his dilemma: was the injury the cause of his dementia, or had the delusions brought on his accident? When Jilly arrived that Sunday morning, he was neither asleep nor awake but in some other realm, like purgatory. "He's obtunded," the nurse said. "That's his primary condition, poor guy." His feet were uncovered, turned inward like Christ's on the cross, and he whimpered in his restraints. Jilly and three nurses were trying to rouse him when the doctor arrived. She entered the room wearing bike-racing regalia, slim and muscled, her bike shoes clacking like spurs on the tiled floor. Jilly instantly straightened her posture, stepped away from the drama so as to notify this doctor that She Wasn't Involved. The Daughter Was Different.

The doctor scanned Jilly and found her apparently dismissible. What part, Jilly wondered, had disappointed the doctor's efficient gaze? Perhaps velvet, as a fabric, should be permanently retired? The doctor had tiny colorful stones lining her ears, Jilly recognized them as opals, the whole array, punched into the flesh like rivet studs, fashionable piercings adorning a functionally shaved scalp. It was she who would tell Jilly the next morning that her father had died. This woman alone of the pack of them seemed like somebody her father might have respected. Trim, serious, intelligent, brutal, in her way. It was Sunday morning and she'd been not at church but out on her bike. Her stethoscope was not covered in a cartoon-animal slipcover. Her hair was the same thick silver as Jilly's father's, she was a dignified woman, a woman whose lover was probably also a woman, her *partner*. Early the next day, she would shake hands with Jilly and express her regrets. She would request permission to autopsy his brain for educational purposes.

"I recommend you no-code him," she said to Jilly, meaning that no resuscitating measures would be taken. "It's time." Her uncle, it turned out, had coded him for everything. But Jilly undid Dan's work with a simple signature, less sentimental, it appeared, than he.

In the motel room Sunday night, she waited for the hospital to phone with the news. The hours passed, she could not sleep. She flopped from side to side in the bed, kicked until she uncovered herself, then remade the bed and tucked herself in again. Turned on the light, switched it off, surrounded herself with pillows, threw them off. Drank water, took pills, read a book, tried the television. At five in the morning, she finally found herself exhausted and lay flat on her back, relieved to sense herself succumbing. Just before she fell off, she caught the sharp whiff of fire in the air. It couldn't be, and yet she smelled the sulfur, as if someone had lit a match in the space between her bed and the empty one beside her. And then she slept.

They'd sold land to send Jilly to college, to buy her a car, to make investments that were supposed to save her. She could feel the waste her uncle believed those sacrificed acres had been, the negligible yield. Encroaching housing developments were far too high a price to pay for a young woman's whimsy, her bad grades and ingratitude. The car had been totaled before a year was up.

Her father had taught her how to drive; her uncle had taught her how to drive drunk.

Jilly pulled into the yard to see a few stray sheep staring blankly at her. The trees dripped water that was turning to ice; the bright red A-frames of her childhood swing set still stood, empty chains dangling from the crossbar. On the hillside adjacent to her father's house, her uncle's place looked abandoned. He would be in Hamilton at the Kokomo, the same excuse he'd had for not finding her father pinned in the shed for a day and a half. At nine o'clock, the sky held the orange of a setting sun, and the faint purple smudge of distant forest fires. Lightning had started the dry timber. You could wish for rain, but then you ended up with fire. That was the story of Montana, Jilly thought.

She hadn't been home for many years, although she'd clearly imagined this place as her father had described cooking mutton here. This kitchen that would have shocked the nurse squad, its masculine fittings, smoke shed, meat hooks, the scent of animal, the stain of blood. Throughout the place, tackle and fishing equipment dominated, heads on the walls, bones on the shelves. It was dusty, stale, grim; with a need to act, Jilly began cleaning. By the time her uncle found her, she was taking apart the vacuum cleaner, cursing, hand held above her head to minimize bleeding. "The fishing line," she explained. It had been sucked into the machine, wound tight as if on purpose around the vacuum's roller. At the end, a barbed hook. Her uncle snipped it out of the web of her hand, squinting yet still not wearing glasses. He was vain that way. He couldn't see her tears, either, which was preferable to both of them.

"They left a message on my machine," Dan said, twisting the severed hook in his fingers.

"Yeah."

"Ah, hell." This would be the extent of his public grief. The two of them would bury her father by her mother in the small family cemetery, under the scattered heart-shaped stones. Her uncle gave her his all-purpose smile. He had not been marked by tenderness. Upon hearing of his only brother's death, he'd drunk enough liquor this evening to lay flat an ordinary man, yet here he was, cordial, contained—no commitments to deplete him, untouched by entanglement of any sort. Was this why it was he and not her father, nor her mother, who was still alive? Was that why he seemed vaguely relieved that his brother, his oldest friend, had been dispensed with? He and Jilly worked in the kitchen together without speaking, then sat to eat. "Hey, good-looking," he would say to her as he left the house after midnight, after their shared meal of elk meat and alcohol, slapping her ass—fondly, flatteringly. This was the man she would be left with, this one and no other.

✐ Rear View

WHEN I WAS YOUNG, our winter wear wouldn't have permitted anyone to look sexy. The look then was like the inflated figures in a Macy's
parade, puffy and down-stuffed, colorful rubber boots, with pom-
poms on the hats our mothers knitted, matching mittens hanging on
yarn from our coat sleeves. Fashion didn't have in mind sprinting
along the highway on a bitter frozen day in muscle-sheathing elastic
fabrics, costumed from head to foot like a superhero. Running hard,
the jogger on the highway shoulder outside Telluride had every straining tendon and ligament, every flex and thrust, defined in his shining
black outfit. His mouth made a white grimace under his yellow bug-
like goggles. Velocity Man, on his way to save the day.

And on a Sunday, no less. I had braked when I saw him, hobbling
my old Saab apologetically toward the center line to be sure he understood I knew he possessed the moral high road, hiding my smoldering cigarette beneath the dash as if he cared. I was wondering if I was
pregnant, banking on a rumor I'd heard that nothing you did during
the first ten days of pregnancy affected the fetus in the least. A grace

85

period, some stepping-down time from your bad habits. God's air lock. And then, amazingly, there was my brother, also on the highway shoulder, but not wearing Lycra. Not likely. He was climbing into the passenger side of his car. I pulled up behind it, assuming he'd stopped to pee or that the car had broken down again. We were two miles from town on the only road into it.

"Beer?" Sonny asked, unsurprised when I opened his driver's-side door. There was a box of cans on the backseat.

"No, thanks. What's going on?"

"I'm taking a break."

"From what?"

"Getting this heap home." His heater blew; the day, mid-April and barely into spring, had begun with rain down in Grand Junction, but up here, naturally, it alternated between snow and hail, soft ice or harsh. On the windshield, the snowflakes melted upon contact. This was the treacherous seasonal moment when it seemed that winter might never end, that summer was a sappy dream left over from a storybook. "What are *you* up to?" he asked.

"Back from the bin." I blushed, but my brother wouldn't ask where I'd spent the night, or who with. On Saturdays, I drove the 125 miles to Grand Junction to visit my husband, then slept at another man's house. He and I went out drinking at the Junction bars, which were different from the Telluride bars. Happier, I thought. Younger, this time of year, while the junior college was still in session, and certainly no dumber. Up in Telluride, the ski runs had shut down and the party animals had gone home. Their hosts were vaguely sour, used and disillusioned. The slopes had turned treacherous, glazed with ice like glass. Off-season.

"How's Larry doing? Close that door. It's a witch's tit."

I tossed the cigarette butt over the car and onto the bike path, then settled into the driver's seat of the Nova. Sonny had bought it just recently to restore, and its interior smelled like hound dog and its prey. "You should drink whiskey, if you're so cold."

"Don't go there," he said, shaking his head, finishing the beer. His gloves were wool, without fingers because he'd snipped them off.

"He's fine," I told him, concerning Larry. "He says he meets really interesting people in the hospital. He says he's still achieving nirvana at least once a day, when they let him have the solarium to himself. He asked me to bring him his bridge books next week so he can teach one of the other patients how to play, try to wrestle up a foursome . . ." I sighed. "I don't think he's planning on coming home anytime soon. He likes it there."

"What's not to like? Nirvana every day?"

"That's what he claims."

"Although I could never get bridge straight."

"Me, neither."

Sonny popped another top and drained half the can. Because it was diet beer, he could drink twice as much. He'd asked me to pick up more for him, down in Junction where it was cheaper, and I'd forgotten. I was forgetful. He said, "You wanna do me a favor?"

"What's that?"

"Drive me back to my truck." He threw a thumb over his shoulder.

I craned around and saw Big Red, sitting a few hundred yards behind, also on the roadside. Its roomy cab and rounded edges made it seem homey, smiling grille and side mirrors like little ears, snow on its roof like a flattop haircut, a jolly destination on a gloomy day. "I like Big Red," I said, "but this car seems kind of cursed."

"She's been manhandled." He patted the cracked dash. Overhead, dusty material sagged. Blond dog hair clung to everything, a few downy feathers, dank undercurrent of dead fish. A hunter had owned it before he had a heart attack out in the woods alone. At auction, Sonny had been the only bidder. Such was the advantage of being so out of step with the rest of Telluride, where the Range Rovers ruled. Today, because the Nova had needed a valve job, my brother had been driving the two vehicles home by himself, leapfrogging the five miles from his friend's illegal garage down the canyon.

"Drive ahead, run on back," he explained, running his fingers like legs. "Drive ahead, run on back."

"In those boots? Why didn't you wait and let me help you this afternoon? Or tomorrow?" It went without saying that his wife wouldn't help; she wasn't finished avenging herself on him for some past bad behavior.

"I needed the car now." Sonny was simple that way; he wanted something, he went and got it, even if it meant running some portion of the distance home in freezing sleet, wearing his logger's boots and ball cap and cut-up gloves. What portion? I wondered. The whole five miles? Ten, since he had to shuttle back and forth? This was one of those story problems math teachers are always trying to persuade you will come up in your real life. "I reckon we could figure a better method," he said, "now there's two of us."

"But now there's three cars."

"Damned if they don't still have us outnumbered."

The state trooper rushed by, heading out of town with his lights on and his siren off.

"Go, Smokey, go," urged my brother, tossing his empty on the floorboard.

The bartender back in Grand Junction hadn't been the one from the night before. I was just glad the place was open on Sunday; I hadn't realized it was also a diner.

"I'm here to pick up my credit card."

He was the daytime tender, too young, soft from TV and Pop-Tarts and higher education, somebody who could handle no more difficult patron than the elders, the early risers who opened the place at ten to order hard fried eggs and red beer. A few of them leaned over the bar, still as wax figures, occupying every other stool, eyes an easy blur behind fudgy lenses. Cigarette smoke, at this hour, smelled somehow fresh rather than noxious, like a bristling campfire at dawn, complete with the odor of bacon wafting about.

"I don't find a card," the youth reported, sniffing. He had a hell of a cold, a bead of clear mucus moving in and out of his nostril as he breathed. His inner eyelids looked drawn on with red ink.

"Well." It was so exhausting, the missing credit card, the long chain reaction. And the place was warm, smelling of fried pork. I decided to delay the labor, the retracing of my steps. "How about a Bloody Mary?" The bartender took a second to decide whether to ask for I.D.; it still happened to me maybe half the time. But not for much longer.

He made the drink with Clamato. "Nautical," I said, settling at an empty stool between two men. "Naughty," I added. "Maybe the card is under the counter, with the bad checks and the lost-and-found? There might have been an altercation?"

The drunk on my right said, "That's a good breakfast drink. It's got food value. Beer has food value as well." He indicated his own glass. "This Guinness, here." We watched the creamy portion roil into the deep brown, mesmerizing as a geologic event. "But food, you know, does not have beer value." He, alone among the group, didn't even pretend to eat.

"No," I agreed. "That *is* the problem."

"Wherever your credit card is, it isn't here," the bartender said, using two fingers to plug his sneeze. I'd left the card to run a tab, then there'd been pool balls flying on account of some college girls and their boyfriends, a town-gown kind of dispute. We'd exited through the back door, the one with the panic handle that claimed to be only for emergencies, into the alley and down the block, laughing, floating. My friend was Jonathan; he said he'd seen enough bar fights to know when to leave. I was trying to fall in love with him. Escapades like this were helpful. The effort required diligence, an active imagination, an ability to overlook. I didn't recall love being so much work. *Falling in* suggested ease, the advantage of gravity. He was fifteen years younger than my husband; close to my age, in other words. Though I saw no evidence of the fracas, I knew this was the place because my car still sat in the parking lot out front, morose rusted Saab. It was remarkable what could happen one night and be utterly forgotten in the light of the morning after. This enduring establishment, named Earl's, like the human body, withstood a drunken brawling assault and resurrected itself, day after day after day. The pool balls sat racked and ready, the cues returned to their case. The trembling hands at the bar, reaching for their drinks.

My brother, Sonny, had once told me he'd rather die than quit drinking. I felt certain I was sitting among like minds.

"You know, you can cancel the card," the bartender said wearily. I could tell he thought he was better than any of the people he served. He probably said "You're welcome" before he was thanked.

"I have to figure out which card it is." I had a lot of credit cards, each with a low limit, because I was somebody credit-card companies thought ought to be spread thin. I paged through them in my wallet while the man beside me, old enough to be my father, gave me discouraging scenarios concerning spending sprees.

"That fella could be all the way to Mexico by now."

"By God," the Guinness drinker on my other side affirmed.

"He could be putting himself up at a swanky four-star motel, getting himself whatever he beck-and-calls, all on your nickel. I once had somebody charge himself airline tickets on my Visa—and you know, that card never even left my billfold, I had it on my person the whole time, in my ass pocket—and here it comes charging me, anyway, some somnabitch flying from Vegas to Boston."

This line of conversation tapped into the computer nerd in the bartender, who proceeded to disabuse his old clientele of their fears concerning fraud. One phone call, he kept saying pedantically, wiping his runny nose. Easy as pie. I made the call after spreading the contents of my wallet on the bar and narrowing the options. There'd been no "activity" overnight on the missing card, not even here at Earl's, according to the person who named herself my representative. Did I want to wait and see if I located it? She, like the barkeep, felt herself superior to carelessness and its consequences.

"Nah, I should cancel that card, anyway." I should. I had debts now that Larry was in the hospital. I didn't want to bother him with them. Part of his trouble lay with overassuming everybody's problems. In his false largesse and skewed lucidity, he believed he was capable of solving anything. He could fix the world, he thought, if he applied the simple lessons of Zen Buddhism to every part of his day. *"Flow,"* he'd insisted to me, a meaningful syllable bestowed like a blessing. He hadn't slept in nearly a week when I brought him to Junction. He'd ridden in the backseat like a pet or a child, lying with his feet up against the window, explaining the inventions he had in mind to patent, the choreography that would transform his restaurant kitchen into a model of efficiency. At his intake, he was asked if he felt like killing anyone, himself or others. "No, no, no," he'd said impatiently, waving at the air. Corporeal concerns had left him; the life of the *mind,* he maintained. He needed time to think. That was four months ago. Our insurance, his insurance, would cover another two before raising much of a fuss.

"Buy you one of those?" asked the Guinness man. My glass was empty but for the pulpy remains, a limp celery stalk, a few lime seeds and their green rind. "I'm not going to make any moves, sweetheart, I recognize you have some problems. I'm just offering to buy you a drink."

"Sure."

He nodded at my lapel. "You been at the hospital?" I looked down to see the guest sticker still stuck to my shirt.

"Yes," I said. And, like him at this bar, I would be there again. Meanwhile, I would spend the morning in the warm, smoky haze of avuncular concern, sipping my liquid breakfast before heading home alone.

The day before, Jonathan had met me at the drugstore across from the hospital, as usual. I kept waiting for my heart to leap, as it was supposed to at the sight of the beloved. He sat looking exhausted—unshaved, hair savaged by his worrying hands—wearing mint-green scrubs, playing solitaire on his laptop computer at a plastic table. The plastic chair below looked ready to give up, legs splayed beneath his massive bulk. Perhaps it was his size that allowed him to be a nurse, the knowledge that no wiseass would taunt his profession. He had the wild good looks of genetic luck and he was indifferent about them, like money he had inherited rather than earned. No doubt he would lose his handsomeness to disregard and intemperance. His muscle, someday soon, would melt to fat.

He smiled when he saw me, a slow spreading that made wrinkles at his eyes. It was a sad smile; he worked with damaged people because he was damaged himself. He was a gentle giant, and there wasn't one of his patients he couldn't carry or restrain in his arms. His job was at the hospital psych ward, but not on Larry's floor. Jonathan's patients were confined to chairs or small padded rooms or the deeply debilitating doze of sedation. My husband, stabilized on a few helpful pharmaceuticals, lived upstairs. His stay was voluntary—necessary, it seemed, but voluntary nonetheless. Jonathan's patients had not volunteered. They'd been abandoned or rescued, depending, but they weren't at Mercy by their own choosing.

Jonathan folded up his computer and tucked it into his armpit. "How's it going?"

"Good." I nodded, nervous, but not in love, I didn't think. I wanted to be in love. I wanted to locate love, as I had known it, and invest it somewhere, in Jonathan, if I could. He was kind, modest, complicated, a good kisser. Why didn't I love him? My love for my husband had burst into discrete pieces when he himself came undone. I could name them—concern, fear, fondness, pity—all separate, like parts of a broken object it was my job to reassemble, an object whose linchpin I seemed to have misplaced. If I'd known he was going to have a psychotic break, I would have gotten pregnant last fall and by now be halfway to a new kind of love, the love of a baby—me for it, it for me, the two of us for its father, and him for us, a perfect, impermeable system, a closed circuit. Pregnant, the barhopping and the overnights in Jonathan's bed would be utterly unthinkable. Pregnant, I'd have installed a little cop, helping me toe the line.

"So it was a good visit?" Jonathan asked as we walked against the wind to retrieve my car. He'd made it his chivalric duty not to meet my husband, not to learn anything of him. *My husband.* When we got married twelve years ago, I could not speak those two words with a straight face. One year ago, when it was clear that my husband was unhappy but before he went completely AWOL, I had given him permission to sleep with another woman, a waitress at his restaurant. He'd gotten as far as her bedroom, as far as a long kiss, before he changed his mind. I had been so proud of us then, me the open-minded, him the devoted, each of us choosing an unexpected course. I naively believed that represented the extent of our married hardship.

"Pretty good," I lied to Jonathan.

He pulled on his sweater and hat as we went, shifting the computer around like a paperback in his large hands. "'Cause there was a suicide on his floor early this morning," he said, once inside my Saab. He sighed, unsettled. His big body absorbed bad news, trapped it inside so that it couldn't afflict anyone else.

"Larry didn't say anything."

"An Italian woman, a transfer from the E.R. They treated her hypothermia over there and then sent her our way. Nobody understood what was up with her because she wasn't talking, not in Italian, not in English, nothing. She was just about to get moved downstairs when they found her. And how she got two belts, I'll never know. One would have been hard enough. I was hoping nobody on the second floor knew about it yet."

"Belts?"

"Buddy Belts. We use them to manipulate paralytics."

"She hanged herself? That seems so . . ."

"Painful?" Jonathan supplied, messing his messy hair. "Desperate? Senseless? Retarded?"

"Difficult. I wouldn't even know how to tie a noose."

"Remember, she had belt notches to work with."

"I see." Italian, I thought.

"And a showerhead. If she'd weighed any more than she did, it wouldn't have held." We rode in silence to our usual first stop. "They called me to come take her down."

"I'm sorry." The car coughed when I switched off its engine, always three coughs before it quit. "Have you touched a lot of dead bodies?"

"I guess. Depending on what you think of as a lot." He breathed audibly, as large people did. "I think more than I could count on one hand, but less than on both."

"That's more people than I've had sex with," I said.

"People?"

"Men. A boy or two."

"Let's drink tequila tonight," he said, shoving the computer under the seat and climbing out. He would forget it there, I thought. It would ride home with me tomorrow. "Tequila," he repeated, "even though the margaritas here taste like Gatorade."

We always started at the Alpine, where the Western co-eds went. From there we would migrate toward Jonathan's duplex, stopping along the way to warm up, to sink further into the drunkenness that would allow me to make love with him later. At Earl's, fifth and final stop, where we'd been waiting for our turn at pool, he swept me smoothly out the door when he noticed the gun inside the jacket of one of the local guys playing against the college boys. The two balls that flew off the table when he took his shot hadn't been intentionally hurled, but they provoked a fight nonetheless.

"I've dealt with enough blood and guts this week," Jonathan claimed as we hustled down the alley. I felt half-carried, him large, me light with alcohol. The last woman he'd held had been dead. It was only two blocks to his duplex; our course had built into it a fail-safe drunk-driving logic. At his house, we started kissing the minute we had closed the door, drama and tragedy adding, tonight, to my attraction to him: the gun tucked in the guy's jacket played a part; the Italian woman hanging from two belts dangled somewhere between us, my husband's ghostly disappearing self. *Love,* I urged myself, biting Jonathan's plump lip. He moved backward down the hall, me on his feet tops like a child, past the second bedroom, where his daughter stayed on the nights he had custody. Stuffed animals. A poster of a singing group, five scrubbed boys of varying skin tones, the United Nations of ballad crooners. They sang the kind of songs I had liked as a girl.

When Jonathan lay asleep and I gazed through his skylight into the clouds, I didn't realize I was dreaming. It seemed real: I was where I was, who I was, and who I was with. But my teeth were falling out, the roots beneath them softening and letting loose one by one. Strange dangerous men, those from Earl's, had broken into Jonathan's house and were wreaking havoc in the kitchen, drawers crashing to the floor, the clatter of silverware, the garbage disposal ready to eat digits and limbs, if need be—a loud fantasy in a home so silent that you could hear a clock tick. A pack of clever wolves waited outside, in case we thought we could escape. And how could anyone love me now, I kept thinking, me without my teeth?

And before all that, Saturday morning at Mercy General. I was still queasy from having hit an animal with my car, still trying to eliminate the image as I crossed the parking lot, when I saw my husband at the rec-room window. I had looked up accidentally, shaking off that highway event, and there was Larry, his face and hands pressed up against the glass. His tortured expression reached into my chest. I wanted to call out his name, shout a warning, make him step back immediately. I ran into the building, passing the fish-mouthed front-desk receptionist and storming up the stairs, hurrying down the hall until I found him. He wore his black cotton pants, chest and feet naked, and stood at the floor-to-ceiling window overlooking the parking lot. I was glad to know the window was reinforced. You could see the fine wires, if you stared closely into the glass, an intricate, nearly invisible web. I stood catching my breath; he hadn't heard me, perhaps hadn't even seen me, down below. Larry had his hands spread reverentially on the smooth, cool surface, smearily, his cheek and chest pressed to it, too, as if absorbing the on-again, off-again sunlight, as if listening for information carried in the wires in the glass, perhaps wishing not to break through but to squeeze into its transparency, to enter the *flow*. I could see his ribs, the loose skin where once he'd been robust. His eyes were pinched shut, and that was the part that most scared me. What was he praying? And why was it so anguishing? He was fifty-two years old but seemed older, the flesh on his face slack, his whiskers and chest hair white. I didn't know how to imagine what he was doing, or why he'd left our home and his business, or why this place, of all the ones, was where he wished to be.

The receptionist from downstairs caught up with me, brandishing the sign-in form on her clipboard. Her annoyance was silenced by the spectacle of my husband. "We need to have a record," she finally whispered.

For months I had entered this place murmuring my own prayer: let him be better. Last December I'd found him on the living room carpet amid a pile of dirt and roots and broken pots, our houseplants pulled from their shelves and destroyed. "I can't take the responsibility," he'd said simply. "The responsibility is plaguing me." Just the need to water them once a week tormented him; he lay in the mess as if to join it, another life for someone else to nourish and encourage. I'd thought his busking at his own restaurant was a joke, him sitting out front with a hat on the sidewalk, strumming his guitar; a week later, he'd fired the entire kitchen staff and given away the contents of the walk-in, thousands of dollars' worth of meat and cheese and chocolate and cream. No telling what might happen next; the head waitress had wisely locked up the wine cellar. His unhinging was erratic, some of it lighthearted. But this full-body press on the window didn't look good. It was as if he wished to sieve himself through the wired glass, disperse like powder into the landscape.

The receptionist was only too glad to retreat to her post.

"Larry," I said. "Larry, what are you doing, baby?"

He pulled himself away slowly, peeling his cheek off like a sticker. He'd left an odd imprint, fingertips, the squashed side of his face. "My feet are freezing," he said, looking down as if he had just realized they were his, wiggling his toes. His nails needed grooming, along with every other gesture of personal hygiene. That had been the first to go, caring about his appearance. And it had played such a large part before, since I was younger than he, and he wanted to feel presentable. Only the young could afford to be slovenly and still attract a mate. Even Jonathan, at thirty-five, would soon have to put out some effort.

I led Larry slowly to a couple of vinyl-covered easy chairs in the corner, grouped there near a lamp to inspire conversation, to suggest normalcy. Nurses and patients passed through the large rec room but paid no attention to us. Nobody really seemed to occupy the same universe here. There was something liberating about being among people so completely unself-conscious. Or maybe it was narcissism that made them seem nonjudgmental—they were too busy worrying about themselves to worry about others. But there was also something terrifying. My plan, as it had been every recent Saturday, was to have sex with Larry. Pregnancy was my only salvation, I believed, and even if I wasn't ovulating, I wanted to have an explanation for when Jonathan succeeded where Larry had failed. These were the lies I lived by: not loving Jonathan, betraying my husband. Put together, they equaled a truth, which was that I needed a child. I was thirty-six and could no longer tolerate the jittery limbo of my life. Once I had a child, I would know what to do. Every move I made would have a glowing imperative attached like a corona, a flare of ambient light to lead me.

I'd been having sex with Jonathan for ten weeks now, the three most recent of them unprotected.

Larry sat, breathing hard, frightened. He searched my face as if I'd just pulled him from the sea, as if he were still in the throes of drowning, desperate, and not quite sure that I had his best interests at heart. Did I?

"Did you take a drug holiday, hon? You know they don't like you to do that around here. Should I run fetch something?"

"Say, Martin," he called out anxiously to a passing pajama-clad man. Here was a familiar, safe harbor. The guy smiled, tilting his head like a friendly dog. A piece of his fine brown hair flopped down like that dog's ear. "You haven't met my wife. Come meet my wife." Martin held out his hand as he approached: shake. There was a gap in his pajama bottoms through which his shadowy genitals could be glimpsed as he moved. I'd met him a few weeks before; it was electric shock that had messed with Larry's memory. Or maybe, in his enlightened state of mind, Larry divined my plan for an accidental pregnancy and was rebelling, deflecting my attention. I did not doubt his heightened consciousness; it just wasn't very useful, sequestered as it was in his mind, feeding like a worm on his physical substance, surrounded for months by these reinforced walls.

Martin was an English professor at Fort Lewis College, in Durango. He'd timed his stay to coincide with a sabbatical. Alarming how thoughtful and reasonable the people on Larry's floor were, practical, in their way. Martin could, and did, recite Shakespeare. He was preparing himself for a summer repertory production of *Hamlet.* "'Give every man thine ear,'" he'd advised me at our first meeting, "'but few thy voice: Take each man's censure, but reserve thy judgement.'"

"Noted," I'd said.

"Polonius," he'd said, as undaunted as everyone else here by sarcasm.

He settled himself daintily on the arm of Larry's chair, his pants gap now completely open, like a grin, guileless. They began discussing the possibility of pulling together a bridge foursome. There were the two of them, and one of the orderlies, and this new admission, a young deaf woman from Italy, where bridge apparently was not just for the geriatric crowd. The only problem was her not being able to hear or speak, yet they were optimistic that they could work around that. Larry held up four fingers, then made a shoveling gesture: this would be four spades. Martin put a fist on his chest, pointed to his ring finger: hearts, diamonds. But what would be clubs? And no-trump?

"I just question how advanced she is," Martin fretted. "You can't overestimate the importance of everyone being somewhere near the same in terms of expertise. And maybe it's *whist* that they play in Italy? Not necessarily bridge?"

"You have to wonder if Jimbo will be able to fully concentrate, with his other duties," Larry said.

The television across the room was muted: another window into another world, this one of commercials aimed at children, Jell-O, Barbie, Play-Doh, an onslaught of action and primary colors. I could still make out the prints Larry had left on the glass of the picture window. You could probably see them from below, outside. I'd come from the windy road into the static recirculation of this room, where extraordinary minutiae made up my husband's conversation with his new friend. He hadn't seemed so banally out of touch, so dotty, a few minutes ago; then he had seemed at the zenith of misery. Which did I prefer? Now Larry took my hand, stroking it benignly, the way he might a flat stone or the head of a slumbering cat. In the midst of their bridge-party plans, I couldn't possibly mention lovemaking—so indecorous, for starters, but also because, for the remainder of my time with Larry, Martin stayed perched on the chair arm. His asexual personality overruled his open P.J. fly. Every week there were different but similar circumstances to help me realize the altered and mystifying atmosphere of my marriage. I was being taught every Saturday the lesson of losing him without losing him. When the buzzer sounded that meant lunch would be served in five minutes, I rose to leave. Relieved, reprieved, ready to go find Jonathan across the street.

"Join us?" Martin asked politely. So mannerly, these nuts.

"No, thanks. You want to come with me?" I asked Larry. I knew he would say no; I asked to offset my guilt, to get away scot-free. "Maybe to a real restaurant? For a real meal?" With real people, I wanted to add. Out there in the real world.

"These are real people," he told me, well aware of how my thoughts worked. And his sudden insight—bittersweet déjà vu—made me burst into tears. A flash of heat, mucus, helplessness. Seeing me, Martin abruptly wandered off, blinking.

Larry took my hand again, stroking. All at once a horrified expression clouded his face, and he clutched my fingers. "I forgot that you played bridge!" he said. "Honey, is that why you're crying? Oh, honey, you of *course* ought to be our fourth! How could I be so dumb, to have for—"

"It's not bridge," I said, sniffling. "Good God. *Bridge.*"

"A *Saturday* game, what was I thinking?"

"It's not bridge." My outburst was over.

"Are you sure?" He cocked his head playfully, looked under his lids, nudged his forehead toward me, as if I were being coy.

"I am positive. Absolutely."

He held my face and used his thumbs to wipe away tears. This role he summoned from storage, comforting me. He still performed it well. He kissed my cheeks, one and then the other, his lips so dry I could hear them chafe my face. This was as close as our bodies were going to come today.

"I love you," he said serenely. In his irises I saw vast space, the blue-green of the ocean, of the sky, of the deep and crippling uncertainty that had landed him here. And I said what every coward says when challenged by that sally: "I love you, too."

Before I left Telluride, I stopped by Sonny's house to see if he needed anything in Grand Junction. Fruit or tools or some other supply. The sky was already beginning to cloud up; my breath came in steamy puffs. He was awake early, as always, today building a dog pen out of scrap metal, old box springs and parts of a swing set, a structure he had not bothered to have sanctioned by the fussy city bureaucrats. His wife's pair of matching dogs sat watching from Big Red's truck bed, where he'd trapped them. They wore sweaters, fat Pekingese with their smashed faces and sputtering outrage. The word Sonny applied was *warthog*: noun, verb, adjective. "That's right, warthogs," he said when they leaped to bark and wheeze at me, "let's just see if you can warthog your warthog asses out of *that*." To me he said, confidentially, "They're starting to piss me off."

Inside the house, a shade slat twitched: his wife, posted at the window.

"You want me to come with?" he asked, pushing back his safety goggles, welding gun pointed at the ground. Sonny wouldn't enter the hospital proper because sick people bothered him, but he enjoyed a trip to Grand Junction regardless. We could drive in Big Red instead of my car, listen to country music, eat burgers and drink beer at Tex's, shop at the AutoZone, and come home tonight instead of tomorrow—a totally other visit, a different agenda entirely—but I knew Jane Lynn wanted him at their house. Her hand was on the blinds not fifteen feet away. They had only recently gotten back together, and one of her chief complaints against Sonny was the time he spent looking after me. And it hadn't helped that for a few months he had rekindled a flame with his old high school sweetheart, she and her four children. I liked the girlfriend better than his wife; I'd said so twenty-some years ago, when Sonny had dropped one for the other, and it was Jane Lynn I'd said it to.

The girlfriend was sweet, the kind of large, happy woman whose bra strap was persistently sliding down her arm, who, out of genuine affection, called everyone *sugar* and hugged you goodbye wet-eyed. She had very sweet children whom her complete loser of a husband had abandoned. He was in jail for manufacturing and peddling methamphetamines. I thought Sonny had made a romantic step forward, coming to her—and her children's—rescue. The first I'd known about his affair was when he'd shown up at my house wearing a nasty wound on his forearm, a dirty hankie held in place with duct tape. This was where he'd sliced off his tattoo, *Jane Lynn,* the wife he thought he was done with. Her name had been excised and the sore was ugly. The arm festered, a sickening green fluid that escaped from beneath a rough brown patch of scab. Every shirt he owned had a rusty left sleeve.

"Didn't anyone ever teach you about infection? Or how to get out blood?" I asked him, pouring hydrogen peroxide over the mess, quelling nausea.

"I can field-dress a deer," he said stubbornly. "I can get out a tattoo."

I'd been jealous of his flushed, renewed love. It was as if he'd reclaimed his youth, gone merrily down that other path. He'd be a great father! I knew from experience as his surrogate child; for years I'd lobbied in vain for nieces and nephews. And the girlfriend had two of each, Daisy, Adam, Melanie, Mikey, their names like a lingering jingle in my head, ready-made little blond tykes young enough to adjust, squint their big blue eyes and view my brother as their father, me the fun auntie . . . Then, not long ago, he'd asked Jane Lynn if he could return to their marriage.

"I got tired of the squalor over there," he said of the girlfriend's home. His arm wasn't even healed when he came back. Jane Lynn had made some conditions for his return. Probably he was supposed to stop spending so much time with me. I knew for a fact that drinking was forbidden, although that was the request he made of me Saturday morning: buy him a few cases of Bud Light. He went to the truck's dash for his wallet, taking a moment to menace the Pekingese with a hissing tongue of flame from his torch. They skittered on their nails across the slick surface of the bed.

"I found this under the seat a while back," Sonny said. He handed me a spent yellow shotgun shell. It held a rolled piece of paper with my name on it and a date more than ten years past: 8–8–88. Since I was born on 6–6–66, I found dates noteworthy. I'd engraved 7–7–77 all over town when that day came; same with the 8s and 9s. I left my phone number on napkins tucked under the glass tops of tables; my initials carved in the soft walls of saunas, in the boards of fences, the bark of trees. A part of a poem, a line from a song, a lovelorn query, moony messages sent into the universe in search of an answer, a responding soul, that alleged prince. At a bar in Junction called Earl's, I'd penned my initials in an equation with Jonathan's on the wall of the women's room stall: J.J. + S.S. = love. This winter I had marked 02–02–02, and for the first time felt a discouraging downward tilt, imagining somehow a gravestone, that other public place where dates were registered. These notes had once been a record of my own fantastic hopefulness. Beneath Big Red's front seat, I'd tucked this one, the reverse side of which read, *All the little emptiness of love* . . . Those eloquent ellipses I'd drawn in, a trail of sentimental crumbs that wished to dispute the claim.

"That's yours, right?" Sonny asked.

"Yep." So far as I knew, he was the only one who'd ever found any of my messages.

"You want me to put that back under the seat?" Big Red was a fixture, could be used like a safe-deposit box. My brother held out his hand, and I returned the scroll in its ribbed tube.

On the road to Grand Junction, I got teary, feeling sorry for myself. The landscape turned an impressionistic mess before my eyes, a set of blurry yellow warning lights, construction cones, slow curves, bare trees furred into ash-colored fluff. My father had taught me to drive on this road, unhappy passenger pulling air between his teeth and clutching the chicken handle, stomping at what would have been the brake. When he and my mother moved away, he told Sonny to look after me. That explained Sonny's consternation when I started dating Larry—a man older than himself—since the match wouldn't have pleased my father. But surely they were relieved that I was finally doing the things grown-ups did. And Larry eventually endeared himself to my family. He had taken good care of me until lately. Then in stepped Jonathan the nurse; the first time we met, he was tending me after I'd fainted. Hospital odor: that nauseating alchemy of blood and antiseptic, the cool fluorescence of the halls, like walking into a refrigerator where half-dead people were stored, living only by the grace of machinery and medical personnel. Why should that place, the epicenter of need, the headquarters of help, send me limp to my knees? Jonathan sat cross-legged beside me on the floor, unalarmed, instructing me to breathe slowly and lower my head. When I told him my name was Sissy, he disagreed, "No, no, don't worry. People faint all the time."

"No, I don't mean I'm a sissy, I mean that's my name." My brother was Sonny, my parents' son, and I was his sister, Sissy.

"Sissy," said Jonathan.

And now, driving to Grand Junction, I thought of how I'd lied to Jonathan. I *was* a sissy. I would tell him so, since it was in fact Jonathan I was going to see. It was Jonathan to whom I'd turned myself over.

Down the familiar highway I rolled, through the little towns and the bigger ones, away from the brooding winter clouds of Telluride and into the mild high desert outside Grand Junction. Down from the ski village to the fruit orchards, the stands selling juice and jerky. On the last long stretch of flatlands, just before the big sign that announced the city limits, a notorious speed trap where you had to drop from 60 to 35 in an instant, I saw the marmot. This was where I'd been cited, three different costly times these past months; now I knew better. Today, instead of a motorcycle cop holding a speed gun like a hair dryer, the marmot sat in the sign's shadow, poised, quizzical, nervy. Whistling pig, big as a beaver. "Don't move, buddy," I murmured, tapping the brake. "Don't you dare—" I had failed to note his partner, who suddenly dashed from the other side of the road, his brown fur the rich thick pelt of a Russian hat. I swerved but felt him bump under the back tire, soft yet fatal. I screamed, braking, putting my fingers in my mouth and looking to the rearview mirror, where I saw the animal thrashing madly on the pavement. "Oh my God, you damn dummy!" Injured, in violent agony, squealing. A fine spray of blood from its gasping mouth. His friend had disappeared; there was no human traffic except me. I'd hit animals, yet never before left a survivor. My obligation was to put it out of its misery, anybody knew that. "Sorry, sorry, sorry," I murmured, looking once more in the rearview, longing to see another vehicle come finish what I'd begun, my brother in Big Red, for instance, its bright rounded hood and headlights and grille familiar as a face bearing down. Some agent of mercy to do the right thing, aim his wheel at the creature's chest swiftly and without hesitation—sparing what suffered, killing with kindness.

But I couldn't do it. No matter how painful that backward glance—and I kept looking behind, long after the animal was out of sight—I couldn't stop myself from driving away.

⟜ Only a Thing

YOU COULD COMPARE a certain kind of love affair to a car wreck. You don't expect it, but when it does happen, it seems somehow inevitable—even overdue. There is the status quo, and then its interruption; a pattern, then variation. Julia had felt a crash coming ever since they had rented the Intrepid in Cancún. What was she doing riding around in a foreign country in what was, in Mexico, a foreign car, with someone other than her husband behind the wheel? Foreign, foreign, foreign. The car had only eighteen miles on it when they plowed into a wall.

The wall, made of ugly cement block, was being repainted. An elderly Mexican man was slowly brushing over graffiti, tracing atop the foul Spanish as if writing it himself, unwriting it, in slow motion. Julia had noticed him before the crash, had thought in a brilliant, lucid flash that having sex with a new man was like tracing graffiti in order to erase it: the same motions, the undoing in the doing. And then Martin had crashed the car into the wall.

The painter guided Julia gently by the arm to a neat pile of rubble, painted white, no doubt by him, to resemble curbing. Of the totaled, steaming vehicle, he said philosophically, his brush held like a torch, "Is only a thing."

"*Gracias,*" she said.

Martin meanwhile stormed around, swearing in English, circling the crashed Intrepid as if to conjure up a repair. He wore his traveler's pants: the legs unzipped so that the slacks became shorts. Good for climbing volcanoes, visiting cathedrals, a fabric so light it would dry overnight, slung over a shower rod. Martin's legs were muscled, hairless because he cycled, red now because he was fair and had burned. "God*damn,*" he kept saying. The front right wheel had been completely sheared from what Julia believed was called the axle. That (possible) axle had scraped a deep gouge into the pavement of the street, the crumbling painted rocks beside, and the dirt just before the front fender had met the wall. The poor painter would now have to plaster as well. Bits of red and silver plastic from the headlight and fender glittered in the sunshine. Atop the wall, pieces of glass sparkled, sharp and alluring, something you wanted to touch with a fingertip just to risk getting pricked.

Martin: he had no title in Julia's life. He was married, too, so Julia was his mistress. But what was he? *Master,* Julia thought—only Barbara Eden in her bikini and groovy genie bottle could get away with that. Julia shivered giddily, relieved to be alive and recalling old sitcoms, sitting on terra firma in the hot Mexican sunshine. An overfilled bus slowed to admire the Americans' bad luck, and Julia observed herself as if from the crowded window, a bottle-blond woman dethroned, removed to the gutter in her goofy pedal pushers and daisy-topped flip-flops.

"You neck?" the painter inquired, peering down at Julia as she massaged herself. It was whiplash, she supposed. Everything else seemed fine, toes wiggling in their rubber thongs, heart beating in its ribby cage, but her neck ached. Not fatally. Whatever flow had constituted her life had simply been diverted. She was interested in what would happen next, but it wasn't a tragedy, just a glitch. A wall had popped up in front of them, like a piece of toast, like a warning shot, like a love affair. That was all.

It could have been the accident that made her dwell that night on the dead brother of her husband, Teddy. The brother had been only seventeen when he died, ten years before Julia and Teddy met. He was therefore a ghost to Julia, dead without her having known him, haunting her life nonetheless. Not unhelpfully, she thought. If he hadn't lost his brother, Teddy wouldn't be who he was, and Julia never would have met or fallen in love with him. This ghost, named Billy, accounted for Teddy's character, for choices he'd made, for people he'd befriended, for places he'd gone, for the man he'd become.

Billy had been Teddy's only brother. Good-hearted, bespectacled, asthmatic, conceivably homosexual Billy, whom Teddy had spent his young life defending and educating. On his behalf, Teddy had mowed the grass, punched the bullies, purchased beer, chauffeured, chided, counseled, consoled. Later, it was Teddy who'd supplied the cocaine and the prostitute, the tequila and the hotel room. Billy had probably died happy, Julia thought, having gone alone to the swimming pool, shed his clothes, left his eyeglasses on the tiled edge, and thrown himself into the illuminated blue water. This, too, had happened in Mexico, Tijuana, San Diego's dark twin, the news drifting up to the States on a Sunday afternoon. It was Teddy who'd gone south by bus to recover the body, to bring it and the family station wagon back across the border.

In the aftermath, Teddy had collapsed into mourning. Wretched in a San Diego psych ward, he had waited for clarity while his friends finished college, married, finagled jobs, and became parents, fulfilling their contracts as adults. But Julia's future husband's undoing was followed by an impressive reassembly. By the time he stepped out of the bin and back into the world, restored, he had developed an unswerving internal compass, one that hovered perpetually at moral magnetic north. Unlike his friends, he had legitimately grown up. He and Julia had met soon after that, sharing classes in a public-health program. Once he had fixed his gaze on her, he never lifted it.

Home in L.A., two weeks after Mexico, Julia waited for a cashier at Walgreens, a pack of cigarettes in one hand, a pregnancy test in the other.

Such a *dumb* problem, she thought, unworthy of her, interesting nevertheless.

The line was moving slowly, and a party waited for her back at her house. She'd pulled away from the hoopla without anyone's noticing. It was that kind of party—raucous, sodden, oblivious. The boys were safely asleep, each with an arm around the neck of a dog who wouldn't let any drunken degenerates defile him. The girl was happily turning pages as Teddy held forth at the grand piano, thoroughly in his element and three sheets to the wind. His friends—students, other professors, secretaries, the whole democratic entourage—stayed later than Julia's colleagues at Fidelity Pharmaceuticals, the few who'd put in polite appearances in expensive black clothing and then coolly slid away for their late dates, their real deals. Even if they'd stayed, Julia wouldn't have had fun; she frequently felt alone at parties, especially her own. Her invisibility sometimes led her to her bedroom, where she lay on the bed among the jackets, listening to the roaring jocularity coming through the wall. All those people and no one to talk to. Martin was that one, and not only wasn't he here, he never would be.

The Walgreens cashier didn't blink at the purchases. She'd seen worse combinations, Julia told herself: Scotch and circus peanuts, condoms and electrical tape, diapers and kerosene, any number of pathetic binaries. Outside, beneath an awning, hung an unlit pay phone, one that Julia had used a few times to call Martin. But at his end of the country, it was very late. Testing for pregnancy was as close to him as she was going to get tonight.

As she left the parking lot, she had to brake abruptly. A group of high school girls all carrying musical instruments had bounded unthinkingly into the crosswalk, laughing, swinging their flute and cornet cases, bonking one another in the rear, strutting their pretty young bodies in the light of colored neon on a balmy Friday night. In a few years, Julia's daughter would be their age, sixteen, seventeen. Billy the ghost had died at seventeen. Julia put her forehead to her steering wheel and suddenly wept. Trooper, her vehicle was named. Most of the time, Julia felt like one, too, but not tonight. The sudden stop had reminded her of the crash in Cancún.

"Is this safe?" she'd asked, joking, as they climbed into a replacement car from the rental agency—a Mirage. But Martin was not in any mood to make light of the accident. He wanted to analyze it, explain how it had happened, again and again. This meant that he had to turn his attention repeatedly from the road to Julia's face, to remove his hands from the wheel to punctuate, to show the distances between lanes. "Did *you* see anything in the road?" he demanded. It was the first time Julia had seen him flummoxed. It didn't suit him. She was trying to adopt the attitude of the old Mexican painter: "Is only a thing." Nobody killed, not even particularly hurt. Money was involved, but not much; Martin was nothing if not insured. Mostly it was his youthful masculine pride that was damaged, and his annoyance served only to remind Julia that her husband was a better man, milder, steadier during disaster.

If she'd died, if she'd been seriously injured, how would it have been explained back home? How to account for the active, aimless sperm still inside her? All these guilty problems, unkindnesses that might outlive her. And what pitiless irony, her husband sent once more to Mexico on a gruesome errand.

"Cars should be named other things," she told Martin brightly. "Like the Ford Spanky. Or Wanderlust, the Volkswagen van. A convertible Picaresque, with tailfins."

"And you would be targeting what demo group?" he asked, taking a curve at far too high a speed.

"The whimsical," she said, clutching the upper side handle with one hand, the shoulder belt over her breast with the other. "Somebody should throw more bones to the whimsical."

When she returned to her house, alive and ordinary, she got rid of any evidence of Martin's presence in her life, letters, tidbits, all of it: trash in a landfill somewhere now. Only the first office voice mail remained, secured these three years in its electronic vault, the combination encrypted by Julia's private set of lucky numbers. When she was lonely, when she wanted to be reminded of why she loved him, she revisited his message and the virgin urge he'd had to reach her. On and on he stumbled, a long and lovely pratfall.

Martin's daughter played the flute, Julia remembered a few days later. That, too, could account for the crying at Walgreens. She had once heard the girl play, over the long-distance line, a thin, sad song in the background at Martin's Manhattan apartment. It had sounded like a professional recording. Satie, that mope. Nothing had made the atmosphere of that apartment clearer to Julia as she stood in a radiantly warm L.A. parking lot. Martin's sadness—taken up in the daughter's perfect lonely performance. His restlessness and duty struggled in the confinement of the vertical city while Julia's sprawled in the horizontal one. Strangers in strange cars rushing by, children playing sad songs on flutes, love in its inimitable, baffling shades. Her affair seemed both random and fated, perfectly scripted and half-baked.

She wasn't pregnant.

The next time she and Martin rendezvoused, two months later, they rented an Intrigue. "Why not a Dullsville?" Julia suggested in the Hertz lot of Denver International Airport. She rested her head on Martin's shoulder. "Those auto execs think like us," she said, meaning Fidelity Pharmaceuticals, its reps who understood the sexy significance of names. It was Julia who'd dreamed up the name Hydra for the miracle anti-inflammatory that also softened your stool, improved your mood, lowered your blood pressure, and didn't eat away your intestinal lining. "It sounds as pure as water," Martin had said gleefully, "but means a riot of snakes!" For the remainder of Hydra's promising patented life, he and Julia would be able to meet at exotic locales all over the world, sell their many-headed product to millions of sufferers. The future of her affair felt secure, like money in the bank, like a nongeneric painkilling wonder drug.

"Martin," she'd said at the gate. She loved to say his name. He covered her ears with his hands, put his lips to the part in her hair, speaking her name into her skull. In the car, she couldn't look at him—he was too much to take in. She watched the landscape fly by, plains, plains, plains, then suddenly mountains, over to the west.

"You mustn't hiss," Martin warned as they merged onto the beltway.

He owned no car in New York, so he did all of the driving, jerkily and too fast. In Julia's real life, she and Teddy shared fifty-fifty. They shared driving and they shared their money. Martin pinched pennies: 10 percent tips. He'd grown up poor and never lost his fear of ending up there again. It surprised Julia to learn of the financial arrangements that prevailed at his home, the arguments between him and his wife about who would pay for what aspect of their daughter's existence. The girl was being tutored in everything, languages, dance, religion, art, etiquette, test-taking, a life the likes of which Julia's daughter would never know. Using scissors and scraps, Julia's daughter made costumes for stuffed bunnies, sang country-western songs at the top of her lungs, strung shiny beads on thread, gave loving names to the kitchen appliances. Julia's family was impossibly impromptu next to Martin's, lumpy, lacking manners and vigilance and sharp facial features. Three children was too many. Martin took the global position: negative population growth. One child for every two parents.

When, five years earlier, Julia had announced her third pregnancy, she'd been met with a kind of slack-jawed wonder. Her friends and coworkers and relatives had realized that she might never stop having babies. But Teddy adored his children; he had started rallying for more now that the youngest was in Montessori. His calling, this fatherhood for which he'd been in training since the birth of his little brother, had come to claim him fully. Now in his care were not only children but students, that steady parade of need, as well as colleagues, neighbors, readers of his letters to the editor. When describing their life, his and Julia's, he habitually used the plural pronoun, but Julia didn't feel as though she'd played much of a role. She had carried the children and she had decorated the house, but Teddy was the load-bearing member. He stayed there, steady as Atlas, while Julia flew away. Her salary was triple his, which was how she justified her transitory relationship with her home and children, her *business travel*. When they cried at her departure, she promised gifts. Over the phone, she assured them that she loved them, applying many terms of endearment: *monkey, sweetness, moonpie.*

It was her daughter, Billie, who'd recently looked up from homework hour at the kitchen table to note in a woebegone way that she and her brothers spent more time with their teachers than with their mother.

"Not literally," Julia said.

"'Literally,'" repeated the youngest boy dreamily, the one with the most words to learn.

The Fidelity convention was in Boulder; the conference rooms were climate-controlled, the personnel identically outfitted no matter where they were shipped to, Mexican beach, European castle, alpine ski slope. But here in Colorado, everyone seemed smugly healthy, in mind and body, which made Julia crave fast food and cigarettes, cellulite and cynicism. She didn't want to step outside because it was too beautiful, the air so painfully clean her eyes watered. This suited Martin, who wanted to simply fuck. And it was simple fucking. Less complicated than sex with Teddy, because Martin didn't care if she had a good time or not. Teddy cared desperately and would do anything to ensure her pleasure, even if it meant sacrificing his own. Teddy had long ago discovered how to make Julia respond; it was an odd kind of power, and Julia faintly resented his possession of it. Martin, however, was a selfish lover, indifferent to her even as they mashed together face-to-face, chest-to-chest, toe-to-toe, and that struck Julia as a strange relief. While he labored away, she let herself daydream.

"I'm pregnant," she said to Martin when he'd finished. A bold lie. She supposed she was looking for proof of his character, support for the thesis that he was worth loving, worth possibly ruining her life for. But, like the car accident months ago, the news appeared to obsess him with his own significance.

"Shit!" he exclaimed, frown lines crimping his smooth forehead, just under his thick, alarmed-looking hair. "*How* pregnant?" He didn't ask if it was his; his arrogance prevented the question from entering his head.

Would her husband have been so obtuse? No. But her husband would have said something worse in his delight, tossing into the air new names—a boy's! a girl's! two of each in case there were twins! "That's what we call a forced-choice question," Julia said to Martin dryly, then added, "Mexico," as if that would explain.

They both wanted out of the hotel room. Blinking like bats, they each took a cellular phone underneath a different manicured spruce tree on the hotel grounds and made a discreet call home to check on the family, the false new weight of their relationship sending them to their other obligations.

"Honey?" her husband said carefully. "Honey?" Julia's heart lurched, all idiocy evaporated. He was going to say something awful. One of her children was dead, injured, lost. Or he'd found out she was not alone. In his voice Julia heard her punishment. She'd pushed her luck too far this time.

"What?" she said, moving toward and then away from Martin, her free hand fluttering before her as if to erase something—to erase it before it even existed. "What is it?"

"We're fine," Teddy said soothingly, deliberately, "we are one hundred percent fine, but there was a break-in here at the house."

"A break-in?"

"Through Billie's bedroom window."

"*What?*"

"We weren't home, honey, someone came in while we were gone." In the tone he always used to calm the crying child or the churlish student, Teddy told the story. Someone—someone small—had broken and then crawled through the casement window the night before. Teddy and the children had been at Knott's Berry Farm when it happened. They'd come home to find the doors swinging in a brisk Santa Ana wind and the three floppy-eared, dumb dogs loose in the park across the street.

"The fish, however . . ." Teddy sighed. Besides the dead tetras, there was a trail of gang insignia spray-painted on the walls, a vivid blue crusade that wound from Billie's bedroom to Julia and Teddy's, where the aerosol had apparently run dry. Detours of destruction had been made in every room: the fridge had been unloaded, the silverware tray upended, two gas burners left on high, some paintings slashed, and the sofa gutted. Their daughter's bedroom had been thoroughly trashed, drawers dumped, stuffed animals stabbed, nail polish poured on the floor, whiskey on the bed, motor oil on the curtains—as if in preparation for a struck match.

Julia was stunned. "Who would do this?"

"I don't know. I've been trying to remember if I failed anybody recently, some vengeful student. I can't believe one of my students . . ." He had no enemies, her husband, none that he knew of.

Julia's mind spanned the western half of the nation, situating herself last night—as if providing an alibi—in Colorado, in a hotel room at the time of the crime. She and Martin, propped up on pillows, eating from a service cart. "Tell me once more," she said to Teddy, pressing her free hand against her other ear as if to fill her mind with what he was describing. He obliged.

"Oh," Teddy interrupted himself. "Oh yeah, and this is the really strange thing. On our bed, laid out like a paper doll, was your *under-wear*, arranged like it was on somebody. Just these panties and bra and hose. Black," he added. "I guess they're yours." He didn't know, because he'd never seen her wear them. One of two sets bought when her sex life had drifted beyond that room, the other on her body right this minute. Shame flushed through Julia, a wave so powerful she had to sit down in the pine needles. Her house: raided, its closets and cupboards and nooks and crannies struck with ill will, a vicious bushwhacking tour of mayhem, ending, it seemed, with the flimsy silhouette on her bed.

The locks had been changed already, the window covered with ply-board; the insurance agent had visited, and a cleaning crew was coming in the morning. Teddy told Julia he had promised their daughter a new comforter and curtains, plush toys and books and CDs and posters.

"And white mice," he finished.

"Why not?" Julia said vaguely. She could see Martin under his tree across the park, talking seriously but with only half his attention into his cell phone, sucking from his sport bottle of Scotch and water, his legs flexed—point, relax, point, relax—in a cyclist's stretch. He was always multitasking. His brain had compartments. She was in one of them.

"The dogs are okay?" she inquired once more, her own sport bottle forgotten, leaking on the ground.

"Everyone is fine," Teddy continued to assure her. "We're all sleeping in the big bed together."

"I wish I were there," she said, and meant it. Her voice shook. But why shouldn't it? She was cold, she told herself, it was November in Colorado, after all.

"I love you," Teddy said. "Tell Mommy we love her," he called to the children, who echoed the sentiment, a three-voice chorus.

Julia withheld the news from Martin. All the long weekend, she bravely didn't mention it, instead listening to him fret over his daughter's prep-school applications, which required essays and shot records and a cumulative GPA and an *astronomical* nonrefundable down payment, and also, as if that weren't enough, there was his secretary, whom he would have to fire because her multiple sclerosis was finally too debilitating to ignore. Could he really be expected to perform her job in addition to his? He paced, he ranted, he anticipated in advance the fallout. Stewing over these problems was aging him in ways that Julia suspected he welcomed, little worry lines at his temples and mouth, proof of his influence and manhood.

Meanwhile, the chronology of the vandalism in L.A. whirled in Julia's head like a shaken snow globe, from breaking glass through eventual departure, those doors swinging in the Santa Ana wind.

"December in the city?" Martin said at the airport the next day, already glancing over Julia's shoulder, on to his next appointment.

Julia nodded, congested by tears. She said what she always did when they parted: "This might be our last kiss." And he looked at her, as always and finally, with warmth, knowing he would not have to extend that benevolence longer than this momentary farewell in a public airport. "December," Julia confirmed. The annual Christmas party was where they'd met three years before.

"Is only a thing," Julia had told Teddy, recalling the Mexican painter as she regarded their belongings.

"Well, several things," her mild husband had responded, standing amid the wreckage.

But he wasn't as aware of *things* as Julia was, and when she'd returned home, she had to revise the list he'd made to give to the police and State Farm, counting out the modest items the thieves had taken, the list oddly long.

And odder what they'd left behind: the insignia on the living room wall bothered Julia, a mysterious metallic-blue symbol, calligraphic and deranged, a snake in a Celtic knot swallowing its own tail, yet something less specific than that. How could the vandals be so talented with paint, so artful and yet still so bent on destruction? Julia found an old can of latex, left over from the last time they'd done the walls, and, like the Mexican graffiti-coverer, she found herself tracing atop the marking, moving her arm in an approximation of what the intruders had done, following the devious twists with her own brush. But the blue spray paint bled through, the image emerging in creepy shadow fashion, like a bruise surfacing on flesh. Professional painters finally had to come and sand the wall, gouge it, prime it, restore it.

It was the neighbor, Linda, who pointed out the other tagging. This was in Julia's sitting porch, where the women looked out over the sludgy L.A. skyline, drinking wine before their children came clamoring home from school. The vandals had not done much damage to this room, dull as it was with rocking chairs and fringed lamps, an absence of electronics, and a preponderance of books. Here the two women discussed their love affairs, Linda's former one, Julia's present one—trading off, living vicariously, taking turns. "Look," Linda said all at once. The smog had shifted, and sunlight beamed briefly into the room, illuminating what had previously been invisible: there in the corner, eye level with a wicker shelf, a set of shining images. An empty can of spray fixative had been found after the break-in. And here was what had become of that transparent aerosol, hidden pictures on Julia's walls, whispers, sighs. You could see them only in certain kinds of light, at certain angles. These, like the conversations in this room, Julia shared with no one else.

The thieves were girls, it turned out, fourteen-year-old gang wannabes. Having no vehicle with which to haul their bounty, they'd made off with backpacks—hence the portability of what was missing. They got busted just around the block a few weeks later, crawling out of another casement window with a litter of whimpering Chihuahuas in a soup pot. They confessed to everything, being girls, sobbing and sorry, one of them with a pierced eyebrow, a gold cross winking there. Everything that had been stolen—other than a few children's videotapes and some jewelry—was recovered. Even the puppies came through unscathed.

Julia's daughter went with her to the police station to recover the family's belongings, housed there as evidence. Together, they examined the heavy plastic bags. There were objects there that Julia didn't remember owning, things she might have been nostalgic for if she'd noticed their absence. To the uninterested cop who had delivered them, she said, "These are my kids' teeth." They rattled like pills in an old Fidelity sample bottle. Why would you steal them? Julia wondered. The cop was probably wondering why you would keep them.

"And you told us it was the tooth fairy!" Billie said, grinning.

Teeth: parts of her children and yet not, expendable as the tails of lizards. Her husband had saved his dead brother's glasses, those smudged lenses that had watched poolside as the boy threw himself away. Kept nowadays in a leather snapcase in Teddy's sock drawer. For a second, Julia grew dizzy, the pill bottle clutched in her hand—had she checked at home for the snapcase?

"It's just teeth," Billie said dismissively, already back to the bags, searching for her CDs.

Another recovered object was the audiotape Teddy had made of each of the children promising to clean up dog shit if they could please please please get a dog. They'd feed and water and walk and scoop. *Oh please Daddy please.* Three times he'd done this, not that he'd ever use their words against them. He was easily amused, her husband, charmed by simple pleasures. Such was the way with people on track.

"*Please* is the beg word," Martin had once said to Julia sniffily. He himself never used it. He hadn't taught his daughter to use it, either, a fact he was absurdly proud of.

"How about *sorry*?" Julia had asked.

On the way home from the police station, Julia popped Teddy's old tape in the Trooper's tape deck and heard her children, years before, pleading, making a promise they wouldn't keep to a man who wouldn't hold them to it.

"She had *her* affair," Martin had told Julia, meaning his wife. It had happened before their daughter was born, and was sufficient excuse, he felt, for his carrying on with Julia. His wife, he claimed, knew about them in some corner of herself. Not the conscious one, of course; he was far too discreet. But they were finally achieving equilibrium, in his opinion. He felt entitled. A lot of his character was marked by his confidence, his overt self-worth. He was quick and decisive and very handsome—so handsome and clean-shaven and fit that Julia often felt frumpy beside him; then she soothed herself with the knowledge that his wife was unquestionably homely. He'd married her for her *mind*, he'd told Julia piously, that worthy intangible. The sole photograph Julia possessed of Martin was on page fourteen of the 1998 Fidelity newsletter, a legitimate document to have floating around the house. There was something misleadingly breezy in his smile. With his cleft chin, clear eyes, and even teeth, he could have been a movie star. Pharmaceutical representation had been only one of many available careers. Elegant, nervous, streamlined Martin, the man to whom Julia could not fully explain her messy Left Coast life.

Not that he asked her to.

He *did* enjoy hearing what Julia's therapist had determined about their affair, feeling, naturally, superior to diagnosis. With a few drinks in him, he could be enticed into skewering their colleagues at Fidelity Pharm; he possessed such an elastic and mean imagination that he caricatured brilliantly, chillingly. Julia had named this trait *edginess*; her husband did not possess it. With edginess, however, came the edge— over which you might fall. Julia trod lightly. She hoped Martin would never make her his critical subject. Concerning her husband, Teddy, Martin held vague and charitable views. The dead brother, the psychotic break, the lesser career, the tendency toward beer and television sports and a spare tire. *Sentimental slob,* he seemed to have decided, *poor bastard*; the community-college teaching job, in Martin's opinion, was of the "those who can't" variety. Simple logic dictated that Julia would need more, other, opposite. What Martin didn't understand, she thought, was that he wasn't really opposite. He wasn't the same as Teddy, true—and no one but Julia would see the similarity, the fact that he was like her husband, dedicated to the life he'd made, tight as a tick with his confidence in its worthiness. And attracted, apparently, to someone like Julia.

Moreover, if Martin knew Teddy, if he were Teddy's friend, for instance, singing around the piano, playing with his children, then he wouldn't be able to sleep with Julia. Period. That was the kind of men they were. Julia, mistress and wife, alone understood the essential, mutual ignorance.

Only after Martin had asked, three separate times over the phone, inflecting each of the three simple words differently—"How are *you*? How *are* you? *How* are you?"—did she recall that he still believed her pregnant. In the aftermath of the vandalism, she'd forgotten to miscarry.

On the way home from the police station, she and Billie sat stalled in traffic. In the pile of recovered loot, Billie had found her old key ring. A real ring with real keys that she had collected as a toddler: skeleton keys, old house keys, skate keys, luggage keys, any random key that was no longer of real use. Having a key ring made her feel like one of the big people. She'd gone around unlocking everything, dishwashers and kitty cats and tangerines.

"Some of this stuff isn't mine," Billie said now, shaking the set. She showed Julia a baby-bottle-shaped eraser token that was not actually a baby bottle, on closer investigation, but a small pink penis. And there was a silver key, thick, square, with the instruction not to duplicate it on one side and the number 818 on the other.

Eight hundred and eighteen was the number of the hotel room Julia and Martin had shared in Cancún, in September, back when they could have accidentally made a baby. Coincidence. And this couldn't be that key, because that key had been a card, two of them, one for Julia, one for Martin, kept as souvenirs, then discarded with all the other evidence of her love affair. Discarded in case she was killed, discarded in case someone was charged with investigating her life after it was over. In case she had the power to ambush her husband and children from afar, the power held in objects, mute and inscrutable things. For a second, she envisioned another car accident, in Brussels or Seattle or New Orleans, in a Mirage or an Intrigue or an Intrepid, one in which her dead hand was clutched by Martin's.

"Do you think you could find the lock if you wanted to?" her daughter asked.

"Doubtful," Julia said.

"I bet I could find it," Billie said. Julia looked at the girl. At the station, one of the cops had stared at Billie, running his appraising male eyes up and down her slim body before casting a glance in Julia's direction. Julia flashed back to the odd arrangement of underwear on her bed, the seeming import of it, in the topsy-turvy house—a message, if someone cared to receive it.

Billie, scrutinizing the third of the mystery objects on her key ring, a long, old-fashioned brass key with something etched on it, announced her findings: "Sally Cummins. I know her."

It was one of the fourteen-year-old thieves. "You know her?"

"I know her." The words seemed somehow proudly produced: *I know her.*

"How do you know her?" Julia asked. But Billie wasn't going to say. She gazed defiantly into her mother's face. She resembled her father, with only one obvious feature of Julia's, a slightly wide nose. Her nostrils flared now, barely perceptible, the breathing flex of will, like a thoroughbred just before its race. If traffic hadn't shifted at precisely that second—brake lights flashing off, movement, horns—Julia might have been able to get her talking. But the moment passed.

Her daughter's secret was safe, Julia thought, and so was hers. She loved a man who was not her husband, a situation against which she was ceaselessly building a case, collecting data that proved her own mistake, only to neglect it, dissemble it willingly again and again. Soon she would need to have an imaginary late-pregnancy miscarriage or abortion. Either way, she had to undo what she had done, even if it was only in Martin's mind that she had done it. There was Martin—whose existence often felt invented, as if Julia, like a child, had dreamed up an imaginary friend with whom to share her life, this man she loved who lived strictly separate from the sunshine and shimmering asphalt around her, who had yet to be notified of the nonexistent fate of a nonexistent fetus—and there was her now-teenage daughter beside her whose former little voice begged on tape to be able to clean up after the puppy she fantasized owning. And there was Martin's unseen daughter and her dooming superiority on the flute, and those girls who'd nonchalantly carried their instruments after playing them at a high school concert one night when Julia had imagined she was really pregnant, and then there was the strange girl named Sally who'd crawled into her house, uninvited, to steal and ransack and mark.

I know her, Julia would remember her daughter saying whenever those transparent images left on her sitting room walls reappeared, ghostly whisperings—*Pssst*—in the rare right light for many years to come. They would outlive her children's childhoods. They would outlive her puzzling love for Martin. They were of hearts, strangely enough, something any girl, good or bad, might idly draw, sloppy valentines to remind Julia of other lies she believed.

Eminent Domain

WHAT CAUGHT PAOLO's attention was the smile, teeth extravagantly white and large, orthodontically flawless. Expensive maintenance in the mouth of a homeless woman. Around the smile was a pale, animated face, around that a corona of wild purple hair. The owner of this gleeful mouth was drunk, her flame of a head swaying on the thin stick of her body, lit at nine in the morning on the front stoop of a condemned Baptist church. Its facade alone remained. The vast skirt of the steps fronted the building the way the smile did the woman's face: behind was a pile of rubble, scatter of boards and bricks and glass, a frightening exploded emptiness.

This neighborhood was called transitional; anything could happen. Paolo drove through it on his way to the theater for rehearsals. Every day she balanced on the church steps, surrounded by a shifting group of men. Always the only girl and, as a result, the center of a kind of stoned, stunned, possessive attention. They surveyed the street, drinking from bags, leaning on bundles, panhandling with plastic cups,

123

124 · A N T O N Y A   N E L S O N

laughing too loudly, ready to attack anyone who made the mistake of approaching their girl. Stripped of props such as cars or homes, they stood aggressively unprotected, brazen wildness in their eyes. Some wore hospital wristbands. They adopted dogs and then took better care of them than they did themselves. Their own habits seemed like those of a stray, the unclaimed, uncollared mutt trotting purposefully through parking lots or along sidewalks, city savvy, jauntily dodging danger, its only objective the next meal or drink, a place to lie down. When inspired, the group catcalled in the direction of the traffic—provoked by an angry driver, a hand gesture or shout, the look of fear in an elderly face or disgust in another, the mere fact of a particularly ostentatious vehicle like the Humvee or Bentley. Other times they collected aluminum cans in grocery carts. You'd see them paired off on recycling day, scrounging through the green bins left curbside. Strange economy, Paolo thought. You could grow so accustomed to their presence that you stopped seeing them, driving the streets trolling for a parking space instead of watching the people. But there they were—everywhere, like squirrels; with routines, like mailmen. The church where they gathered was being destroyed to accommodate the new freeway, a ramp that currently jutted raggedly into the sky, a road to nowhere; eminent domain.

But Paolo felt he must know the woman. His attention to her was riveted, every morning anew. Her animation most likely had to do with her high, with being the only female and therefore the source of a kinetic sexual friction not only among the men in her circle but among the men in the passing cars, and among the ones wearing hard hats and safety vests, operating the raucous city equipment erecting the freeway. She presided in the manner of the stripper before a paying audience. Still, Paolo stared with what he knew to be special interest, something about her that he alone perceived . . . Then one day he knew what it was. He squealed to a halt in traffic. The street people looked at the source of sound, the lazy, blinking regard of lizards, zoo animals. And there, showcased among them, was Bobby Gunn's girl. Sophie Gunn. A Houston River Oaks Country Club girl. Not a woman at all. Debutante, she should be, by now. Through the steamy window of his convertible, Paolo took her in, the furthest thing from a debutante he could imagine, and she gazed upon him, a taunting expression that said she was high, protected, superior. Her glance said, *You fear me; you may even envy me.* He felt as caught as he had by her smile: snared by a corresponding flash of embarrassment from himself, irrepressible, as if she'd snapped his confused face in a photograph and therefore had a record. Then her smile faltered. She staggered backward. Now she understood that she knew him, that he had ties to her past. That he might leap from his car and reveal her spoiled origins. She was slumming, while her companions had no other options. Was that it, simply threat, exposure both here and to her parents? She and Paolo held the gaze as if connected by an invisible filament, across traffic, through the windshield, as if time had gelled.

Then it jerked forward—horns blared all around him. Houston drivers were patient, to a point—their Southern manners, maybe the languor that humidity encouraged—then just as surly as their counterparts in New York. He hadn't been a driver in New York, and his skills were still rudimentary. He sometimes forgot he was in charge of the car and drifted, foot ambivalent on the pedals. He lurched away now, sure, and saddened by it, that Sophie Gunn, having been recognized, wouldn't hold court on the steps tomorrow.

Paolo was having a sort-of secret affair with a patron of the arts who was ten years older than he and divorcing. *Sort of* because it seemed that most people knew. Her husband the heart surgeon had been charged in a recent scandal at the hospital—a dull scandal having to do with billing rather than with botched surgery or drug trafficking—the details of which he'd kept from his wife. It was the intern mistress, his new confidante, who would have to appear in court, in the pages of the *Chronicle,* implicated. The hospital escapade was just another in a rash in Houston of police bungling and energy intrigue and insane ego; reading the daily news could be like following a few different soap operas, each its own genre, its cast peopled by types. The surgeon's wife enjoyed the installments of the hospital saga starring her husband. Mary Annie, her name was. She had such a tendency toward laughing herself to tears that she couldn't wear eye makeup. She referred to herself as *well preserved,* which meant she had blond-streaked hair and tennis-ball arm muscles, minimal wrinkles, snappy fashion sense. She'd grown up in West Texas, tough from her childhood ranch rearing and larger-than-life father. Pampered in a peculiar way, she was expected not only to perform all of the typical female functions but to cultivate an additional set of skills, the bawdy, tolerant sense of humor, the whiskey voice, the distinct and disarming impression she left of knowing your weaknesses and forgiving them in advance. Intelligent by nature, a horse handler, a tea drinker, a student of nursing, formally educated in the East, and now curious about the creative arts. Cautious in love for having been wounded by her husband, that coward, that man whom her father had enthusiastically offered to come shoot dead. Texans: they were a breed apart.

Paolo had been seated next to Mary Annie at one of what he'd named the Rubber Chicken Events. They came with the visiting-artist territory; this year was his last as actor-in-residence, the fifth. How many fund-raising dinners had he attended? Round tables of benefactors who wanted to meet the talent. Each table sported a performer and seven others; for these affairs he fortified himself with Scotch. Mary Annie had been the odd uncoupled one across from Paolo; she'd smiled into her plate when he was asked how he prepared for his roles as, well, such *lowlifes.* His calling was malfeasance. Iago, for instance.

"Assholes are easy," he said. The dowagers and their husbands liked to be scandalized; it was part of what their thousand-dollar-a-plate meal bought for them. Profanity from a man in a rented tux. The flinch in Mary Annie's face when he spoke brought Paolo up short. He hadn't meant real offense; the fund-raiser was becoming its own specific role, for which he had stale lines that revealed impishness and mock insouciance. Alternately, he could drop clues about his drug-tinged past, his modest forays into oblivion. It was this self he used to redeem himself with Mary Annie. Later, they became true intimates; not when she'd undressed for him in a hotel room, nor when they'd kissed in her car, but when, on the telephone, she had confessed that she was puzzling over the problem of her daughter's pregnancy. She didn't want to be called *Granny* or *Nana* or any other fossilizing term of endearment. She was only forty-four, for God's sake. Then Paolo knew he'd truly been let in.

Mary Annie wasn't Paolo's first affair with an older married woman. The last one, Louise, had contracted breast cancer during their involvement; recovering had led her not only back to her husband and children but to her forsaken Catholicism. She'd struck a bargain during treatment, and since God had apparently held up His end, she'd done the honorable thing herself. "You aren't very good with weakness," she'd told Paolo, tears in her eyes, prosthetics in her blouse. With effort, he kept his gaze on her face. "I loved you, but I've realized it wasn't a very healthy love. It didn't include damage. It didn't go deep." She touched her throat. "I thought you were like an insurance policy, or maybe like a Plan B, but while I was in the hospital, I saw that it was a really weak thing, us, just a flimsy connection with no power at all."

"None?"

"Not really." She'd seemed sad to have to confess it, but she no longer had time for frivolous chitchat, lightness, the idle phone calls they'd shared when her family wasn't home, making puns and relating their childhoods. Time had turned into hard currency rather than, say, flower petals or fireworks.

"Or maybe," she said, her eyes clearing with new insight, "maybe the affair was like the cancer, just a sick secret that needed to be wiped out. I told my husband. You must never contact me again." She'd pecked him—yes, *peck* was properly the word—on the cheek and disappeared from his life.

At lunch with Mary Annie, he did not mention the girl on the church steps. Already he'd decided.

He might have first met Sophie Gunn at Mary Annie's house. There could have been a function there once upon a time, the child brought along in a dress with a bow in her hair, or perhaps the reluctant teen in her outfit of chains and denim. For five years, he'd gone to these houses and shaken the hands of a parade of youngsters. Whatever she'd been, she'd shed it.

"Head's too tall for your roll bar," Sophie said to him there at the curb, after which she coughed ferociously, making a fist and hacking into it. He'd parked before the church and she'd stepped forward automatically, the representative of her crew, a pack of cigarettes squashed suggestively behind her metal-studded belt. He was glad to see that she hadn't been scared away by his recognition of her. It was a sunny February day; he had the roof down, sunglasses on.

"Beg pardon?"

She repeated her cryptic statement. Was she crazy? Flirting? Clever? All three, he decided, certainly under the influence; yet what she said was true: his convertible's roll bar didn't quite reach the top of his skull. He patted his hair protectively. Given a chance to do it over, he'd have chosen a less ridiculous vehicle. You did something for the first time and you went a little mad. "Hey, *you* could give *me* a ride," she was saying, pantomiming, pointing at him, back at herself.

Knowing her name, he should have delivered her straightaway to her parents' home. Maybe to Mary Annie's. But he had never seen himself as a savior. He was an observer at best, a bad influence or an attractive nuisance at worst. A stringer-alonger. An actor, for God's sake, hungry for the disreputable, the late hour when the good people slept, the bright pill to pull surprises from the head as with a magic hat, the accomplice met only after the precise stages of descent. Dark impulses were almost never denied, wending as they did toward trouble.

"Get in," he told her.

He took her to a Taco Cabana and bought her beans and rice and guacamole. She was a vegetarian, which made Paolo laugh. She joined him; it was as if the same silly slogans ran through their minds, *Sleep in the street, don't eat meat. Smoke pot, not pigs.* Her wits were still about her. How long would they last? She knew everyone at the restaurant and greeted them extravagantly. She was indulged; the neighborhood had not yet turned its gentrifying back on her ilk. And she had not yet acquired the look of derelict. Her skin was intact, mostly clean, exposed with such randomness that you kept seeking the neglected nook or cranny. The clothes seemed fashionably ripped, held on to a pretty girl's body with safety pins and zippers, a rivet-studded bracelet that Paolo was alarmed to recognize as a cock ring. She wore combat boots, which maybe would never go out of a certain style. Every few days, she told Paolo, she went to a high school friend's house and watched television, took a shower, sat on a sofa. "And dye my hair," she added thoughtfully. The color was eggplant, tipped in jet black. Her vanity about it interested Paolo; some product had been used to make it flare up rather than lie limp. He stared for a long while at her beautifully smooth arms until he realized she had to have shaved them, and recently, to achieve the look. Style: how it has a hold on us.

He needed to know if she was eighteen yet. The wholeness of the number signified something. But she wouldn't say. He pretended not to know what that meant.

Without asking, without promising, they struck some bargain—the kind made between people who would eventually sleep together, whose business was mostly of the subterranean, unspoken variety—that he would not tell her parents where she was. Her father was Bobby Gunn, who had slid out from several investment and oil businesses just before they'd toppled; he was the minorest of minor players in two of the newspaper soaps. "Wily," Sophie said of her dad. "Daddy," she referred to him. Either it was an affectation (and it *was* charming) or, as a Southerner, she was unaware of the word's perverse disharmony when she used it. "Daddy," she said, as in "Daddy once called the police and had me arrested for pawning Mama's jewelry." She'd also summoned the police to come get him; he'd beaten her when she set fire to the playroom—shot the garden hose at her after extinguishing the blaze, then whipped her unrepentant, grinning face with the hose's metal-banded nozzle. They went tit for tat at that household, apparently.

All that Paolo could recall was Bobby Gunn's habit of mumbling. He'd tucked it away as a curiosity for future use in a character study. The under-your-breath aside, the meanness most people kept to themselves rather than muttering aloud. You could never be sure what Bobby Gunn was saying when he engaged in conversation. "Fuck you," Sophie had said, sotto voce, instead of "Thank you" as a girl her own age wearing the Taco Cabana paper hat had disdainfully taken her order.

"I used to Magic-Marker *I want to die* on my arms during tests if I hadn't studied. *Bada-bing,* down to the counselor's office." She was providing him with tips for a kind of survival. She was entertaining him. She was trying not to lose the urge that was uniquely her own, brattiness, joy, jokes, willfulness. The need to shock. "When I was a baby, I would bang my head on the floor until they gave me what I wanted." Paolo noted how tidily she ate, etiquette lessons still coursing through her system like the blood of a feline, fastidious and sexy.

"Didn't you used to ride horses?" Paolo said, an image returning to him like a forgotten dream.

"Yep," she responded. Bobby Gunn's daughter had been wearing jodhpurs when last Paolo had known of her. She had stepped into a living room party when all present were lulled by liquor into a dreamy observation of her garments, the strange grand uniform, part English Regency, part Vegas showgirl, the boots, the helmet, and—especially— the crop. She'd been teenage scornful, eyebrows arched, lips twitching as if to hold back a derisive snort. She had a knowingness beyond her parents' and their friends', a skepticism—a fringe-factor affiliation— that Paolo shared, wide enough to allow him to recognize her otherwise unrecognizable self on the steps of the torched Baptist church three blocks from his garage apartment. Without it, he wouldn't have been able to unearth her in that smile.

"Aren't you supposed to be in school?" Stupid, stupid, stupid, he instantly berated himself. But she wasn't listening. She was expanding her eyes as if to hypnotize him.

She leaned across the lunch debris. "What would you pay me to suck you off?"

"What?"

"Not *what,* how much? *Cuánto?*"

"I wouldn't, at any price." Paolo hated the heat that infused his face, the repulsion that accompanied it. Hadn't he just been looking at that flesh in full possession of unclean thoughts? Her confidence wasn't complete; he told himself she didn't know what she was doing, that she was trying on vulgarity rather than genuinely inhabiting it. "I'll lend you money."

"But I can't pay you back, so I have to do something for it. I have to earn it."

"It can be a long-term loan. In ten years, it'll come due."

"I'll be dead," she said breezily. "Daddy says all debts are forgiven in death." She took twenty dollars. "I won't buy drugs," she promised boredly, anticipating his next stupid statement. She withdrew a foil-wrapped half-stick of chewing gum from her jeans pocket and poked it in her mouth. When Paolo delivered her to a tattoo parlor a mile away, she gave him a kiss on the cheek that left a small minty tingle.

He didn't see her for a week, although he looked. Had his twenty dollars bought her oblivion? Then there she was, outside the Starbucks he sometimes frequented. He locked his convertible with his usual sense of futility; anyone with a knife—screwdriver, ballpoint pen, sharp fingernail—could hack through the roof.

"What are you up to?" he asked nonchalantly, hugely relieved to see her. He understood that from now on, he was the owner of a small gnawing anxiety with her name attached to it, an irritation that only her living presence would soothe.

"You can't believe how nervous people get when you walk into their place of business carrying one of these." She brandished a red plastic gas container like a lunch box.

"Well, yes," Paolo agreed.

Over coffee—she ordered a large sweet beverage full of whipped cream and caramel, a kid's concept of coffee, consumed with a spoon— she proposed a few favors he might perform for her. Her cohorts in the world of the disenfranchised, while often fun and generally supportive, couldn't render all required aid. Listening, Paolo was already justifying his attraction to her. He would save her, he told himself as he nodded along. Surely he was better for her than the boys she was currently hanging around. Boys? Men. And more adept at the traditional manly functions than Paolo was, decidedly. Fighters. Hunters, gatherers— after a fashion. Addicts, scroungers, streetwise. Paolo wouldn't last in that world, that odd cosmos out there. He was the pampered dilettante, supported by the gifts of women who were starved and bored and eager for a cause, his patrons. Sophie could be his cause as he was theirs. He was like them, he thought, discreetly nudging the gasoline container beneath the table. Not so different from those do-gooders.

People at Starbucks looked at Sophie surreptitiously; they didn't want to be the staring sort, but her outfit demanded it, the holes in the shirt, the low ride of her filthy pants, the absence of underwear. The piercings in her face—a new one, maybe, in the eyebrow?—and that mass of wine-colored spiky fluff on top.

"This is a school day, right?" she asked suddenly.

"Thursday," he said. "No, Wednesday."

She sent him into her private school to clean out her locker, abandoned several months ago but still full of stuff.

"They're afraid to disenroll me," Sophie explained. "It's too hard to get back in, you sign up for this shithole, like, in utero, so instead they just put me *on leave.*" She said the last words like a phrase in French.

He was old enough to be her father, more or less; only old enough, he told himself, if he'd fathered her when he had been in high school himself. And that helped. The woman at the attendance desk did not blanch; she sent him with a prissy aide who made a point of looking away when the locker door swung open to reveal its decoration of broken mirrors and slashed photographs, everything held in place with duct tape. Paolo had the feeling that much of what he removed from the locker did not legitimately belong to Sophie.

He could hear his stereo, practically see the poor little car throbbing, as he hustled across the parking lot. Sophie snapped the radio off before he complained, greeting him with "No one in that building has ever set foot in a public school." And, anticipating his next remark, added, "Including the janitor."

"Nuh-uh."

"Uh-huh," she hummed confidently. Her locker made her seem more deeply disturbed than Paolo had thought. She was a liar, a thief, a beautiful, broken, fathomless girl. She had acne in her eyebrows, which were still blond. When he handed over the locker's contents (the aide had fetched him a box), she immediately separated the salable from the personal and sent him back inside to the bookstore to redeem the goods, including her textbooks, uniform jacket, padlock, calculator, and transferable St. James patch emblem—yellow cross, red ribbon, blue justice's scales.

He was sweating by the time it was over, unnerved in a specifically immature way. This was the business of adolescence. What was he thinking? An alarm was sounding, he believed, alerting all the parents and law-abiding citizens.

"Tell me your name?" Sophie said as they drove away from the scene of the crime.

"Paul," he said automatically, reverting to the lie; he was legitimately Paolo but, as a child, had adopted Paul for use in school or on the street, leaving it and childhood in Milwaukee when he moved to New York. His mother had given him his name; from her, he'd also acquired the habit of crossing his fingers, knocking on wood, making wishes, and looking for portents. On his forehead was her same worried V, entrenched right between his eyes.

"You're cool, Paul," said Sophie Gunn, thanking him, blessing him; again her lips against his cheek. Back at the church steps, she took her box of goods and cash and waved goodbye. And like a functionary of a kind of church, he'd fed her, he'd listened without judgment, he'd given her money; what more could he do?

At his garage apartment, he took advantage of the rare sunny afternoon to lie on his deck and tan, gauging his moral temperature. Would he have attached himself to a runaway boy? To an ugly girl? And why was he trying to imagine bringing her here, to his home? What did he have in mind? Below, in the backyard of the main house, a pool shimmered. Once it had been for swimming, but not anymore. It had been altered by the current owners, Paolo's hosts, filled with concrete except for the top eighteen or so inches. A giant shallow pool that attracted clouds of mosquitoes and wandering rodents—Paolo watched from his garage quarters the evening show of possum or raccoon or rat as they approached the body of tepid water cautiously, then slipped in their snouts, alert to all around them. The rustle of frogs or snakes in the leaves. The maniac hum of bug at your ear. The prodigious steamy output of tropical plants. The atmosphere was insidious, suggestive. He drank beer as the sky turned city pink.

His hosts were patrons of the arts; his quarters came to him free of charge. Yet there was a cost. It was his privacy, of which he had none. A steep price, actually, all things considered. You wouldn't know the cost until you had something to hide, however. He assessed it now as he acknowledged his desire to bring Sophie here, to give her a place to sleep for the night. His thinking took him no further than seeing her safely on his futon, beneath a borrowed bedsheet, wearing a pair of his soft shorts. In a little while, his hosts would be home from work, standing on their deck, waving up at him with drinks in their hands, the way they did every evening, beaming at their pet.

It seemed wise to fill her Ritalin prescription for her, picking it up from the safety of the Walgreens drive-through lane, his eyes skidding wildly for spies in the parking lot. The pharmacist probably wouldn't sell it to her, or would phone her parents since she wasn't an obvious adult. Her shabby, hostile clothes didn't help, nor the scary stud in her nostril. The plan charged her twenty dollars a month for her supply. It kept her from losing focus, she told him. It interacted well with cigarettes, marijuana, alcohol. Not so well with cocaine or Ecstasy. He took in this information without expression. "And I can always sell a few of them," she added. "Some people think it's a trip."

On a weekly basis, he delivered her to therapy in a building without windows. This seemed sane, choosing therapy. The office was for the indigent; there wasn't even a parking lot beside it, just an open door and a steady stream of runaways and homeless, people who endured an hour of questions in order to recline on a padded chaise in refrigerated air. Sophie enjoyed her doctor, who was a young, idealistic man who had himself run away, suffered a kind of free-floating angst having to do with entitlement and disillusion. Out sweating in his car, Paolo had several less-than-noble thoughts on the topic of Sophie's therapy. For instance, was the doctor attracted to her? And if so, was Sophie mutually inclined? What really happened on that Naugahyde surface? Was Paolo perhaps a subject? He didn't inquire, Sophie didn't reveal. He, like the therapist, was careful never to seem like a probing parent; a younger beau might have been able to scold her for being high, for endangering herself, for eluding her mother and father. But Paolo couldn't. If it weren't for those very things, he wouldn't be with her at all. If she were still a senior at St. James High, living in her wallpapered girlhood bedroom, preparing for prom, he wouldn't be anywhere near her. There would be no virtue in seducing her as her parents' child, only reproach and judgment, banishment. Instead, he enjoyed the luxury of being better than the alternative, those filthy men and boys. They were a lost tribe of person, citizens of a fantasyland they kept vivid by ingesting, or failing to ingest, mixtures of chemicals. They slept in the bayou and ate out of Dumpsters, stood on street corners with signs and cups and occasionally a musical instrument. They talked to themselves and others about Jesus, whose story, for whatever reason, continued to strike a chord in the community. The oddest Paolo had known about was the one with horns—a stump on each side of his forehead, surgically installed—a man whose ambition it was to become a troll. Paolo was preferable, by far, over him; this was the ongoing argument he made to Sophie's imagined parents, the Gunns.

Whenever they parted, she kissed him. First it had been on the cheek; now it was on the mouth. What, he asked himself, would that tongue stud feel like, slipped between his teeth?

During rehearsals, he imagined her observing him from the depths of the dark auditorium seating, her clunky shoes hoisted onto the seat before her, the bullshit-detecting gaze leveled through her knobby ankle bones and booted feet at his performance under the lights onstage, and he addressed himself to her skeptical expectation, to prove himself worthier than her fantastical doubt.

"You were on fire," his director praised him, and Paolo, still spellbound by Sophie, waved it away.

Her name came up by accident with Mary Annie. Paolo's blood surged—in his face, his heart, his groin. They were vacuuming her SUV at a self-serve car wash, sucking up the Irish-setter hair. Over the noise of the suction, she mentioned that the Gunns had been through three different private investigators before deciding Sophie must have left the city. Mary Annie and the Gunns were social acquaintances, on many of the same boards and members of the same country club. The older Gunn daughter had gone to school with Mary Annie's girl Meredith. The families weren't close friends, but the gossip of their lives circulated through their ranks. They'd all had problem teenagers. There was a lot of support in the system. Mary Annie was stretched across the carpeted cargo cabin, jamming the nozzle of the machine into the crevices, when she said, "I really feel for the Gunns. These kids are like terrorists. They hold their families hostage, basically. They make threats, they break negotiating promises, they aren't afraid of the occasional suicide bombing. Tell me how they're different than these other people we've declared terrorists."

Paolo had no answer. She supplied her own, sighing as the machine abruptly ceased. "We love them," she said. "That's the problem." Her eyes were moist; her own daughter, the one due to deliver the first grandchild in three months, had been a wild girl. She'd had to go survive in a camp in Utah for a few weeks, detoxing on a cliff top, rappelling and rafting and eating nuts and berries around a campfire with a bunch of other druggies. The cost for such restoration was astronomical; Paolo thought it sounded like a racket, but wisely kept this to himself. "If they could find Sophie, they could take her there. You can even pay a person to transport her."

"Sounds harsh."

She blinked up at him, then slammed the back hatch of the SUV. "Teenagers steal years off your life," she said. "I myself developed an esophageal disorder due to stress. I still can't use Ziploc bags without thinking of Mere's backpack full of them, of her getting kicked out of St. James for dealing pot."

"But she came through okay," Paolo said, needing it to be true. "She's fine, right? Husband? Baby?"

Mary Annie used two cupped hands to push back her hair, reattach a silver barrette held between her teeth. "Maybe. But my marriage started to go downhill because Tad and I couldn't agree what to do about her during those years. We took all of our confusion and anger at Meredith out on each other. We went at it like tigers. It's terrible to care for someone more than she cares for herself."

Mary Annie's words, these last ones, ran inescapably like a banner through Paolo's mind. He did not think he'd felt this way before, and it alarmed him to guess that it was going to soon be true of his affection for Sophie. Mary Annie often reminded him that, despite the juvenile zipping around inside of himself, he was in fact an adult. Parental concern felt more honest than that thrilled sensation he had entertained at the theater, imagining Sophie out there sarcastically clapping.

"Did you know that your mom and dad hired private eyes?" he asked the girl later, on the church steps.

This news surprised her, which was gratifying. Very little surprised her. "How hard could it be?" she asked. "Here I am."

"The point is, they're looking."

"They're doing a piss-poor job," she said, spreading her arms. "Anyone who wants can see me." But that wasn't quite true; she didn't look like her old self. His recognition of her hadn't been the same as a parent's. What they were looking for was dated, buried deep.

Couch-surfing, she called her living arrangement. But surely not on a couch in a house with mothers or fathers. Paolo bought her a cell phone because she'd thrown away hers after its battery had run down; moreover, her parents had known the number and filled the voice mail. He purchased two chargers because he was certain she would not be able to keep track of the one he provided her. The other waited in his car cigarette lighter for him to pick her up, plug in her phone as they cruised the sultry city in the comfort of air-conditioning, stereo sound, the throbbing intensity of urban youth. Sophie dozed in its rhythm. Mouth partially open, eyes closed, she could have been ten or twelve years old, an ordinary pretty child. Then the phone would ring, she'd abruptly startle awake, take her call in the savage, secret fashion of her transformation.

A few times Paolo panicked because the phone was on his plan, a cheaper alternative but an implicating one should, say, the unit be found on her dead body. He tried hard not to imagine her body dead, dead instead of sleeping against his passenger headrest. He fed her. He compromised, buying her cigarettes but not liquor. He'd wanted to hold on to the Ritalin, but she'd threatened to jump from the moving vehicle. He didn't doubt her commitment to the idea; this was the terrorist behavior Mary Annie had mentioned. He considered it progress when Sophie allowed him to care for her on a weekend night, because that was when the clubs were busiest, when the kids she knew from St. James were released and sneaked out into the dark. All the worst things happened then.

The weekends were when Mary Annie's soon-to-be-ex-husband was most likely to be pulled from sleep for an emergency transplant; the organ donors died then, then and during holidays. One family's tragedy led to another's miracle; they might meet in poignant scenes in the hospital lounges and waiting rooms. The divorce was in the works, but the terms were complicated, given his other pending lawsuit. Separate bedrooms. Mary Annie stayed in the house, waiting for the phone to ring so that her daughter could let her know she had become a grandmother. Sophie had ruined Paolo's nascent love for Mary Annie, eclipsed her elder easily, without even trying. As he sat with Mary Annie—at restaurants, concerts, movies, between the sheets of her very comfortable bed—he resented Sophie's power. And why had he given it to her, anyway?

"Hey, tough girl, don't you worry about getting busted?" Paolo said peevishly as she lit a small metal pipe in his front seat. She never asked permission. "And if not yourself, at least think of me, the adult driver." He hated to feel so threatened by rule-makers; what had become of his "question authority, fuck you" attitude?

"I was already arrested," she said, as if the event were like a baptism or an inoculation, singular and prophylactic, thereby making her currently exempt. "Dude, it's so funny." She'd been caught smoking hash in the bayou one night. The cop had cuffed her—she held her wrists together as she took a long toke from the plumbing-supply-like pipe—and dragged her to the downtown station, where he threw her in a cell. She phoned home and reached her furious father, who, on his outraged way across town, was stopped for DUI *and* resisting arrest. He wasn't allowed to drive her home, so her mother had to be called. Her mother was too sedated on pills to answer the phone, and her father was too embarrassed to call his own friends, so they ended up reaching a cousin, Mina. "Mina's a total fuckup, so we figured she wouldn't tell the rest of the family. It was our secret, me and Daddy's. We didn't fight for a while after that," she finished a little nostalgically, offering the pipe to Paolo, who declined. "And the weird thing? It happened on my mother's birthday, just after midnight on her birthday."

"That's some family you've got there," Paolo said, retracting a previous wish to see her suffer remorse. Regret, like sleep, made her look considerably younger. It was accompanied by doubt, a flitting uncertainty followed by a sigh. At even the smallest possibility of reprimand, she changed before his eyes, grew slack-faced and beaten-looking. She agreed, in advance, to deserving her punishment. Now she abruptly opened the passenger window and rapped the pipe on the exterior, where Paolo would later find a ding. Instead of dropping her off in front of the church, he suggested a long ride around the city's belt loop. Sophie took the opportunity to curl up against the headrest and take a nap, her hands in fists at her chin. That she so wholly trusted him made Paolo afraid; what if he wasn't who he—and, presumably, she—believed he was? That is, what might he do, if he were other?

In April he gave Sophie a ticket to *Othello*. The production, set contemporaneously, traded freely on the O. J. Simpson story, the national soap opera that had filled the news a few years ago. Like a high school boy, Paolo expected Sophie to materialize in the audience, to be in the seat he'd designated, to be for real where he'd installed her in his imagination these last months, and wearing an outfit suitable to the occasion, because his desire was so large as to ordain this particular impossible bit of magic. And, as in high school, he was simultaneously disappointed and validated; no girl, no adulation, no fantasy fulfilled.

It was hard, then, a week later to receive her desperate call. She phoned him from a McDonald's on Westheimer. "I feel hot," she said—not passionately but listlessly. As far as Paolo could tell, this was accurate; her forehead burned beneath his wrist, though he had no notion what he was checking for: another of his mother's gestures. At his guesthouse drive, he ascertained the absence of Clem and Sheila, his landlords and hosts, before hurrying Sophie up the rickety steps, following her lurching bottom, the painful pinch of her flesh as it met her metal belt. Once indoors, he drew the shades and opened the oven door to provide mood lighting, hiding inside his own home. She lay on his futon with a wet compress on her forehead, three aspirins, and a slug of whiskey for her cold symptoms, bare dirty feet splayed out. Her toenails were painted black. Or maybe all ten were badly bruised.

"I can't sleep," she said. "It's been two days, and I just can't fucking sleep!"

"What did you take?" Paolo asked.

"Nothing," she claimed. But later revised, a few unknown things, not much, nothing new, that was for sure, and far less than usual. He was afraid to ask her to change her clothing, though it wasn't fresh-smelling; the sheets wouldn't conform to the bed, slipping off under her twitching anger to be constantly realigned. At his sink, he took a hammer to a bundle of ice cubes, turning them into something palatable and cool for her, shards of slippery water passed from his trembling hand to her pink tongue. He thrilled sickeningly as she closed her lips around his fingers. He promised himself that if she showed just one sign of hallucinating or seizure, he'd rush her to the E.R.

"My mind is racing," she said. "I just can't relax." This made her cry, that despite her exhaustion she could not let go of consciousness. Paolo knew the feeling. He sat beside her on the futon.

"When I was young," he said, remembering it as he spoke, "my mother used to do this thing." He cleared his throat, lifted his voice, trying on his mother's cigarette-tinged steadiness, her words like a rich note sustained on a saxophone. "Imagine lying in a field," he began, reaching into a very distant past. A field of grass, he said, the ground below your head and hands, and the sky above. A little wind, the sound of . . . he improvised with wind chimes, because Sheila's were tinkling faintly from the yard. "You think you're relaxed, lying in your field, but not yet, you aren't. Squeeze your toes, squeeze and squeeze, and then let them go, just let them go, they might feel like they want to float . . ." The ankles, the thighs, the hipbones, the clavicle. Up the body he went, from toes to knees to ribs to face. The ground, his mother said, was warm with dirt and cool with grass, hard enough to support you, soft enough to forgive. Paolo's breathing slowed as he took Sophie through the incantation. He'd been his mother's youngest child, her only boy, his three older sisters wild girls who disappeared into the night laughing, leaving Paolo and their worried mother to wait for them at home. When he couldn't sleep, when his vivid imagination that would become the source of his later success undermined and plagued him, images flashing before his closed young eyes in a fearsome beating pattern, he called for his mother, who sat beside him and summoned the field of grass, the easy breeze, drifting clouds, sunshine, sleep.

"Whattarya, Yoga Man?" Sophie said, a smile in her voice, obeying his commands to clench and release, seize and relinquish. Calm overtook them both. The oven light flickered. A distant siren cried. And finally she slept, her fists as usual near her chin, her limbs still randomly twitching, the drugs firing and ricocheting inside her despite her essential absence. Paolo sat breathing as deeply as his guest, more peaceful than he'd been in months. Either it was the sureness of her safety, here with him behind the closed gate and the locked guesthouse door, under the influence of sleep, or it was his dead mother's sudden presence.

"Let him have it," she said later, from inside a dream. "He can have it, I don't want it." She followed through with a dismissive swipe of her hand, which flopped off the futon to the floor.

While he waited for morning—for light, for the disappearance of fever, for whatever shift toward optimism was going to occur—he switched on the radio to a jazz station, a reminder of another past, this time New York and his mature youth, the nights he'd sat before a window apprising the landscape and his satisfying melancholy in its secret heart. Out this Houston window flowed the humid street below, the shimmering pool, the lights at Clem and Sheila's after they came home, his view of their house like a dollhouse, the windows that revealed their move from downstairs to up, ritual, ablutions, the absentminded passage through doors and halls, lights flaring and extinguishing, objects shifted from one room to another, keys, mail, laundry, glass of water. Sheila habitually visited each closet to check for vandals. Would his life ever resemble that life? House, pool, wife, routine? This garage apartment was designed for their children's visits, those eventual adults who'd implicitly promised to provide the gift of grandchildren. When Sophie rolled to the far side of the futon and fell into a heavier, unromantic sleep, Paolo shut the oven door, lowered the radio's volume to a vague hum, and removed his outer layer of clothes. Wearing boxer shorts and a T-shirt, he carefully positioned himself beside her, moving so stealthily as to become one with the furniture, another comforting feature of her curative evening. Her back was turned to him, her hand on her hip. He rested his head beside her pillow, shaping himself to complement her shape, breathing in the complicated odor of her head, hair product, smoke, sweat, something metallic, perhaps from her various ring hardware. He lay a long time inching his hand toward hers, at last covering it, where it made a fist in his grip. She arched herself backward against him automatically, her reflex one of welcome rather than repulsion, an attraction to the source of heat. And for a second, Paolo reacted without thinking, pressing his instant erection along the seam of her pants, the tip creased painfully by her studded belt. If he shut his eyes and let himself pretend, he could have followed through, told himself she had done much more with many worse, and later, she most likely wouldn't even remember.

Instead, he turned himself over, planting a friendly backside against hers. His eyes were wide and he was aware of his blinking them, yet soon enough he returned to the grassy field they both inhabited, watching the clouds, drifting with her by his side.

In the morning, she was gone. He could have dreamed the evening, for all the evidence it had left. After trying her cell phone—"Hey, muthafucka, leeme a messssssssage"—he drove to the church, but it was an act of hope rather than reason. Now he was like her parents, he thought, seeking her at a disadvantage, lagging two steps behind, berating himself for having let her slip, literally, through his fingers.

"Where's our friend?" he shouted to the troll, who, along with his horns, had a terrible hunched back that he kept hidden beneath a cape. Maybe the one disfigurement had led to the urge for the other. He did a kind of "You talking to me?" routine before he limped reluctantly to Paolo's vehicle and scowled in at him. "Our friend Sophie," Paolo clarified. The man's forehead sprouted two inch-high protrusions, each of which, although bluish in color, clearly had veins of blood circulating just under the tight, thin skin. "Wow," Paolo added, unable not to comment. Without thinking, he touched his own forehead. Though Sophie had patiently given him all the names of all of her comrades, Paolo had instead assigned nicknames, the Troll, the Rooster, the Slag Heap, Mr. Natural. Others were moving slowly toward his car. If they decided that it was he, Paolo, who was responsible for Sophie's disappearance, what might they do to him?

"Fuck off, man," said the Rooster. He was older than Paolo had realized, a tense man with a bright orange Mohawk razored straight up the middle of his head. His features were tiny and sharp beneath it, jammed in the center of his face, ears off alone on either side, filled with safety pins and fish hooks. Tattoos crawled up from his shirt collar. When he walked along Montrose, he kept up a purposeful pace and swung a car antenna before him as if bushwhacking. He and the Troll and a half dozen others virtually surrounded Paolo's little convertible. Someone put an anchoring foot on the rear bumper, creating an ominous sag. "Loose change, my brother?" asked the Slag Heap. He was a toothless black man, huge and harmless-seeming. He was always attended by two younger black men, not always the same ones, but always boys whom Paolo could imagine as members of the Slag Heap's family, sent on a rotating basis to guard their uncle's alcoholic meanderings.

"How's it going?" Paolo said to them, looking for allies among the group. "You guys seen Sophie? Purple hair?" He searched for other descriptors as the two teenagers waited, nonplussed.

"Last I saw, she was with you, Miata." So they had named him, too. Well, that was only fair. The Rooster reached into his pocket and Paolo flinched, fearing a gun or a knife. Instead, he pulled out a cell phone. "You the one calling?" Paolo stared at Sophie's phone. "'Cause she asked me to take her calls." He put the little device to his cheek. "Hold, please."

"Where is she?" Paolo asked. But none of them was saying. He felt as if he'd been sent back to elementary school, to the circle of taunting children who did not play by the grown-ups' rules. If he got out of the car and grabbed for the phone, they were going to toss it among themselves. Abruptly he popped the car into gear, shooting out from under the foot on his bumper.

Why this urgency? he asked himself, shifting to third, then fourth. He'd gone days and weeks before. Yet he felt he had to share with her one important fact: *I didn't do anything,* he would say. *I was good, nothing happened.*

At the end of Paolo's time in Houston, on the very evening of the final of his going-away parties, she called him and said, slurrily, "Hey, I'm in jail?" His had been the only number programmed in her cell phone; he'd done it himself when he bought her the thing. While it was in possession of the gang, he'd received a few accidental calls, shouting and singing and odd bits of street noise coming over the line. Tonight, still reeling—not drunk, just achy, regretful—he dressed among the boxes holding his belongings. Before he had time to leave the house, she phoned once more, telling him she'd been mistaken: hospital, not jail. She'd been picked up riding the bus, passed out and in possession of a few controlled substances that had poured from her pockets. After she'd ridden the route twice, the bus driver had delivered her to the downtown station, where she'd been thrown in a cell before fully waking. She'd refused to tell them who she was. Her school photo, Paolo assumed, the one her parents had submitted to the cops last fall, looked nothing like her.

Someone or something—a fight, a fall—had knocked out one of her two front teeth. Her eyebrow had bled, probably because a ring had been torn from it, but the amount of blood, its flow over her face, plus her confession that she'd been thinking about killing herself, had made her captors nervous enough to send her to the emergency room rather than keep her at the station. And that was where Paolo drove, at four-thirty in the humid May morning, to retrieve her.

"Paul," she said. "You aren't wearing gloves."

In the grim green light of the basement hallway, he looked at his hands, as if he'd forgotten what was or wasn't on them. "Why would I be wearing gloves?"

"The others did." In addition to her slur, she had a vague lisp. Her inability to stand up further frightened him. The orderlies found nothing new or interesting in their situation; Paolo was allowed to sit beside her in the busy hallway as paperwork was undertaken. She wore two thin hospital gowns and an I.D. bracelet that named her as Jane Doe.

"You have to say who you are," he told her.

"No."

"Then I will. Sophie Gunn," he told the passing uniformed cop. "She's a runaway." He had joined the other side, he saw, turned into an adult. He hadn't felt such relief since a visit to a church confessional box, easily twenty years before.

"I'm eighteen," she lisped. "On May first, I was eighteen. May Queen," she added, smiling raggedly.

The cop waited for the two of them to get their stories straight. Being eighteen meant that the parents wouldn't be notified, but the possession charge would be lifted from juvenile to regular court. And then if she wasn't indigent, there was this emergency room bill to reconcile.

Beside him, Sophie started to gag. Both men shifted away instantly; she covered her mouth and looked around, following the hand gesture of another woman who sat across the hall, toward the women's room. Paolo and the cop watched her disappear behind the door. "Her father's Bobby Gunn," Paolo said. "I'll phone him if you can't."

"If she's eighteen, she doesn't need her daddy."

It was Mary Annie whom Paolo phoned. The Gunns, naturally, were not listed in the directory. She answered unsurprised, expecting a call from the hospital in the middle of the night, her daughter having recently gone through several false labors.

"It's me," Paolo said. "I'm with Sophie Gunn." His explanation was brief, uninspired, suspect, no doubt, but he was too tired to embellish, too close to leaving Houston to really care what Mary Annie thought of him after all. Maybe that was another grown-up trait, not caring. She found the phone number and wished him good luck. At the Gunns', it took a lot of rings to rouse them. Their expectation of hearing from their girl had apparently waned.

"Wha'?" said her father the mumbler.

"I've got your daughter," Paolo said. "She's with me."

But this wasn't true. For she had not returned to her seat beside Paolo after running to the restroom. The officer came back, a sheaf of papers in hand, calling her name as he passed through the hallway of the bleeding and bandaged and sedated and sad. "Gunn," he said, in time to his heavy echoing footsteps, "Gunn. Gunn. Gunn?"

There was a time, earlier in the strange relationship Paolo had with Sophie Gunn, when he should have given her up, turned her in, ended his part in a questionable business. This was at one of the ubiquitous fund-raisers, not a Rubber Chicken (sit-down) dinner but a cheese-cube, shrimp-in-its-tail, stuffed-mushroom (stand-up) affair. At this party, Paolo was paying careful attention to the Gunns, the Mrs., whose smile clearly pained her, its hollow origins no doubt her anxiety about her daughter, and Bobby, who had a talent for attracting people in a circle around him. They leaned in, scowling to make out his murmuring anecdotes. Paolo found a place on the second ring of the circle, listening, holding a wineglass like a mask before his face. Bobby Gunn, having reached a few too many times for the champagne floating by on the caterers' trays and not often enough for the hors d'oeuvres also circulating, was discussing his missing daughter. In the gathering of glamorously dressed friends, parents themselves of teenagers and young marrieds, he told in his notorious mutter about his heartbreak, the all-star-equestrian, straight-A-student daughter who ran away, who got into drugs, who was lost to them on the streets. Paolo flushed, longing for the strength to either walk away or confess. At least the father could know that the girl was fine; how could Paolo communicate it to this man, whose eyes were damp now, whose leaning listeners all reached to pat his arm or felt their own eyes fill sympathetically. They were so easily sympathetic. Really, the rich in Houston, those who believed in art and culture and putting their money where their mouths were, they seemed so civilized to Paolo, so genuinely *good*. He had developed quite a fondness for them.

"Teenage girls are the canaries in the coal mine," one of the sincere party guests posited. Paolo hadn't seen her until she spoke; her gray hair hung unfashionably long, her eyes shone with discomforting passion. But he saw her when he heard *teenage girls*. She went on, "We think they're so hard to live with, and yet just think how hard it must be to *be* them."

"Just think," one of the other listeners responded drolly, a former beauty in her husking late middle age. What she'd do, Paolo thought, to be seventeen again.

"Yet it's the boys who drive up your car insurance," said a father.

"Still, they're easier than the girls."

Such was the conventional wisdom concerning delinquency, youth: the wildness that hadn't yet been harnessed, the bad habits still blatant instead of hidden, the obsessions and addictions that would in the future be channeled, put to good or at least profitable use instead of ill and unsightly. Paolo felt distinctly his place in both worlds, the young and the old, and yet his committed belonging to neither. Now the crowd began offering their own evidence. Teenage girls: This one stole her grandmother's silver. That one drove a car into the swimming pool. Another left the children she was baby-sitting to go to the liquor store with her boyfriend. Or she let the children watch as she screwed the boyfriend, sex ed in the family room. She'd leaped from a roof. She'd run naked through the mall. She'd set up an Internet porn site featuring herself and her sisters. She'd said to her mother, each and every day, "Die, you psycho cunt!" These girls. These lessons they had taught their parents and that their parents recited. They were presented like poker hands, wagered and outdone, one-upped.

But Bobby Gunn raised his voice over the general din. His story was not over, he'd been cut off.

Apparently he was offering advice—solace, warning?—to one of the circle of listeners, a newcomer, the parent of a girl eleven years old, just now entering a rebellious, rocky terrain. This man had bowed his head, and Bobby Gunn had reached to touch his shoulder. "You've done all you can do," he said with certainty. "Sometimes it just comes down to luck. We got unlucky with ours. The worst thing you can imagine just keeps getting worse. You find yourself doing and saying the most unlikely things." He related, in his increasingly choked voice, the rest of the story. This daughter had not only disappeared but been incarcerated. While there, in psychiatric care, she'd hanged herself. Paolo gasped, his heart seized. He reached for his chest as he lost his breath, his body believing the story even as his mind swiftly contradicted. *What?* Sophie had been lounging on her stoop just that very morning, no better than yesterday, true, but certainly no worse. Incarceration? Why, that was the hash-smoking incident, with Bobby Gunn's DUI to complicate the matter. Was her father using Sophie as a way of eliciting pity? And how, exactly, did he think he could get away with it? These people had been baby-sitting and hiring and marrying and nominating and showering and cuckolding and roasting and eulogizing one another for generations; anyone besides the newcomer in the small circle would immediately learn of this lie; the community was a closed, busy, busybody buddy system. Or was this father insane with grief?

"Laurel," Bobby Gunn said then, swilling the last of his drink. The circle of friends bowed their heads. And in the time of a single breath, Paulo realized that there had been another daughter. Sophie's big sister. His mind stumbled into chaotic sync with his heart.

This was what should have forced him to end his secret life with Sophie. To retrieve his silly car from the valet service and drive three miles east to the scary rubble of the transitional side of town and pull the girl out of it, drag her by force, the nape of her neck, into this clubhouse. It should have impelled him to action. But it didn't.

Paolo returned to New York, which greeted him, as always, with precisely what he required. The city had a capaciousness, an ability to accommodate whatever mood you happened to be in when you went there. Haven. This time the form it took was anonymity. He didn't call his friends; he didn't go to parties. He walked the streets, drawn especially into the East Village, thrilled now and then by a head of hair that reminded him of Sophie Gunn's. He would turn as if to embrace or converse with her. But it was never she.

Paolo had been restored to New York for almost a year when he heard about Sophie's marriage. His old friend Mary Annie sent him the *Chronicle* picture of the girl and her fiancé, the two of them no different from any of the other photographed couples, sitting in an arbor in the usual costumes, his hands on her shoulders. Paolo didn't see her when he first scanned the page, looking for that trademark smile. But the unremarkability of the image was, of course, what made it remarkable. Her hair—could it be a wig? Surely she and all the king's hairdressers wouldn't have been able to tame that nest of singed straw and dye, nor grow it out so hastily to the blond coif she now wore. And there were no visible punctures in her eyebrows or nose or tops of her ears; airbrushing? Or had she simply healed that quickly? Credit the notorious resilience of youth and its flesh? He stared at the photo overlong, oblivious to the fiancé, the man whose hands bore no tattoos on their knuckles, whose brown hair swept over a forehead that might still be spotted with pimples but certainly not horns. That person was inconsequential to Paolo. And Paolo realized that he himself was as inconsequential to Sophie as any other reader of the newspaper, any other Houstonian who happened to page through the Lifestyle section last Sunday morning.

Through the photo Paolo gazed into Sophie's clear, smart eyes until he saw what he had missed all along: this girl had prevailed. Her triumph was in the tilt of her chin, the provocative parting of her lips, behind which lay the promise of that stunning naughty smile, the knocked-out tooth that would have been repaired. All along he'd misunderstood the role she was playing, the drama she was enacting. The story he'd been constructing for himself when he was with her, the intense duration when he wasn't turning her in to her parents or to the authorities, the length of what he'd considered his moral quandary and journey, had been another story altogether, and Sophie had been fashioning it for herself and for her mother and father and their well-intentioned, grieving friends and for her own friends still in school and, most significantly, for the memory of her sister. *I have survived,* she had concluded the tale, victor. Paolo wondered if others understood the amazing and unlikely thing she had done, the treacherous gauntlet she'd run and come through, intact, on the other side.

This same paper had announced the arrival of Mary Annie's first grandchild early last summer, a little girl named something fanciful and trendily ridiculous, something her parents, particularly her mother, Meredith, former dope dealer and hell-raiser, had fantasized and prayed would suit her as she emerged into the world.

⮑ Some Fun

SUMMER

Her little brothers don't mind when things begin going to hell. On its castors, the television comes rolling from the closet and takes a more permanent spot against the living room wall. It puts forth warmth like a fireplace and friendliness like the painted face of a clown. While Claire holds the remote control, the two small boys sit watching the hot circus of possibilities scroll by.

"Can you grow up to be an orphan?" the six-year-old asks scientifically.

"Can *I*?" responds his sister.

"No," he says. "Can *one*."

"Maybe."

He nods once, the way their father does, eyes and lips mashed in a deal-sealing pucker.

To Claire Pratt, the house feels crooked and wrong, like a house in a nightmare, as if the lightbulbs are all mint-tinted and sickly, as if the floor slants at a deadly angle down. One Sunday evening, Claire's mother lies in bed in her clothing, as if catnapping rather than coming to. She's been asleep more than twenty-four hours. When she finally wakes up, she raises her head and asks, "Do you know what I dreamed?"

Claire says she doesn't.

"I pulled a handful of rust from my ear, just crumbles of rust."

Imagining her mother's dream causes Claire to remember her own from the night before: she'd been wheeled around her neighborhood on a gurney. The boy driving the gurney was Michael Angel, the boy she loves at school. But school has ended. Michael Angel isn't the kind of boy you see over the summer.

It is a desiccating June dusk in El Paso, Texas; sweat dries before it has a chance to surface. Claire has prepared yet another meal for her younger brothers, tacos and peas. "*Frozen* frozen peas," they explain. They eat on a plastic shower curtain she's spread over the couch, their faces lit by the television screen, their hair fluttering in the damp breeze of the swamp cooler. An inferior Sunday kind of cartoon plays. Next to them on the couch sits Mr. Man, the pillow-stuffed, life-size figure wearing their father's clothing and baseball hat, a scarecrow designed to keep away bad guys, a decoy dad. Her mother asks for a can of cherry cola and some ibuprofen; after she swallows the pills, she rises and moves through the house as if testing gravity, grasping the backs of chairs, steadying herself in doorways.

"You wake up!" crows the youngest boy, the one they call Beano, who is three. Claire watches her mother all evening as the sky fades to black, waiting for the moment when she realizes how long she's been sleeping. While she napped, nestled up behind her eyes in a selfish dream, the sun has rolled slowly over her town and her house, has burned into and around the objects that cast rising and falling shadows, her three children wandering without her knowledge, at the mercy of all the harmful fates. She has lost an entire day, and that day was Saturday, the good day, leaving her abruptly dumped into the sinful dull thud of Sunday. And when she does realize it—reading the clues, the dishes Claire has washed and left in the drainer to dry, the tidy pile of mail on the glass coffee table, the condition of her own sweaty clothes, the way her two sons cling to her legs as if she's just returned from a trip—she looks straight at Claire, who has not told her. And Claire feels herself on fire, blushing red from toes to temple, guilty.

She aims for confession but comes up with a lie: "I tried to wake you."

Then she tells what is at least true: "Dad came by to get his video-tapes." Their father moved away three months ago. This morning Claire led him into his old bedroom, showed him the sleeping form of his wife, who lay propped on two pillows, an open book on her chest and a wineglass balanced miraculously on the novel's wide spine.

Valley of the Dolls: she reads it every few years. If you ask, she'll explain that she knows it is not well written, but still, there is something arrestingly honest about its women and their destinies. Claire has seen the movie; Patty Duke's hair is hopeless. She knows her mother wants her to read *Valley of the Dolls* so they can talk about it.

Yesterday afternoon, in the hot doldrums, her mother fell asleep while reading, then slept without moving, her breathing quiet and uneven, as if she were pretending, in the glass a scant slosh of wine that evaporated overnight, leaving a smooth red skin. Left long enough in the desert air, the skin would crack and flake away. Claire has seen it time and again in the kitchen, milk, juice, wine, the ants and roaches not quick enough to capitalize. Her father reached out his cupped palm to cradle the fishbowl-like snifter, setting it on the nightstand, then gently lifted his wife's hands from the two sides of the book. He crossed them over her chest and covered her with a sheet: a corpse; or perhaps a mate for Mr. Man, Mrs. Woman.

Her father, James, glanced forlornly around his former bedroom. Over the bed Claire's mother has taped a sign, one that six-year-old Sam made for his endless zoo: *Loins*, it says in orange Crayola, *I woud rather that you didnt touch them.*

"Lions," Claire explained. Her father nodded once.

"I'll take the boys," he said, back in the living room.

"You don't need to," Claire told him. "I've been doing fine."

His eyes were wet, and he wore several round Band-Aids on his cheeks where skin samples had been removed. Before leaving her mother, Claire's father had discovered he had melanoma, so Claire doesn't have to hate him for abandoning them. He is already being punished.

"I'll take the—" he started to repeat.

"Don't!" When her mother woke, Claire wanted the evidence of her own saintliness nearby. Also, she wanted her brothers' company; during the night, she had taken the baby monitor from the night table by her mother and put it beside her own bed, listening to their wheezing and sniffling over the humming white noise, to the click of the dog's toenails as he wandered down the hallway to the toilet for a drink. All night she had been accompanied by raspy, needful racket.

On his first pass through the house, her father had not noticed Mr. Man. Now he said, "You don't have to tell me whose lame idea that was."

But Claire lied and said it had been hers, acting hurt so that her father would apologize.

"I'm sorry," he said. Claire has learned the trick of making people say they are sorry; sometimes she misuses her power.

Her father finally was convinced to leave without his sons. "I'll just take these and go," he said, clasping the yoga videotapes he'd come for. One of the tapes showed a swami swallowing a nine-foot-long strip of gauze. After he swallowed it, inch by inch, he would pull it from himself. "Gizzard flossing," Claire's father had said the first time he saw the tape, illustrating by pretending to pull a jump rope back and forth through his own body, mouth to tail. Claire gagged; just to watch the swami's calm, measured ingestion made her throat contract, her stomach clench. Good riddance.

Claire's brothers were glad to see their father, but soon they were busy with another cartoon, resting their heads on either side of compliant Mr. Man, whose brown corduroy face pillow had seams that might be smiling, a jolly round button nose. Up until recently, television has been dispensed in doses like vitamins; the boys now seemed to be making up for deficiencies. Their father studied their identical profiles, Dutch-boy haircuts hand-scissored by their mother, two inverted blond tulips.

He wrote a number on a Post-it and pressed it to the telephone. "You call," he told Claire at the door, "if she doesn't wake up soon."

She quickly memorized her father's mistress's phone number. *Gweneth.* She couldn't deny the pleasure of her own stoicism as she slid the bolt behind him, then circled the house once more, securing the other doors, which hadn't been touched since her last tour a few hours earlier. In the boys' room, Sam's animals rustled in their cages, ferret, mouse, guinea pig, hamster, gerbils, parakeet, and snake. The goldfish and guppies darted in their bowls; green slime clouded the water. The room smelled of rodent, cedar chips, and urine; this was one part of his Endless Zoo. In piles on the bed and floor were the others, stuffed toys. Claire longed to turn all the living animals loose on the patio, let them squirm away, survive by their own wits, especially the bird and the snake, both of whom seemed utterly unfit for captivity. Why did her brother love them, these undomesticated creatures? She did not know. He named them all Sam, after himself, as in Sam bird, Sam mouse, Sam guppy. Outside there was a graveyard behind the swing set, full of Sams, stones and sticks and bricks set in the desert dust, each bearing his name in chalk or nail polish. Only the dog, who predated Sam boy, had eluded this ritual naming. He was Napoleon, the Nap Meister, Nappy-head, Mr. Complex. Barrel-chested, short-legged, smash-faced, he gimped from room to room wheezing like a busted squeeze box.

From his mistress's, her father phoned. "A sleep that deep has to mean pills," he said. He insisted that Claire go to the medicine cabinet while he was on the line and tell him what she found. Because Claire didn't want to disturb her mother, she went into the second bathroom, hers and the boys', and, after squeaking open the cabinet, reported her findings.

"I'm sorry," her father said. "I'm being ridiculous, aren't I? I'm projecting the worst. It's a bad habit." Claire's father could be difficult to have a conversation with because he often took both sides. And sometimes he was terribly easy to have a conversation with for the same reason. He wasn't very definite, as a rule. The Post-it note, still on the phone when Claire had answered it, was missing, stuck somewhere else. Claire picked up each foot to check her shoe soles.

So she waited through the rest of Sunday, and at last her mother woke. Eve recounted her dream, treated her hangover, spoke gently to them all. Claire doesn't enjoy the triumph she had imagined. When everything registers, her mother simply looks at her with her naked face, and Claire feels ashamed. Her mother won't say she's sorry because she isn't sorry. Indubitably not. Instead, she joins the boys on the couch before the television, tasting the congealed cheese and ground beef they've left on their plates, drinking can after can of soda, allowing Sam and Beano to fall asleep between her and Mr. Man as if camping out. Claire supposes that if you were walking by outside and glanced at the shaded window, you would see the shape of a happy family.

Not too long ago, in the fall of last year, Claire's aunt Lolly was killed. *Murdered,* Claire sometimes realizes, and all over again she feels wakened into a disembodied stasis—shock, she assumes. It's like walking into a tree branch, being whacked in the head every now and then, left dizzy and seeing stars. Among people she knows, she is the only one related to a victim of murder. It isn't as common as you might think. Aunt Lolly, her mother's wild sister whom everyone in the family worried about and murmured over. She lived alone in a bad neighborhood and she never thought ahead. Left her windows open and didn't replace the flimsy locks on her doors, didn't go often enough to the doctor or the dentist, trusted strangers, picked up hitchhikers, got involved with the *worst* kind of men; Claire had grown up with her desultory aunt's example hanging over her. For Lolly, there had been narrow escapes and strokes of luck, both bad and good: abortions, car crashes, arrests, restraining orders, rehab. She might as well have lived in the third world, Claire's mother sometimes said, exasperated. Claire's grandmother Mamaw had always said she couldn't believe Lolly survived high school.

And Mamaw didn't know half of what had gone on, according to Claire's mother, who seemed to think she herself *had* known.

One morning last October, Lolly's luck ran out. Claire woke alarmed, drawn without thinking toward the noise, toward her mother's wailing from the kitchen, where she found her parents in frightening positions—her father on the floor because he had fallen upon hearing the news, fainted dead away, and Eve over him, screaming, yanking at the two ends of her bathrobe belt as if to keep herself from more dangerous gestures. "Get up, goddammit, get up!" she screamed into his face. Her father lying on the kitchen floor made it seem to Claire that he was the victim. It might have been the beginning of the fatal rift between her parents.

It also seemed to Claire that she had been promoted that morning, from one of the three children in the house to one of the adults. She'd changed sides instantaneously, as easily as stepping through a door, standing tall while her father lay prone on the floor, next lodging her hand under his other elbow to help her mother resurrect him.

Her aunt had been killed in her bed in Brownsville, shot with her own handgun, an ancient gift from her father. Ivory-handled, it had come through an old war, from Claire's dead grandfather to his errant daughter, who'd somehow managed to have it aimed at her temple one terrible night.

Or day, Claire supposed; not all the bad things happened at night. She and her friends had discovered the best hours to be bad were the daylight ones.

Her little brothers were not told anything except that there'd been a tragic accident, that poor Aunt Lolly had died. Bean couldn't remember her but started crying regardless, just because everyone else was. Sadness: it was general. Sam scowled; he had never particularly liked Lolly. She had a habit of putting her face too close to his and criticizing his humorlessness. "Who died?" she would say, poking his ribs. "It wouldn't kill you to smile." But he wasn't ticklish and he didn't like people. It wasn't on purpose and it wasn't personal. Had one of his animals died, he would have mourned, made a grave, and said a prayer. A prayer to Mother Nature, his only god.

Since Lolly's death—still unexplained, still an active case on the other side of the state—Claire's mother has not been the same. And then Claire's father's skin cancer surfaced quickly after. Mortality has set them on separate courses, sent them hibernating in their own bodies, in search of their own cures. They've proved not to be so compatible in disaster, what Mamaw would call *fair-weather friends.*

Summer has come to the desert and wrapped the daylight around the dark like a hot fist holding a cool bullet. Something seems about to happen. Claire and her brothers are waiting.

They move Mr. Man around the house, sometimes in the kitchen with his thick handless arm resting on the table, sometimes in the living room, perched before the television, his eyeless, Oreo-like, maybe-smiling face benign if not pleasant. Claire wonders if it is perverse to enjoy the little shock his authentic heft gives her every time she encounters him, a willing fright she brings on herself.

The grandmothers arrive for long visits, as they do every summer. The food improves. Eve gets off the telephone and quits drinking cherry cola for breakfast.

First the good grandmother comes, Eve's mother, Mamaw, from Kansas. Claire loves Mamaw, who is big and soft as an easy chair, and who never believes the worst of you. She trusts you when you tell her things aren't your fault. She is on your side even when you are wrong. Her delights are uncomplicated, like eating sweets, working crossword puzzles—"cross-eyed," she calls them—or watching detective shows. A few years ago, Mamaw went to California and found James Garner's house, just walked right up to his door and rang the bell. She told him she thoroughly enjoyed his shows, each and every one. He served her cranberry juice. "In a *glass* glass," she marveled. Right in his foyer.

Will Claire ever be so fully satisfied by something this minor? Moreover, Mamaw has in the recent past had an ongoing relationship with a real detective and a real mystery: Lolly's death. Detective Newsome is on the case. Maman is not as charmed by him or his ways, which are time-consuming and, so far, inconclusive. It's hard to get on Mamaw's bad side, but Detective Newsome has succeeded. He has terrible grooming habits—yellow teeth, greasy hair, body odor—and a lazy, insinuating nature. Foul to behold, and not one suspect: what good is he?

For Mamaw's visit to Claire's home in El Paso, Claire's father moves back, too afraid to disappoint her, even though she isn't his mother. He tells Claire not to mention that he's been away.

"It was only a few weeks," he says, smiling grimly, as if smiling hurts. Plus, he's lying: he was absent a few *months,* the entire spring season, the season of the winds. "Mamaw has enough on her plate, what with Lolly and all." *Lolly and all*; this refrain echoes faintly in Claire's ears wherever she goes, like a haunting song lyric. Mamaw sleeps in Claire's room; Claire sleeps in Sam's bed, right above Bean, among the animals; and Sam sleeps in his parents' room, on the chaise longue, witness to the reunion.

"Did Mama and Daddy talk?" Claire asks him after the first night.

Given to sulks, Sam spoons his breakfast without answering her. He says, "This cereal has bugs in it."

"Those are oat grains," Claire tells him. "You didn't hear anything Mom and Dad said?"

He just eats, breathing through his nose. Their housekeeper is an automaton at the sink, feet planted while she rotates at her thick waist, shifting dishes from wash to rinse to drain. Her varicose veins are long blue worms twisting down her calves and into her shoes; why does she wear shorts? She likes to be in the same room as the family and organizes her cleaning routine to keep company with somebody, which makes her the opposite of discreet. Every once in a while, she stops to strain over the sink and peer out the window at her delinquent son, Oscar, who is supposed to be mowing the lawn. "*Ose*-car," she calls him, but if you happen to pronounce his name that way, he will quickly correct you: "Oscar," short nasal vowels, the American version.

Michael Angel, the boy Claire loves, does the reverse, emphasizes the Mexican pronunciation: Miguel Ahn-hell.

"*Permiso,*" Chacha says, swiping her soapy hands on her apron and heading bow-leggedly out the door. "He is forget the dog poo *otra vez.*" Last time Oscar mowed, he ran over the piles, spraying dry shit in all directions. He is a year older than Claire and attends her school, West High; part of the arrangement worked out with Claire's family is that Chacha will use their street address in order to send him to an American school rather than one in Mexico. Oscar enjoys scaring Claire. He scratches his initials in the thick pulpy leaves of the century plant like a message for her, *OH.* Chacha returns, apologizing, smiling, pointing to the oat grains Sam has left beside his bowl.

"For your *patitos,*" Sam tells her under his breath. He won't feed his own pets anything but the approved chow, yet he hates waste. In Mexico, Chacha keeps ducks and geese and chickens in a clucking hutch beside her trailer. It is an ancient trailer, a tiny tin vehicle like a rusty lunch box.

Chacha thanks Sam, then bends to hug him, an urge she can never resist. He has giant blue eyes set in a large bony skull, a translucent complexion pulled over the evident peanut-shaped framework, blond hair, and a sorely sour disposition. Sam pushes her away.

"Oof!" she says.

"Don't be rude!" Claire tells Sam, thinking of Chacha's trailer, her scary son, her absent husband, those geese with their foul prehensile tongues.

"I don't *want* her to touch me."

Every now and then the topic of autism is raised concerning Sam. His teachers like to have a name for his unfriendly intelligence. So far nothing more conclusive than speculation, a threat that passes through Claire like heat, shame and protectiveness at once.

Chacha smiles sadly, taking Sam's dirty bowl to the sink, caressing her midsection. Chacha's husband and son take advantage of her good nature, too. Her husband drinks and often disappears deep into Mexico, and Oscar is in a gang. He calls it a posse. Claire is always tempted to laugh—a posse. He makes her scared but also scornful. His sister, Chacha's teenage daughter, Teresita, died a few years ago in a car accident. Chacha's affection for Claire has a tinge of sentimentality attached to it, that and barely noticeable tartness; after all, Claire isn't her daughter. Chacha probably thinks God's ways are mysterious, taking angelic Teresita and leaving someone like Claire.

Chacha is the one who discovered the cache of stolen trinkets in Claire's bedroom. Claire steals them and then sort of forgets she has them, stored away in the empty space beneath her dresser. In the moment of theft, it seems imperative to possess them. Having them, the urgency evaporates. Stealing is an impulse like eating sweets: afterward, she can't quite account for the greedy need, in fact feels a little ill. Under the dresser, those things disappear as if into a void. But Chacha cleans with a vengeance—she literally has scrubbed holes in the rug and washed the color right out of the towels—and when she found Claire's stash, she left it on Claire's crisply made bed, strange lustrous matter like pirate booty, the accumulation of which kind of shocked Claire: she hadn't realized there was so much.

Grandma Mamaw doesn't like to inconvenience the housekeeper; she's been straightening up before Chacha arrives, stacking and folding, patting her own soft white hair. "I look like something the cat drug in and the dog wouldn't eat!" she often says of herself. Now she comes into the kitchen for breakfast and insists on Chacha's joining her at the table, pouring another cup of coffee and offering up the Pecan Sandies. "*Pee*-can," she says. The two of them sit expectantly across from Claire, their mutual topic, who studies the newspaper. *Climb Out of the Lunch Meat Rut!* the headline reads.

"She is pretty girl," Chacha offers.

"She takes after her mom and her aunt Lolly," Mamaw replies, melancholy as can be. It isn't true; Claire's skin and hair are like her father's, like her brothers', fair, pale, washed out; her aunt Lolly had called the three children James's clones, declaring that her sister, Eve, was nothing but an incubator. "Lolly used to only wear the jeans, too," Mamaw informs Claire, her voice intended to sail over the newspaper.

"Oh, jess, the jeans," Chacha says.

"Lolly was a tomboy. Eve was the belle, and Lolly was the boy we never had. You'd think girls like that wouldn't take to one another, but you'd be wrong. You never saw such good friends as my girls." Mamaw draws a long, tragic breath. "Do you know that the police have not, to this day, found the fellow who did it to her? It's so awful, I can't think of it."

"That detective calls here," Claire says. She does not say that just last week she pretended to be her mother, listening and agreeing on the phone as Detective Newsome reported his lack of progress. Some men—not many—enjoy the difficulty of Claire's mother. The hippie electrician who stops by every month or so. A soccer coach of Sam's from some brief, reluctant foray into the world of real boys. Her boss, Clyde, who takes her to happy hour every Friday afternoon. This detective apparently is another of them, Eve's small fan club. Claire's father, once upon a time, was its president.

"That detective ought to be shot," says Mamaw. "He hasn't done a blessed thing." Mamaw herself has posted a reward, ten thousand dollars for information. Dead, Lolly sometimes seems more vivid than she did when she was alive, ongoing.

"My girl, she also pass away," Chacha explains eagerly, leaning forward over the table so that her breasts are mashed. They are spotted with a thousand little red moles, those breasts. Tears pop instantly into her eyes.

"Oh no!" Mamaw cries.

"Jess, is so!"

Mamaw pushes the cookies over and pats with her plump, pale hand Chacha's arm. She, like Claire, must be thinking of the child Chacha has been left with, Oscar, who earlier flashed a quick smile at her, displaying his silver tooth like a hint of weaponry.

"Where's those babies of mine?" Mamaw says, rolling out her bottom lip dejectedly. "I need my little boys right quick! Sam? Beany Boy?"

"They're watching cartoons," Claire tells her. Mamaw sometimes looks lost, blinking and afraid, as if her senses take brief leave of her bulky plush body. Perhaps this has always been part of her personality and only lately has Claire noticed it. Perhaps it's because of Lolly, or because of Claire's promotion to grown-up.

Bean shuffles into the kitchen, his footed pajamas droopy with sodden diaper. He is an amiable boy and suffers the affection of both Mamaw and Chacha without complaint, lets them hug him longer since his brother resists them, speaking over their shoulders to Claire. "I need drink a water," he declares. "And dinosaur cookie." Claire has learned that it is easier to wait on her brothers than to teach them manners. And she feels sorry for them; they are confused with the comings and goings of their father.

"Daddy," Bean calls his father; "*other* daddy," he calls any other man.

Mamaw says, "I'm going to give that boy a haircut directly."

"No!" Bean cries, clutching his shaggy blond hair in fright, as if she's threatened to snip off his nose.

Mamaw stays for two weeks; it is all she can spare. She has to get home to her cocker spaniel puppies and her duplicate bridge clubs and her soup kitchen shift. "And those *awful* kitties." Lolly's Siamese; they probably should have come to Claire's family, but Sam won't allow predators in the house. And how could you put them down? Your dead daughter's cats? Before Mamaw leaves, she buys Claire sensible underwear and rearranges the kitchen drawers. She alphabetizes the videotape library and has the vacuum cleaner repaired. She does these things as if she can train the house into a more functional shape, as if it might flourish after her adjustments. Claire's parents continue, up to the moment of departure at the airport, to act as if they are still living together; Claire's father hugs his mother-in-law tight and says, "We'll talk to you soon."

We.

Next, *his* mother comes. She drives down from Albuquerque in her Cadillac, the backseat a kind of closet for her wardrobe. She has a cellular phone, a laptop computer, a one-cup cappuccino machine. Her plastic surgeon lives in El Paso, so every summer she kills two birds with a single stone.

"Mama drinks a bottle of vodka every day," Claire tells this grandmother. Is it vodka? Claire thinks so; it's clear as water, turned a thick, oily clarity in the freezer, like liquid glass.

"Gin," her grandmother corrects. This is her father's mother, Frankie. She stays for a month and does all the shopping, replacing ordinary food with organic substitutes that look worse and rot faster. Claire finds her one day in the garage, crashing the brown paper sacks full of bottles into the trash bins. "You can't even park the car in here!" Frankie tells Claire. Claire, who is already five feet nine inches tall, has a frightening urge to kick her grandmother. What can be wrong with her, that the sight of her grandmother, so crumpled and baggy, looking like an old grocery sack herself, makes Claire angry instead of sad?

"Doesn't bother to hide her habit or even throw away the bottles, what do you suppose you children are to think?"

Claire likes these bottles, square-bottomed, adorned with men in kilts—they seem too nice to throw away. You could arrange a couple dozen of them and make a giant chess set, a squadron of solid pawns.

Her grandmother squawks, but Claire has already headed into the house, where the air is cool and damp and smells of furniture wax. "Your brothers," her grandmother goes on, "they aren't normal . . ." Claire hears the sound of a laugh track in the distance. Good thing they have unlimited TV. The boys follow it like sunflowers in the sun.

They both wear overalls, shirts like the American flag. Grandma Frankie has brought them boys' outfits. But Claire's mother sometimes dresses three-year-old Beano in girls' clothes, flowered pants, puffy cotton dresses with smocking at the bodice, Claire's old baby things. "Doesn't he look like a girl?" her mother once asked Claire.

Claire agreed, he did, a beautiful girl child, more beautiful than he could ever be as a boy, more beautiful than Claire had been. "I'm big girl!" Bean said proudly, looking down at himself, and Claire and her mother laughed. Drinking made her mother happy. Drinking made her want to do things with the children. Why does Claire feel a need to tattle?

Now she falls in with the boys and lets the bright cartoon images of television absorb her, her remaining fear and fury smudging away like erased words, like forgotten daydreams.

Claire's father moved out again before his mother arrived.

Grandma Frankie pulls Bean's pacifier from his mouth and hides it. She takes off his diaper and sets him on the toilet. "This child is a cry for help," she tells Claire. Maybe he should be wearing underpants by now; maybe he should be on tiptoe before the toilet bowl, thrusting his little penis over the cool ceramic lip the way his older brother did. They had the first boy circumcised but not the second. Everything is slacker the second time around.

"I don't love you," Bean tells his grandmother, chin trembling, eyes filling; a declaration that is against the rules, yet Claire doesn't correct him. She doesn't love this grandmother, either. Ironically, the household seems more normal with her there. Everybody goes back to being who they are. Claire's mother confesses one night that it is easier to live with Frankie than with her own mother. "At least Frankie knows what it means to have bad habits."

"She thinks you should hide yours."

"She would think that."

Frankie is tall and thin, her skin loose. She makes Claire uncomfortably aware of how much food Claire eats, since Frankie barely consumes anything; her son claims she photosynthesizes. She promptly joins a health club and takes Claire to work out with her. On the treadmills, Claire is fascinated by the flaccid skin around her grandmother's knees. The bodysuit she wears, which should be skintight, bags at the arm- and legholes. In the wall mirror, Claire watches their respective thighs come forward over and over again. Her grandmother might be the oldest anorexic in America.

Like Mamaw, Frankie disapproves of having a maid; unlike Mamaw, she is critical rather than embarrassed. "I keep fit doing my own housework," she tells Claire sniffily, scrutinizing the driveway, where Chacha is already busy beating rugs. Summer mornings, the doves ask each other, "Who *are* you, who *are* you?" repeatedly. Sometimes, in the right mood, Bean will imitate them.

"Does your mother intend to throw these away?" Frankie demands, pulling a pair of her son's khakis from a box by the stoop.

"She gives them to Chacha." Her mother likes giving things to Chacha; Chacha is always grateful. She never says no. Claire thinks it is Chacha's gratitude her mother likes—that and buying new things to replace the old. And perhaps the sensation of having shed waste.

Lolly's belongings all went to Kansas, to Mamaw's attic. Presented with them, Eve blanched, horrified.

Chacha pulls the rolling garbage bin to the curb for pickup. Inside it, bottles clang. Chacha crosses herself and exclaims in Spanish to Claire, hating the sound of glass against glass. Claire does not know how she knows that Chacha's husband drinks, but she does know it, and also that he does foolish things with other distant family relations when he is drunk. *Borracho,* the Spanish word is, one that the Spanish teachers like to offer up as proof they are fun, loose. That, and *loco* and *perra* and *cucaracha* and others.

Frankie picks through the box of clothing, removing all items that belonged to her son. These she returns to Claire's bedroom, where she is staying, where she leaves them when she goes home.

Then Claire gives them to Chacha, and in the fall, she will see Oscar wearing her father's T-shirts around the halls at West High. He will pinch the fabric on both sides, saying, "See my titties?"

There ought to be other children between Claire and her little brothers. Sometimes Claire imagines them, a stairstep squadron, sisters to mix with the little boys, Claire their leader. Her mother miscarried four times before the pregnancy with Sam took tenacious hold. Claire remembers Sam's development, the tender trepidation that hung over the house, her mother the invalid, the delicate queen wearing the bed jacket atop her enlarging belly. After so many miscarriages, her mother took nothing for granted, held no confident faith that this one, at last, would survive. She lay and sat with her feet propped up. She ate raw spinach and drank milk. "Babies. Are. Fragile," Claire was made to recite, when Sam was brought home intact. Every night her mother watched over him, convinced he would cease breathing if she left his side. She was forever prodding him from sleep just to hear him shriek.

And Bean, a few years later? Bean was extra, a backup baby, accidentally conceived, a fetus who for a few months went undetected. He arrived like a gift from a stranger, vaguely confusing his family: Had they asked for this? Would they keep it? After Lolly died, Claire's mother began to leave Claire in charge of both boys, defeated by the merciless, thankless labor of worry.

Last spring Claire counted on one thing every day: the same white dove flying over the used-car lots and taquerias and pawnshops on her way to school. While at her house everything fell apart, the daily sighting of the bird both excited and calmed her. Happiness, she guessed. Over the vehicles it flew—cars parked, cars in lurching motion— sailing above them, oblivious, diving. The dove was part of a flock, the only white and beautiful member, the others plainly pigeonish and crude, living atop gas stations and billboards. They swooped stupidly over traffic, landed stolidly on wires and signs, held their wings close to themselves as they looked down dumbly at the street, swaying. What was their agenda? It had nothing to do with clocks or money or rage; they didn't know English or Spanish. Or French, for that matter. The single white dove made Claire remember France, where she'd gone when she was eleven with her mother and her aunt Lolly. Girls' trip, a fun fling before her mother's last pregnancy began to show.

The trip came back to Claire differently. Occasionally, as with the dove, it made her aware of the ugliness of her hometown, the garish colors of the businesses, the disregard for beauty in general, the litter and noise, rocks that weren't even actual rocks but busted concrete and asphalt left around, unfinished business, El Paso's brown emptiness and its clutter, its poverty and desperation, its smoky yellow sky. In France, when there was clutter, it was ancient and covered with moss or engraved with the names of the dead. It had gargoyles or curlicues or was gilded; the stone of buildings held indentations from the steps or fingertips or tears of a long line of ghostly human presence. Here, on the street off the interstate, the one that would eventually carry Claire to West High, everything looked as if it were made of LEGO, knockoff LEGO, primary-colored plastic set down in the sand and scrub, a basket of a poor child's toys tossed in a barren ditch.

If she hadn't gone to Paris, she wouldn't know how ugly her hometown was. Had that been the point? Had that been why her mother had taken her there, to demonstrate the inferiority of their lives? Was Claire supposed to be glad she'd learned of it? She wasn't. She would have preferred not knowing.

In the subway, a man had stuck his hand inside Lolly's underpants and made her shriek, then laugh. "Mother*fucker!*" she screamed after him in English as he walked away, completely nonchalant, brushing his hand beneath his nose. "Stuck his finger in!" Lolly told Claire, stomping her feet, grinning. That she found it amusing also alarmed Claire, who didn't want to know that, either.

There must be a word for this desire to not know, to unknow. *Innocence,* she guesses, although that seems simpleminded, the stuff of lambs and babies. *Ignorance,* her mother would provide, as in *Ignorance is bliss.* Her mother's voice goes on and on inside Claire's head, nattering and annoying, continuous fodder for contemplation, for sneering, for sorrow.

Overhead, without words, a white bird casually sailing like a cloud, like something from heaven, if you believed in heaven.

FALL

On the first day of school, the bus driver has to stop on the highway outside town. Migrant workers throw heads of lettuce across the road at one another, a great flurry of flying green. Once Claire understands what is happening, she begins laughing and cannot stop, convulsing in her seat while her friend Dana quietly pinches her and recites a list of items sure to sadden: "Dead kittens, dead puppies, your brothers with ice picks in their heads, your mom dies, your dad dies, Michael Angel dies . . ."

Already the temperature has reached 93 degrees. The sun shines over the desert, the air has not yet filled with refinery exhaust from Juárez, the powdery hills of Mexico shimmer like a mirage. The houses there are low, painted the colors of Easter eggs, set in the sand randomly, linked by winding dirt trails punctuated by tire fires. A few field-workers step onto the highway asphalt from the rubbly shoulder to get better purchase on their aim, then lob the lettuce heads at the opposite side.

"They can't even hit each other," Claire manages to say, still hysterical; the pale green heads float, peeling as they arc. She is sitting in the middle of a food fight.

"Lettuce moves too slow in the air," a boy behind her says. "Resistance. Man, I should lend them my gun."

"You have a gun?"

He nods, meeting Claire's eyes. She's never given him a second thought; now she feels herself take interest. His blond hair is shaved along the sides of his head and long on top, slicked back and tied in a small tail. With a gun, this wouldn't look foolish.

Dana says to Claire, "Thank God you stopped laughing." She squeezes together her thumb- and forefinger nails as if trapping a flea. "I pinched you so hard your skin came off."

Mavis the driver—she describes herself as "rode hard and put away wet"—leans on her horn, nudging through the leaf-covered battle zone. Now Claire feels uneasy, watching the flat brown faces go by. The men's eyes find the bus passengers' faces, registering the presence of Claire and all the other clean children being driven to school. The bus glides through solemnly. Then there is a volley of thumps on the rear windows, both sides united against the bright orange bus. Claire flinches as the lettuce hits. Heads, she thinks, an image before her of human ones smacking the vehicle.

After that, Claire begs her mother to drive her to school. She tells about the boy with the gun, and that convinces her mother, who hated guns even before her sister got shot with one.

Claire's grandfather had offered his gun first to his oldest daughter, Claire's mother, and then gave it to Lolly when Eve declined. Claire saw this grandfather, the soldier, for the first time at his funeral. She was four; he was covered with a flag. Lolly had been his designated hell-raiser, the girl who should have been a boy.

In the morning, Claire's mother is groggy. Claire has to dress and feed her brothers, feed the Sam fish and bird and rodents, lead Napoleon out to dispense his trickle of urine on the ice plant, turn off the lights. All her mother has to do is drink the coffee Claire makes, slip on her scuffs, and then sit behind the wheel of the Volvo in her sunglasses. Even hungover, her hair looks great.

"Your breath is gross," Sam says when she kisses him goodbye. She is the only one permitted to touch him. He runs to the front door of Vista Elementary without looking back, as if escaping. At their next stop, Claire carries Bean into the church Montessori—"*Benjamin!*" exclaim the Montessori ladies, the only people who call him his official name—and signs her mother's initials as she hands over his backpack of diapers and toys and crackers and juice and a tiny square cut from his mother's nightgown that he still uses to fall asleep. Naptime. A dim room of dozing babies. Bean wads the satin rag under his nose, held there over the thumb he sucks. To lose the piece of cloth is to lose full nights of peaceful sleep, to live in family anguish; it was Claire's idea to cut up the nightgown, tattered backups stocked in her mother's hosiery drawer. That drawer smells faintly of cedar, of Chanel No. 5, of Safeguard, of, in short, their mother.

After Montessori, the two of them take the interstate to West High.

By now, traveling at a higher speed, two of her three children effectively deposited, strong coffee flowing in her system, Eve usually has something to say, mostly mutterings to other drivers—who annoy her—occasionally to Claire. Moving, she is reminded of all that worries her: on the driver's side, across the river, Juárez. It used to be a place where the family went on Saturday afternoons to shop for piñatas and masks and spices, to hear mariachis, to eat dinner at their favorite fancy restaurant. But now it is a place where hundreds of young women have been discovered in shallow graves, murdered on their way to or from the *maquiladoras* where they work. Claire's mother shakes her head at the pure horror.

"I won't go there," Claire promises, knowing what comes next.

Abortion, she remembers: the billboard featuring the forlorn teenager and the hotline number she should have called, the trouble Claire can avoid, according to Eve, if she takes good care. "Condoms, condoms, condoms." Or Eve will say something like: "I'll tell you the facts of life. The facts are, number one, someone always gets hurt. Someone always cares more. There is no equal relationship. Either you love him better or he loves you better. Either you're getting dumped or doing the dumping. And even if the leverage shifts, you can count on it to shift back the other way someday. The other fact is: everyone has a secret life. It's the only thing you absolutely have to hang on to. Someone's always trying to get at your secret life. Don't let them. Those are the real facts. Or did you want to hear about sperm and ovum?"

"Move, moron," her mother murmurs now to the ponderous Riviera in front of them. "Hel*lo*, Grandpa. *Six*ty miles per hour, not forty." From the passenger seat, Claire watches the old man's face as he navigates his car. He's terrified, clutching the steering wheel like a ring buoy. Ahead, hitchhikers positioned like mile markers. They heft their thumbs as if they want to launch the cars that won't stop for them right off the highway, as if they are holding up an angry middle finger instead of a thumb.

"Assholes," her mother says. "As if."

"As if what?"

"As if a woman and girl could be expected to pick up every fucking felon and scum on the highway. Please. What sort of fool do I look like?"

Sam was right; her breath is gross.

There are regulars among the hitchhikers and homeless. There is the *What If It Was You?* woman under the overpass; *Why Lie, I Need a Beer* stands by the first exit; and the teenager with the yellow no-eared dog has his own stop sign where he chains the animal with only a few inches' hobbled mobility: *Please Help My 4-Leged Friend! Will Work,* one cardboard sign announces. "Work doing what?" Eve says. "Who's gonna hire that guy?"

The man looks bad, no doubt about it. Crazy eyes and dusty hair, unshaved face full of lines and grit. His sign says he loves the Lord, which is also guaranteed to get Eve going. One day she offered a woman ten dollars to pick up litter on the corner where she stood begging. When Claire's mother returned later, the street still looked filthy. The woman said the wind had blown all the trash right back after she picked it up. Eve gave her a tube of lipstick with an SPF of forty, a freebie from the Clinique counter, and the lady called her a cunt.

"That word is like being slapped," Claire's mother said to Claire, looking slapped.

Eve provides the panhandlers with PowerBars and sample-size sunscreen. Bottles of water. Apples. "If I gave them money, they'd just buy liquor," she tells Claire. She holds up her hand, anticipating Claire's comeback. "That's *all* they'll buy." But she does not pass the homeless as if they weren't there, which is what most drivers do.

Along with the hitchhikers and panhandlers, Claire often sees a man riding his motorcycle, a big Chicano, or perhaps he's Indian, with long black hair. He is very beautiful, scarily so. He never wears a helmet and he rides very fast, so he is dangerous as well as beautiful, his hair flying straight out behind him, his teeth bared, his sunglasses like black holes in his angular face. She is a little in love with the motorcycle man.

"We'll see how gorgeous he is with his brain on the pavement," her mother says, pulling up to the West High parking lot. Spooky, the way she sometimes seems to read Claire's mind.

*   *   *

In the fall, the vultures come.

A big white-skinned tree died outside the Pratts' kitchen window last year, and nobody cut it down. Now vultures settle in its branches. They circle the yards of the neighborhood at dusk, a gloomy spiral in the sky, descending like tossed black capes into Claire's yard, landing in the dead tree, tucking their ugly red heads into their hunched shoulders as if ashamed of their hideousness. Or as if sneering at having chosen her house, laughing up their sleeves. Scavengers, they are; their part in the food chain is to sit and wait while others act. If Claire kneels at the kitchen sink, she can make out their Dracula-like forms in the early morning. She went outside once in her pajamas and waved a broom over her head, beating it against the tree, knocking off the few remaining brown leaves. The vultures stared down at her; one had lifted its wings as if to fly away, as if to indulge Claire's need to create flight, then changed its mind, too sleepy to comply. She wasn't much of a threat, it seemed to say. It just left its wings outspread, suspended midway to frighten her.

"There's nothing *dead* here!" Claire screamed up at the birds, surprised to find herself in a fury. A woman out walking her greyhounds stared from the street, first at Claire, then at the vultures. There must have been twenty of them, perched like ornaments or gargoyles, as if Claire's family were cursed, as if their house were the site of a horror show.

"Are they always here?" the woman asked. The chilly air made her words come out with smoke. She wore an ugly red sweatsuit that tempted Claire to say something unkind to her. "Tomorrow I'll make my husband come. He's a bird man."

Claire ran into the house, dragging the broom behind her, filling the hem of her nightgown with the little burrs that negligence had brought to the yard.

In Peer Leadership, Claire is instructed to write a story. Without thinking, she creates a girl with a gun in a bed, contemplating killing herself. Shamed, Claire destroys that attempt, makes several other false starts, eventually asks her mother what to write about.

Her mother has on her wailing opera music, a glass of wine in her hand. Her boss, Clyde, has given her the next day off. The room fills with the high soprano warble; tomorrow is the anniversary of Lolly's murder. Claire lifts the remote control from the table and rolls the volume down. "Write about the vultures," her mother says.

Claire hasn't known her mother was aware of the vultures. Further, she hasn't known her mother knew *she* is aware of them, or of how they torment her. "I hate those vultures. I'm not writing about them."

Her mother launches into the reasons why writing about what Claire hates might be useful, educational, about the virtues of confronting fears, which are what hate masks. Eve has read books advising—

Claire interrupts, saying, "I hate opera. I could write about that."

"You don't hate opera in a very interesting way," her mother says, snatching the remote out of Claire's hand and rolling the volume up again. "You aren't afraid of opera."

"Sure I am." Claire makes a frightened face.

"Show me what you write," her mother says. "I'd be curious to see it."

"Uh-huh." But Claire might show her mother what she writes. Unlike other mothers, Claire's won't demand to see work, won't shock easily, won't lie just to be encouraging. She truly believes in privacy. If Claire kept a diary and left it out on a table, her mother wouldn't pick it up and read it. She likes her mother for that; she also finds it contemptible: what kind of lazy, uninterested mother is she, anyway?

The next morning Eve refuses to take anybody to school—the boys will have a day off, too, and Claire can ride the bus if she doesn't want to stay home. October 18; they aren't even 100 percent sure Lolly died on this day, it might have been the one before, or the night before that. In Mamaw's police shows, the time of death is always more certain. Detective Newsome has managed not to find even the simplest clues, fingerprints or fibers, tire treads, semen—nothing. The gun was in

Lolly's hand, but anybody could have put it there. The angle of entry, according to Detective Newsome, was awkward.

Claire closes the back door behind her as if on the memory, as if she is escaping, her step light down the street. Waiting at the bus stop, she watches a little brown bird huddled under one of the big trees shading the bench. The tree is a type her father dislikes; it is hairy, and its roots greedily suck at the water table. What is it called? Claire steps forward, too close to the little bird, and it hops backward, its heart shaking its whole rib cage. "Oh you," Claire whispers. "You little you." She envisions herself holding the bird against her chest all afternoon at school, other girls circling her to avoid detection, the secret society of girls doing good deeds with sick animals, Claire taking it home with her, scrounging up a medicine dropper and some warm milk. Her brother would name it Sam brown bird, since there is already a red finch named Sam bird, and they would oversee it until it died, at which point they would bury it in a shoe box in the Sam graveyard. Then the bus comes, the brakes hiss and squeal, the door thwumps open, and Mavis yells out, "Good morning," gruff as always. As Claire pulls away, sitting up high in one of the front seats, no longer able to detect the small brown bird beneath the salt cedar— *that* is the tree's name—she watches a rusty old tomcat pad through the brush. She foresees the real scenario in a flash, the pounce and the blood and the devouring. Maybe that will be her story. And then, without warning, she is sobbing into her hands and everyone around her is looking away.

Uncanny is a word Claire sometimes hears in her head. This is when, for instance, she has a dream about her aunt Lolly in which Lolly dies again, or doesn't die, gets lost instead and is waiting to be found, and then later on, on the way to school or grocery, Claire's mother says, "I dreamed about Lolly last night," and Claire doesn't confess that she, too, dreamed of Lolly, only grunts or looks out the car window, but behind her eyes, that word, *uncanny,* goes scrolling through.

*   *   *

Claire's father landscapes highways, which means he sometimes drives a mower or plants trees, but most times he collects trash and kills weeds, a tank of poison strapped onto his back with a nozzle in his gloved hand. With this he probes along the roadside. He also supervises DUI offenders, who have to wear fluorescent orange vests and pick up litter on the highway as their public service. Their names are printed in the newspaper, along with the number of hours of public service they have to perform. It seems a supremely humiliating system, but her father says that is the point.

Claire fears her mother will someday end up out on the roadway in a vest, stabbing at the fast-food wrappers and drink cups with a spiked stick.

This is how her father developed the skin cancer. Now he has to dress for work in long sleeves even when it is hot, like a beekeeper or a soldier. His skin is red, his thinning hair a bleached chlorine green; his ancestors lived in cold, cloudy climates. On his head, he hides a sunburned bald spot with a company hard hat that he thumps with his own middle finger as if checking a melon.

"Your father's sense of humor runs toward the slapstick," Claire's mother says disdainfully.

He used to bring home oddities he found roadside, limp houseplants whose containers have burst, with their naked veiny roots dangling, or clothes left clinging on the paloverde trees and yucca spines, or money or scratched cassette tapes, occasionally animals. Box turtles, injured birds, a dead boa constrictor longer than James is tall. The dogs he avoids, armed with his metal pole, radioing Animal Control.

Sam started his endless zoo with a few creatures their father brought home. Sam lizard. Sam duck. More recently, the house finch with the bent wing. He has that rule against predators, so the litter of starving kittens had to go to the pound. Only prey in his collection, the pitiful and weak; the losers.

Their father once found a single rubbery breast, a nippled meatlike thing made from the gelatinous stuff of bike seats. They all handled it squeamishly, threw it around like a hot potato, then let Napoleon bury it.

Now that he has moved away, her father must bring his odd treasures to Gweneth. Gweneth, Claire thinks, then mouths. There is no way not to mock that woman's name. It is also difficult not to mock her appearance, because she isn't striking, and Claire's mother is. Claire's mother has thick dark hair and high cheekbones, long legs and large eyes, tragic European looks. She wears clothing the colors of red wine, dark chocolate, rich cream, and in a style of another century, elegant, adult. Gweneth, in contrast, is like a gymnastics coach, perky and bottle-blond, ponytailed, freckled, her nose upturned rather than Roman, her clothing the palette of fingerpaints. She bounds when she moves; she makes a profession out of supervising self-improvement classes. That's how Claire's father found her, when he signed up for yoga.

Yoga. He tried other ways to fight his sadness, pills and a road bike and hobbies in the garage. Yoga, he claims, rescued him, but of course he means Gweneth. He means love.

He tries to explain over lunch one day. He drives his state vehicle to Claire's school and picks her up. In the truck, they eat hummus and bean sprouts, which, according to Claire's mother, smell like semen. Claire has no direct experience with semen, but she knows she doesn't like bean sprouts. She pokes at her portion. The truck cab smells of garlic and sunscreen and dust. Her father says, "I can't afford not to be happy, do you understand? Your mother is incapable of being happy, and I'm not strong enough anymore to counteract her negativity."

"That sounds like something the boys would hear on television," Claire says, holding up her wrist to talk into her watch: "Captain, big counteractive negativity field down here. Over." But she remembers riding in a cab in Paris, her mother looking dreamily out the window and the driver gazing knowingly into the rearview, saying in his thick, sexy accent, "Excuse me, why you are so sad?" Eve swung her sad face slowly from the window and didn't dispute his observation.

"Your mother depresses me," her father says. "Now that my life is on a clock, I . . ."

"What?"

He looks into Claire's eyes, his own blue ones suddenly red-rimmed, red-streaked, allergic-looking. Her father's handsomeness has become frail, pitiable. "I can't save your mother," he says. "She'll have to do that herself."

"What do you mean?"

"First she needs to stop drinking."

Claire nods absently, folding her moist, tasteless lunch into a napkin. Trucks blow past; in the desert, the air is so dry you can see miles and miles away. The Mexican *maquiladoras,* on the horizon, factories where furniture is made, or cheese, the empty, undulating sandy surface between there and here beneath which lie the bones of undiscovered dead girls.

"What after that?" Claire asks.

"Huh?"

"You said *first.* What next? What second?"

"I don't know."

His melanoma has made her father cautious; Lolly's death has rinsed Eve free of hope. Once upon a time, they were different, happily incautious. Now they both fret about Claire, that she will feel the overwhelming need to take risks, run away, say, or overdose on drugs, or steal a car and drive it very fast. And although Claire occasionally will wander her own neighborhood at night, or swallow a pill or two just to get dizzy, or steal small things, things that fit into pockets, she cannot imagine making the grand gestures her parents anticipate. Stealing something as sizable and public as an automobile is the purview of somebody like Chacha's son, Oscar, and his posse. Nevertheless, her parents agree, she must learn to drive. To drive well.

Her father takes Claire to practice in the Mexican Catholic cemetery, a ratty sandpile decorated with faded plastic flowers and clacking pinwheels, colorful santos and candles, a place her father calls the boneyard. Tumbleweeds cover the fence as if clambering to get in; broken bottles glint in the sun. The occasional cluster of grieving family some-times looks up, perplexed, to see a white girl steering slowly through the sand. Claire sometimes gets stuck, the truck tires spitting up grit.

Her mother won't drive with Claire. "You do that on your own time at school, with the guy who's getting paid to be scared witless."

Behind the wheel of the driver's ed car, the seat tilts Claire toward the dash like a sledder on a hill. Mr. Casenberger sprawls beside her, his little flesh pouch of a lap lifted over the seat belt, tasseled loafer ready on his brake pedal. Three other student drivers sit in the backseat. Devils, those boys, loitering just behind her shoulders. Some days they drop Vicodin before class, then just sail the car around El Paso, smiling.

Mr. Casenberger has a perverse side that likes to exhibit itself partic-ularly when Claire, the only girl in the bunch, is driving. He makes her drive on Valley, where the *cholos* and low-riders slide along the streets, bass speakers warbling the windows. At intersections, the drivers of these cars make hand-job gestures—open-fisted pumping, goggled eyes—as Claire waits for a green light.

Once, a urine yellow Toyota halted in front of her, and all four doors swung open. Four heads leaned out, bowed over the street, and four streams of tobacco juice flew. Claire, without thinking, nudged the driver's ed car into their rear bumper, an impact that did no mate-rial damage but earned her an F for the day. The boys in the Toyota at first hopped from their car, but then hopped right back in when they saw the warning sign and lights on the vehicle. "Dude!" the riders in Claire's backseat congratulated her.

She hates that plaque on the top announcing student drivers. From a distance, you might mistake the old sedan for a taxi, but up close there can be no confusion. Sometimes Mr. Casenberger grabs the dashboard and puts on a terror-stricken face, as if his driver were about to cause a pile-up. *Mercy!* is his favorite expression. He likes to cross himself. In her parents' car, Claire used to pretend she was a dead passenger, go limp and bloated, tongue hanging out and eyes crossed as if murdered, being driven to some abandoned site for disposal by her evil abductor. Nobody ever intervened on her behalf, no horrified driver in the next lane with a sympathetic bent or, it seemed, even mild curiosity.

Mr. Casenberger says, "Let's blow the carbon out, boys," which means a stretch of interstate.

When Claire isn't driving, she sits in the back with the other two students, passing on her mother's driving philosophies: the underuse of the left lane, the inability of El Pasoans to merge, the erroneous impulse to honk at their friends rather than at the troublesome slowpokes and idiots.

After she ran a red light in front of a sheriff, Mr. Casenberger accused her of having an attitude. Claire temporarily forgot that only right turns are permitted at red lights. When everything seemed clear after her stop, she just drove through. It *was* gratifying to see Mr. Casenberger grab the dash sincerely, in real fear. And it wasn't *Mercy* that he uttered then. But then the sheriff appeared out of a Whataburger lot, wagging his finger at her as he passed.

"Asshole," Claire said, the way her mother would have.

"You've got an attitude, chickie," Mr. Casenberger told her. But Claire *likes* hearing it. She decides she will cultivate her attitude. Later, she mentions that her mother makes phone calls to report truck drivers, the ones with bumper stickers proclaiming their safety, soliciting comments on it. "So she's one of them," Mr. Casenberger says. "I used to be a trucker."

They are driving to meet Claire's father for lunch. Her mother is speeding, as usual, driving with her knees. Today a cop pulls them over. "Shit," her mother declares, braking, whipping Claire forward nearly to the dash, then back.

"Come on, fat boy, pick up the pace," her mother mutters while waiting for the cop, who takes a long time getting out of his car. Claire watches him talk on his radio, then bend over his lap writing something, then simply stare at them.

"Whattaya, scoping our auras? Giddyup, porky," her mother says.

When he finally arrives at her window, she says, "Hello," in a friendly yet firm way, as if *he's* misbehaved but she's willing to forgive and forget.

"Ma'am?" he says. "You aware of your speed?"

"No, although I *was* aware of the semi that passed me just before your lights came on."

"That semi's no concern of yours."

"Oh, I know that. I just mean his large load displaced so much air that my vehicle was sucked along, the drag between us lessened by that displacement, so my compression on the accelerator never increased, just my speed did. Purely a product of secondhand velocity."

Claire cringes.

"Uh-huh." His sunglasses prevent anyone from reading his eyes. He tears a flimsy from his little clipboard, tucking the other copies behind.

"Don't you see?" her mother persists. "My speed was influenced by his, much like a paper cup in the wake of a passing vehicle. Eventually it would have decreased—"

"That there's a warning," the cop says, flapping the yellow tissuey paper into their car. He leans over and looks beyond Eve at Claire. "Afternoon," he says to her.

"Hi," Claire says. He seems to smirk; her mother's pseudo-physics isn't getting her anywhere. Her father, in happier times, had named it *Cosmo*-girl science, a tolerant stance toward frivolity.

"Yokel," her mother says as they drive off. "Look how he starts doing eighty."

"He's a cop."

"So what?" Later, her mother calls in to the "Shout Out!" column in the *Times* to complain. Claire hears her leaving her message. "My small son asked me recently why police break the speed limit even when their sirens are off. I had no good answer. *Is* there a good answer?"

Of course her message will never appear in the newspaper. They never run her messages, even the ones in which she complains about their not running them.

* * *

Some nights Claire leaves her mother and brothers before the television and visits the side yard, sitting in the grass beside the wall. Her friend Dana provides pills from her household full of them; her family has a lot of pain to kill. Drowsing, under the influence of whatever white or yellow or blue tiny tablet, Claire enjoys simple sensation. The sprinklers come on in the evenings, so the lawn is cool, damp, while the wall still holds heat from the day. On the other side of it, where Claire can't see, the night proceeds: voices, tires at the intersection, sirens. Above her, mourning doves, grackles, settling for the coming dark, humming and hacking. Claire hears the boys ride down the street, the pulse of the car stereo bass, then the opening doors, the sound of their boots. The rattle of the pellet in the can, *tonk, tonk, tonk.* Then the aerosol spray of the paint as they reach high, the sticky vapor misting over the wall and falling on Claire's forehead, a freckling of silver, sparkling in the bathroom mirror later. The wall says nothing legible. It reminds Claire of comic-strip expletive, a mangle of symbols meant to express rage, a public curse upon her home.

It could be that Chacha's son, Oscar, is responsible, and that the rumbling automobile belongs to Chacha's no-good husband, his paneled station wagon with Juárez plates. Oscar and his friends have begun marking cars lately, which the community won't tolerate. Other things—walls, homes, drainage canals, street signs, play equipment—yes, but cars? No.

Chacha is beside herself. In the halls at West, Oscar passes Claire with his tongue peeping out between his lips, as if on the verge of revealing a secret about her, as if he knows something he is capable of saying. What would it be? she wonders. Her home, she hopes, is no less shameful than anyone else's. The advantage of El Paso is precisely that: you can't sustain high expectations of anyone's private life. Claire only briefly envies her friends; she doesn't really wish for other parents. So what does Oscar mean to hint at with that knowing lip thing of his?

"He is going bad," Chacha cries, "with his shhhh-shhhh!" She pantomimes the spray can, the looping arm gesture. Their posse tag is *WAW*: "We against white," Oscar told Claire once, grinning so that she doubted him.

Claire smiles sympathetically, moving around Chacha's cleaning operations to locate snacks. Maybe Chacha pretends the house is hers when no one else is home. Maybe she lies on the couch with her bare feet raised, watching television, admiring her own hard work on the carpet and windows and coffee table.

"*No sé*," Claire claims, shrugging mournfully when Chacha questions her on Oscar's behavior at school. Claire sincerely does not want to discuss his delinquency. She does not want to be quoted.

Chacha wears headphones around the house, studying for some sort of naturalization test, muttering the English names of the recent presidents and their vices. "*Al*cohol," she mumbles. Claire's mother thinks it is some sort of indictment, but Claire knows it is just Al Gore, *Al gol*.

For her part, Chacha does not appreciate the naked-lady paintings on the walls. Nor does she approve of the photographs on the mantel, and refuses to dust them. She often lays flat the picture of Eve breastfeeding Sam, and sometimes one of Claire as a toddler. Claire supposes she should be bothered by having a nude photo out on public display, but she likes it, herself running through a sprinkler with her mouth wide open, feet flying off the ground, wearing not a stitch. And where is a photo of Bean? she wonders. Poor Bean, born third, redundant baby and now a toddler during their mother's sadness and their father's illness. What will become of such a boy, with his nightgown tatter in his fisted face?

"*You* can say *fuck*, but *I* can't say *fuck*," Beano says over pancakes, hands disgusting with syrup, dog hair, grit.

"That's right," his mother tells him.

Claire says, "I can't say *fuck*, either."

"You can't even say 'I can't say *fuck*,'" her mother informs her, butter knife aimed to punctuate.

"Can," says Claire, "but won't."

"Oh, I bet you will," her mother says, resuming her task of cutting bites for Beano.

"I don't eat boogers," Bean tells them, shaking his head ruefully. Little liar.

Claire and her mother laugh.

Now that their father is gone, Claire's mother has to work harder to make the boys love her. She plays with them in the yard, pushing them on the swings, pitching them balls, sitting in the sand while they drive trucks and build tunnels. But always she is glancing at her watch, always shifting her wineglass from one perch to another. An oleander blossom falls into her drink one evening, a pink flower floating in the pinker wine. Sam quickly knocks over the glass, spilling out the wine and the bloom, knowing the flowers are poisonous, and Claire's mother grabs his arm. "What do you think you're doing?" She jerks him upright, even though she is sitting.

"The flower fell in," Claire says. "The oleander."

"Dangerous," Bean adds.

"Sorry," their mother says, releasing Sam's arm, rubbing the place where the fabric of his shirt has wrinkled in her grip. She tries to pull him into a hug, but he resists, standing crooked, as if he's been hung on a hook, and still in the position he was yanked.

"Stop," their mother says. "Don't make me feel bad. I refuse to feel bad." She gets up, brushing sand from her skirt, and hurries into the house. Both Bean and Claire hit Sam on the knees.

"Stupid," Bean says.

"Brat," says Claire.

✶ ✶ ✶

When the news came that Aunt Lolly was dead, it was Claire's father who'd taken the call from Mamaw. First he drained white, then he fell onto the kitchen chair, which tipped him onto the floor, unconscious. Next he denied that the murder could have happened. "No," he insisted, shaking his head. Claire's mother had to convince him, repeating again and again that her sister had been killed. Throughout this nightmare in the kitchen, the two little boys slept. Claire had stood in the doorway, cold, shaking—shaking so hard it was as if the house were moving. She would never forget her father inert upon the floor, knocked down by the news. Eve had driven to Brownsville within the hour, and when she phoned home, it was Claire who took the calls, Claire who knew what to cook for Bean and Sam when they grew hungry. Her father refused to think that his sister-in-law's life had become one that somebody else felt necessary to extinguish; in her own bed, naked, shot through the face, the bloody pawprints of her Siamese kitties all over the spread as they had come to investigate, again and again. It was their noise that had driven the neighbors to complain.

At the precise moment when Claire was poised to ask what would happen to the kitties, her mother warned her over the phone, "Do not mention those animals in the presence of Sam."

So Mamaw took the cats to Kansas, and later, she had Lolly's ashes mailed to her. Eve returned to El Paso with nothing, not one object from that bloodied apartment in Brownsville. She came home utterly empty-handed.

As in every year since third grade, Dana is Claire's best friend. This will be true only until one of them finds somebody better. Dana claims to have just one layer of skin. She is always going to the hospital for stitches and grafts. Coincidentally, her name is contained in the name of the illness, though her family, when they assigned her a name at birth, hadn't known that she had the illness or that it had a name. Claire wishes she had an illness with her name embedded in it, a claim so poetically tragic.

On many afternoons at home, after school, Claire can be found with her back against the hallway wall, feet up the other side, phone warm against her ear. Today Dana, with the thin skin, is crying. Claire is comforting. After an hour, she hangs up. Her mother, who's come home from the law office where she works, changed into her lounging clothes, made herself a drink, and begun tripping through one of her piano pieces on the Casio, says, "I used to want people to confide in me. I used to think it meant something."

"What are you saying?" Claire asks peevishly. Dana has a new set of stitches on her leg; she is bored and depressed and eating a lot. If she gains too much weight at one time, her scar tissue will burst.

"I used to think I was special because I knew other people's secrets. I spent hours and hours giving advice, a big sponge for weepers. I'm just trying to spare you, that's all." Her mother continues playing the piece, stumbling along.

"Dana just got out of the hospital for the *twenty-third* time for stitches." Claire loves Dana's tenuous skin, her complexion like skim milk.

"Oh, sure," her mother says. "Yak on the phone and offer solace." She flaps her hand as if working a sock puppet. "Just don't go thinking it means anything to have people calling and confiding in you, being their keeper. Big. Waste. Of. Time. That's all."

"You're so cold!" Claire accuses, something she's heard her father say about Eve, and then storms off into the bathroom.

Her brothers are arguing over the toilet bowl.

"Some floats," Sam explains, "and some sinks."

"Mine will float," Bean announces. His face is proud, Sam's worried. Peevishly, Claire asks Bean when he plans to actually use the toilet and find out what his stool will do.

"For my birthday," he tells her.

She turns to her other brother. "And why don't you ever flush? Every time I come in here, the toilet needs flushing."

"It wastes water." Sam leaves the bathroom haughtily.

"Oh, please!" Claire says, "You and your Mother Nature." Sam subscribes to an irritating brand of spiritualism: he knows how many miles per gallon their Volvo gets; he stands at the window when the sprinkler comes on and bemoans the amount of potable water pouring into the ground.

"It's scary," Bean tells Claire confidentially as they watch the toilet water swirl. "It makes a big noise."

The day after Halloween, as they pull out of the driveway, Claire notices a pair of shoes, tied together by their laces, hanging on the phone line outside their yard. The shoes—women's running shoes with purple wings on the sides—sway in the wind. For three days, they dangle there. Then, when it turns out that the girl they belonged to had been raped in the park, they disappear. The image of the policemen who must have ridden in a cherry picker to lift them off the line is nearly as chilling as were the swinging shoes.

Dropping the three of them home in the pickup truck, their father asks, as usual, "You want me to come in with you guys?" His face shines red with embarrassed white blotches, a kind of blighted apple.

"No, thank you," Claire says, also as usual. But she takes her brothers quickly into the house and, after slamming the door behind her, bolting it three times over, then checking the others, sits in the middle of the boys' bedroom, comforted by their toy cars and the tedious scritching noise of Sam's rodents. The bedroom smells like a real zoo. When their mother gets home from work, they watch the news to see the brief flash of their white wall as the camera shows the shoes, a white so brilliant that a shining orange octagon flicks onto the screen, as if the camera has been aimed at the sun.

"You don't go out at night, Claire, do you hear me?"

Claire nods.

"We went trick-or-treating," Sam points out. He was a spider, extra legs made of Eve's black panty hose. Claire took her brothers around while their mother answered their own door. She might have passed that raped girl early in the evening, still wearing her shoes.

"Candy," Bean says dreamily. For Halloween he was an eyeball, his own bizarre idea. Now he is nuzzled up to Mr. Man, lingerie scrap at his cheek.

Her mother scoots over on the couch and drops her arm around Claire's shoulders. "I can't stand how dangerous the world is. It makes me crazy." Claire suffers the arm around her for a count of one hundred, then slides out.

Her mother is preoccupied by danger; she sees it everywhere. Danger, and negligence, and idiocy of all stripes. Walk with her through the neighborhood, for example, and you will have an utterly other experience than if you walked it alone. The Magic House—a home that keeps getting built, although no one ever actually witnesses its construction—through her mother's eyes is a haven for crackheads. During the day, no one is on the job site, but there are improvements, a new roof, another layer of bricks around a future wall, and scaffolding that seems to sneak stiff-legged at night from spot to spot around the perimeter.

"It's an open invitation to derelicts," Eve will tell Claire sourly.

Beside this is the house where an old man and his even older mother live, their windows plyboarded and then decorated, ivy and pink flowers surrounding *Home Is Where the Heart Is,* the graffiti of grandparents. Rumor has it that mother and son once saw, from their easy chairs in their living room, two men having sex in the park across the street. After that, they didn't want to look out anymore.

"I can't blame them," Claire's mother says. "I've been tempted to board our windows." But Claire often peeks out the shades toward the park, hoping to catch someone having sex. Who wouldn't want to watch? Especially from the safety of your own home, the comfort of your own easy chair.

Then there is the Baptist church, two blocks away, with the prodigiously large parking lot that just keeps growing. The Baptists knock down a house every few years to pour more asphalt. Most of the neighborhood joins Eve in complaining about the Baptists, but Claire likes the big smooth surfaces for riding her bike, for Rollerblading. Without gaps or rubble, you can ruminate as you roll along, glide like butter on a hot pan. They even installed trees, circles of carved-out dirt for saplings to stand.

On the other side of the railroad tracks: the Sweeper, a man whose job it is to sweep the cotton from the gin out of the street. All day long he sweeps around the train crossing, cigarette tenuous between his lips, reversed baseball cap, patient rhythm of his lifting elbow. Cotton arrives in big basket trailers, which are pulled in a circle to blockade the parking lot of the gin. Men use pitchforks to unload them. The Sweeper will rest on his broom and relight his smoke while they toss the cotton fluff into the gin. Then, when they drive away for more, or park for the night and go home, he begins his job, sweeping and sweeping.

Eve is in the habit of honking at him to hurry his stoned ass out of her way.

And, of course, Mrs. Ono's shop, which Eve has forbidden her two young sons from entering. Claire is too old to be forbidden. In front, Mrs. Ono keeps little glass objects, nut dishes and crystal wineglasses, figurines and antique clocks, a big display case of glittering costume jewelry. But in the back, behind the counter and two closed doors, Mrs. Ono keeps a taxidermied screaming monkey and a polar bear, a two-headed calf and a three-legged pig, a Kodiak bear, an owl and an eagle, ferrets and squirrels and a wildcat and a porcupine with his quills extended. These had been executed and stuffed in the early 1900s; they are scabby and ferocious, pathetic, molting, terrible, fascinating.

You can walk around the block, in the heat, and not burn your bare feet by the time you get to Mrs. Ono's Curiosities, that's how close her business is located to Claire's house. Mrs. Ono always offers Claire a clove cigarette when she comes to visit, shaking the pack impatiently until Claire takes one. Then they stand in the bright sun that pours through the display window and reflects off the crystal dishes, blowing perfumed smoke into the air, Mrs. Ono ever ready to marvel at

Claire's height and heft as compared to her own. "You two times me!" she cackles gleefully, as if in challenge. "Bring you brothers," she always calls out when Claire leaves. This is perhaps the threat Eve feels, the opium-den atmosphere of the smoky front, the dead animals waiting in the rear, that her boys might meet some calamitous fate at Mrs. Ono's.

What else? The white rabbit that hops through the yards and in the park, a thing both placid and terrified at once, a thing perhaps in shock. Glassy-eyed, nervous, a fat Easter gift turned loose by a child who'd grown bored with his pet, now another neighborhood institution sitting demurely among someone's tough orange marigolds, eating, unbothered yet twitching. Sam claims there are actually *two* of these freed, doomed bunnies; you can tell, he said, because one has a black spot on its behind and is slightly smaller, one ear folded sideways as if made of cardboard.

Sometimes the neighborhood air smells of chili peppers, sometimes of onions. It depends on what is being loaded into the train freight cars, what crop is in. Eve will sniff and sigh; El Paso's rural qualities exasperate her. But the odors comfort Claire; they mean that time continues to pass in its traditional ways, seasons signaled by fruition, by the sound of the Sweeper and the pervasive scent of crops. For the rest of her life, these smells—in restaurants, in produce lanes, in her own kitchens—will make her hungry not for food but for the sunsets of her childhood neighborhood, roller skates, boxcars, rabbits, raw cotton, fragrant cigarette butts ground out in crystal saucers, and the swish of a lonely broom.

"You should quit drinking," Claire says. "You drink too much."

"What makes you say that?"

Claire opens the freezer, standing back as if demonstrating its capacity to an audience. The frosted gin bottle waits. "Other people don't have big bottles in their freezers."

"Who says they don't?"

"You know they don't."

"Maybe not," her mother says. "And maybe I drink too much. But I think it's temporary. I think soon I won't be doing this. And furthermore, I think it's better to go all the way with something, to let it crash and burn, than to go at it in *moderation*. God, I hate that word. A person could moderate her whole life long, until she dies, and no one would have said she drank too much. She just moderated. That would be the worst."

It is on the tip of Claire's tongue to mention her aunt Lolly, who had apparently also not moderated, somewhere, somehow—how else to merit a fatal gunshot to the head? But her mother's expression looks wounded enough, near enough to tears, that Claire refrains. She slams the freezer door so hard that the bottom compartment, refrigerated, burps open briefly, then suctions itself shut.

Returning that night on foot after a party from which her mother was supposed to pick her up, Claire is so busy composing a rant that she doesn't notice, at first, the car easing along beside her. If she had a leash, she could be walking it. A black low-rider following her under the streetlights, humping the road on her behalf. It will serve her mother right if these *cholos* decide to abduct her. But they seem content to heel alongside. Claire sighs. Sometimes, like now, she wishes she lived in Paris. Surely no girl in Paris has to tolerate low-riders. The driver and passenger stare straight ahead as if they aren't shadowing her, as if they aren't contorting their car on her behalf. Simultaneous with humiliation at being targeted, Claire feels pity for the boys who think this behavior worthwhile. Not unlike her reaction to Oscar, both frightened and frustrated.

A French girl would feel only disdain.

As she approaches her house, she thinks the place is on fire: the flickering light that comes through the front blinds looks like flame, flashing randomly red and white, like a revolving police cherry light. She had three Coors beers and believes this is what she deserves: her home aflame. She picks up her pace, face flushed, heart speeding yet feet unnaturally sluggish. Beer. The boys in the car slide away, forgetting her at the same moment she forgets them. Then she thinks perhaps her mother has lit a fire in the fireplace, despite the fact that it is not nearly chilly enough. She would not be surprised to find a fire in the fireplace—and this worries her, that her mother has become someone whose actions cannot astonish her. And now, standing before the windows, dizzy with alcohol and adrenaline, Claire realizes that the licking glow comes from the television, nothing more. She is back to being pissed that her mother failed to pick her up.

It won't be the rapist's fault if Claire gets raped.

Inside, Bean sleeps on the loveseat wearing a diaper, and Sam sits on the floor, maybe a yard from the screen, shirt pink with Kool-Aid. The volume has been turned too high, as is Sam's habit. Their mother sleeps on the couch, a half-empty bowl of popcorn on the glass coffee table. The table, which Chacha cleans with Windex every other day, is cloudy with fingerprints and smudge and drink rings. The dog has shed clumps of white hair on the red rug, and the room smells of him and burned kernels of corn. Claire mutes the commercial, then carries Bean to his bottom bunk, which stinks of urine. Sam begins crying when Claire tells him he has to turn off the set, it is late.

"This show is rated R," she tells him. He butts his head, hard, between her legs, which causes her eyes to tear. Claire grabs him up by his skinny arms and shakes him, biting her bottom lip in a way that makes her remember being much younger, enraged like an animal, without words. "Shut up," she tells him, "shut up, shut up!" She carries him at arm's length to his room while he thrashes and kicks, landing another blow between her legs, and more water springs to her eyes. She throws him onto his top bunk, where he screams, and then she rushes to cover his mouth, her palm firm over his teeth. "If you wake up Bean, I'll slap you hard!" she hisses. "Shut the *fuck* up!"

He tries to speak beneath her hand. Claire fears he will bite her, but instead she feels his tongue, more startling than a nip, warm and damp and faintly nubbed. And then she pins him, her fury utterly spent, leans over and holds him close. His resistance is only fleeting. He hugs her around the neck and cries. He hadn't wanted to watch an R-rated movie any more than she wanted him to. Despite a full bladder, Claire steps on Bean's bunk and climbs up into bed with Sam, knocking his stuffed creatures out of her way, ignoring the stench—boy pee and creature cedar chip—and there they sleep.

In the morning, their mother is making coffee when Claire, still wearing last night's jeans and blouse, head aching and mouth fuzzy, finds her. On the last three of her right fingers, her mother wears white gauze and tape.

"What happened?" Claire asks.

"I don't know," her mother says. She has a little pile of vitamins and ibuprofen beside her empty coffee cup. There are two empty soda cans at the sink, waiting for somebody to store them for recycling.

"Well, when did it happen?"

"I woke up with these huge blisters on my fingers," her mother says. "Right at the knuckles." She illustrates on her other hand, running her finger along the inside of her ring finger, where, Claire notices for the first time, there is no longer a ring, just the pale indentation, a fading tan line. "The only thing I can figure is that I burned myself making popcorn and didn't feel it."

Claire sits at the table, wondering if this headache is a hangover. "You should quit drinking," she says idly.

"I know." Her mother's water begins boiling. As she pours it into the cone full of coffee, she tells Claire that her father wants the children to come live with him.

"I won't go," Claire says. Her first vision is of her mother's closet full of clothes and shoes. She would have no interesting outfit options at her father's. Next is her realization that her father's apartment is far too small for the four of them—five, counting the girlfriend—and her final reason for not wanting to go is that she doesn't want to leave her mother alone. *Gweneth,* she mouths, she can never resist, that name so prissy and faux-royal on the tongue. "I'm staying with you," she says.

Her mother looks her over as if discerning a hangover besides her own in the room. "We'll see."

WINTER

Every season has its drink; winter's is heated in the microwave, equal parts milk and vodka in a cup, with a splash of vanilla. After this has rotated on the platter for three minutes, Claire's mother adds a package of sugar-free hot-chocolate mix, floating two marshmallows on top and stirring gently. The spoon makes an echoey *thunk* on the bottom of the cup, as if a loose bass string has been plucked. Winter.

The boys move to their father's apartment and take hardly anything. Refusing to visit, Claire can only imagine the place, generic and sanitary, free of history. It is she and not her father who remembers to retrieve three squares of nightie from her mother's drawer for Bean. "Here," she tells her father. He frowns momentarily as he recalls why she is handing him the little rags.

Now it's finally chilly. Claire closes the windows. Chacha brings Oscar to service the swamp coolers and light the furnace. Claire can hear his feet on the roof, thudding above the rooms like fate, deciding where to drop in. She goes where he isn't, and then he thumps there, mimicking like a magnet, right over her head. The ceiling, like the walls, is made of adobe, an enclosure resembling a cave, a hundred years old, house of sculpted mud. The air smells of burned dust, of insect corpses and animal fur roasted in the heat vents and then blown throughout the rooms. Chacha is armed and ready with the vacuum.

When Oscar climbs down the ladder, he emerges boots first in Claire's view, then knees, thighs, belt buckle, shirt, face. His smirk is painted on; he knew she was watching his descent. His hands are black from work; he places their pads gently on the window glass, leaving his mark, as usual. He leers at Claire. Eve is drinking her hot chocolate and vodka, watching the news. "Go to the mall with me?" Oscar asks, coming through the door.

"No," Claire says.

"Girl, you afraid?" he asks, grinning. His silver tooth makes him look dangerous, damaged. He lifts the long pistol-like lighter in his hand. He flicks its trigger, ignites its tongue of flame.

"No," Claire lies. When he walks out, he seems to know she is watching his pants pockets. He wants to have sex with her, Claire thinks. With her permission, it would be called one thing; without, it would be called another, a fact she turns over in her mind like a coin, trying to decide how to spend it.

Claire finds her mother in the hall, crying on the telephone, one day after school. She is hunched over with one palm capping her free ear, which is how Claire knows she is talking with Mamaw. Mamaw has never quite gotten the hang of speaking directly into the receiver. She would be sitting in her Kansas kitchen watching bread dough rise. Perhaps it is snowing there. In the winter, in Kansas, it snows. She would be sitting in her chair at the table, gesturing as if Claire's mother were seated across from her. She's lived in her house for fifty years. Claire's mother claps her palm over the receiver, snuffling. "Nothing's wrong," she says to Claire, who looks at her own concerned face in the hallway mirror. Her mother wipes her running nose on the back of her hand, then says, "I just heard Mamaw's doorbell ring, and it made me homesick." She presses Claire's fingers for a second before covering her exposed ear again to listen. Claire wanders into the living room, where the boys used to sit in front of the television. Its screen is dark, cool to the touch. Her brothers have left this house, perhaps forever. She knows what Mamaw's doorbell sounds like, too, a long tune with two notes missing at the end, flat rasps sounding as if someone is holding the cylindrical chimes to suppress them.

The bathroom off her parents' bedroom has a wall-unit gas heater, the odor of which, when lit, comforts Claire. Sometimes she takes baths just to breathe in the warmth, listening to the whistling little song the heater whispers: on and on, steady and calm. Her mother claims the

196 · ANTONYA NELSON

fumes are noxious, but hey, she's one to speak, her with the alcohol intake, and moreover, Claire doesn't care if the sum total of her brain cells die. Might she be happier not knowing things? "Ignorance is bliss," her mother says, referring to the contented idiots she encounters every day. Claire's government teacher likes to say it, too, lips pinched priggishly. He doesn't seem to know that he is gay. Bliss, indeed. Though her mother and Mr. Maxey mean it sarcastically, Claire thinks it is true. The evidence is overwhelming.

"He married me because he's an optimist," her mother says on the telephone. "And he left me for the same reason. I think it means that I won." She laughs corrosively. She looks at Claire as if her daughter were transparent; she's listening keenly to the person on the other end of the line. This would be her long-distance friend Anabeth Buess. Claire's mother has two lives, Claire thinks, one here and now, one there and then. The bridge between is bitter. Or maybe, more accurately, burned. Someday Claire will have another life. She will talk to some girlhood friend she has yet to meet, certainly not Dana, and recall this very time, or the one destined to follow soon, in the same wistful tones her mother uses to remember her girlhood. "You're the only one who knew us both," her mother says at a later point in the conversation, meaning herself and her sister, Lolly. Anabeth Buess had been their friend forever, still living in Wichita, still there to rekindle memory when need be. Anabeth Buess, who has visited a few times, doesn't like Claire. She thinks Claire is spoiled, Eve's first baby, born in an atmosphere of adoration, indulged. "Why don't you just whimper?" she said to Claire when Claire was eleven, not getting her way. "Just pull your little act."

"She hates me," Claire told her mother later, feelings bruised.

Eve considered the news, ultimately agreeing: Anabeth Buess didn't like her daughter. "I hope you won't be hurt if I keep being her friend," she said. "She's never liked kids, but I think she's just jealous you're getting more of my attention. *Just* is a weird way to describe jealousy, isn't it?"

"I can't believe you would choose her over me!" Claire cried, tears bursting down her cheeks in a grand self-pitying display.

Her mother hugged her, not saying anything, letting whatever information Claire needed to learn filter through their shared silence.

Now, on the phone, Eve's eyes change expression, they grow mournful and sweet, deep and abstracted. They deny the existence of her adult self, the one that moved to the Southwest, married a man, and made some children. She resembles her mother, Mamaw, in these moments, the person in whom time has collected regret, nostalgia, softness.

But her mother doesn't like to dwell afterward in that region. When she hangs up, she snaps back to the other side of the bridge, her El Paso self, the busy, wry mother with a teenager, a first-grader, a toddler, and a wandering naïf of a husband.

"Didn't I tell you not to wear those?" Eve demands of Claire, who has on a pair of her mother's clogs. Listening to her talk to Anabeth Buess, you'd think a pair of clogs couldn't matter in the least.

It could be the disappearance of people; it might be simply age. But Claire suspects that the dog is intentionally forgetting English. She has to kick at him to make him move. "Napoleon!" she yells. Is he deaf? No. He still hears when the drawer is opened and the can opener is clamped onto a Mighty Dog can. He still hears the mailman drop letters into the slot. He hears the fish flakes being shaken over the bowls on top of the Casio. Not deaf, just obstinate. He misses Sam and Beano. Sam loved him, and Bean was sloppy with his food. Neither Claire nor her mother pays much attention to the pets. This becomes another of Chacha's jobs. Feeding the creatures. Claire's father, in his sanitizing-his-life campaign, outlawed pets from the apartment. That Sam agreed to these terms is terrible testament to how much he had missed his father.

"*Viene,*" Claire tries on Napoleon, luring him outside. He is reluctant; he'd rather dribble on the kitchen floor than head into the cold night. Claire isn't sure she has the proper word, anyway. "*Get,* you big asshole," she says, shoving his dusty rear with her foot. When Napoleon screams, Claire screams back. What has she done? Her mother is not home. "Out," she said when Claire asked where she was going; her boss, Clyde, sometimes liked to share a secret drink. What should she do, the dog whimpering at her feet?

"Dad?" she says into the phone. Her father answered after one ring; no screening over there. Everything in the open. "The dog is making this noise." Claire holds the phone to Napoleon's face. He instantly stops, blinking nervously at the receiver as if, to follow up on kicking him, Claire now plans to bludgeon him. His eyelashes move feverishly. A puddle develops under his back legs. "Oh, never mind," Claire says, and presses the *talk* button off. She knows he will call back, so when the phone rings, she doesn't answer. Instead, Detective Newsome comes on the answering machine. In his slurring, unattractive Texan voice, he leaves a message for Eve. He says that there's some paperwork he'd like to fax to her, some things he'd like to pass on, if she has a chance to phone him. He stays on the line, clearly hoping that Eve will decide to pick up, making enough tantalizing yet indefinite references for her to think he's discovered something about her murdered sister. Even Claire knows this is bullshit. He is a lazy cop with a crush on her mother, that's all. He's probably been drinking and is lonely, ready to fantasize over the phone with an attractive and vulnerable woman.

"Give a ring," he concludes. Claire erases his message.

"Fuck you," she tells Napoleon, who has slid into a sleeping position on the damp, stinking kitchen floor.

"You're so cold," Claire's father would say to her mother. He would sound near tears.

"I'm not cold," her mother would respond coldly.

Claire wonders what a test for coldness would look like. How could you decide? One of Claire's teachers called Claire *aloof*.

When she tells her mother, her mother says, "That's okay, the world needs more loofs." When Claire cries, her mother insists on pulling her onto her lap—ridiculous, Claire the same size as her mother, like those obscene *Pietàs,* Christ as big as Mary, lying there like an infant, Claire and her mother mashing their breasts together, feet on the furniture—and petting her hair, the way she'd always done when Claire's feelings were hurt.

"You're not aloof," her mother says. "You're shy. You're sweet. You know how to keep your mouth shut."

Claire imagines herself shouting at her Spanish teacher: "Not aloof, shy! Do you hear me, *shy*?!?"

Next her mother gets food poisoning. This is Thanksgiving, and they go eat Mexican, just the two of them, something they do more often now. It is cheaper, easier, more jolly for Claire and her mother to eat out; they are forced into conversation, as if to convince the people eating around them that they are normally fully conversant. Claire, who has turned vegetarian, eats beans and rice and guacamole. Her motto is a bumper sticker: *My food doesn't have a face.* Her mother has turkey enchiladas and a pitcher of margaritas. Then, in the middle of the night, she cries out from the bathroom, where Claire finds herself before being even completely awake.

The bathroom smells of vomit. Her mother sits near the toilet, an arm slung across the porcelain. She says, "I feel so sick, I'm afraid I'll drown." Claire tries not to gag; the odor is awful. "I've been hallucinating," her mother goes on. "I keep imagining your father dies, I keep seeing him shot, and he keeps saying, 'It doesn't hurt, really,' while I try to scream." Claire stands above her frowning, chewing the inside of her mouth, where tomorrow she will find a canker sore. "I just want some company for a minute, sweetheart."

"Okay." Claire glances at herself in the mirror. This is a good mirror, the bathroom lit by a low-watt bulb that reflects the faded peach wallpaper. Claire looks tan and seductive, fuzzy and rumpled. If only Michael Angel could see her now . . .

"Just as your father comes through the back door, a shot explodes," her mother says, holding her hair away from her face and leaning over the bowl. She spits twice, then continues. "And I start trying to scream, and there's this other sound, like someone throwing coleslaw on the floor, and your father is standing there with a bullet hole in his forehead and another in his knee. 'It doesn't hurt, really,' he says." She arches suddenly, like a cat with a fur ball. Claire gags reflexively, her spine, her neck, constricting into a question mark. She sends imaginary Michael Angel away. Her mother recovers and says, "I ache everywhere. There isn't any part of me that doesn't ache. I would have thought tequila would kill salmonella, wouldn't you? And that hallucination is playing in my head like a Mob movie." She begins to cry like a child, wiping at her eyes with the backs of her hands. Claire hates herself for not being able to offer some help, but it really doesn't seem possible to kneel there on the floor and embrace her mother.

"What can I do?" she asks, crossing her arms but making her voice quivering and afraid so that her mother won't expect tenderness.

"Nothing, honey. I just didn't want to drown, and I was shaking so bad I thought I might, but I feel less crazy with you here. So maybe just talk to me."

Claire sits on the cool rim of the bathtub, willing away the smell of sick. "I could light the gas," she says, glancing first at the box of wooden matches on the windowsill and then at the long-toothed expression of the wall heater, as if combustion might take place before her eyes. She doesn't have the energy to light it. "You should quit drinking," she says.

"I know," her mother answers, gathering her hair once more in preparation for leaning over the toilet bowl.

Since the cold weather has settled in, the vultures have disappeared. Instead, you can hear the mourning doves. Claire lies listening in her brothers' treehouse, which is still only half-finished because their father moved away during its construction. The cooing tune of the birds reminds Claire of Mamaw. She has a voice like mourning doves. The treehouse floor is slick with a thin, icy dew; beneath hang abandoned wasps' nests, rattling.

Over Thanksgiving break, her friend Dana has asked Claire to come feed her cat every day while the family is in Florida. "Don't let her outside," Dana instructs. The whole family has a phobia about the cat's getting run over; apparently every other kitty they ever owned had been smashed flat in the busy street out front. "You have to open the door with your foot aimed like this." Dana illustrated by holding her boot sideways, as if to karate-kick somebody. "He's dying to bolt, aren't you, Felix?" The cat is spoiled; Claire has to fight her temptation to let him escape. In her experience, neglect goes a long way toward making a good pet. Before he went crazy, Napoleon had flea colonies all over his broad white back and spent most of his time lying near the grease puddles in the garage. He was the friendliest animal Claire knew, perfectly content to see his owners only as often as they got in and out of the car.

Claire unlocks Dana's front door and wanders around the house, listening to the wind chimes and fountains. Dana's mother is a decorator; the house is cluttered, the floors spongy with nice carpet, wall-to-wall, each room papered in at least two different designs, many of them seeming to create busy, distracting optical illusions: is that a pair of kissing people or a flower vase? Big bows tied on bundles of dry vegetation. Floral chairs. So many pillows on the couch that you have to throw some on the floor in order to sit. Same with trying to lie in any of the beds.

She finds a hundred-dollar bill in Dana's jewelry box. It is folded up in a triangle, ends tightly tucked, the kind the boys made to play football during class, punting the triangle over each other's spanned hands. Claire turns it in her fingers. She has a few days to return it, she tells herself, poking it into her jeans watch pocket. From her back pocket, she pulls a single dollar bill and folds it in an identical triangle, substituting it in Dana's jewelry box. Maybe Dana won't notice for a while, like those poison-filled capsules that cunning movie villains hide in prescription bottles: you never knew when the death would come.

A week later, the hundred-dollar bill still rests in her pocket. Dana's family is back, so she's missed her chance to return it unnoticed. It bothers Claire. She leaves it in her pants and lets Chacha wash it with the other blues, thinking that if the bill is missing after the laundry, that is fate. But the little triangle—squishy, damp—stays put. In the Kmart parking lot, she gives it to a beggar, just slides it into his dirty hand. "God bless," he tells her, bowing.

"What'd you give him?" her mother asks. They are buying Christmas presents for the boys, decorations, strings of plastic white beads, tiny lights, rocking-horse ornaments for Bean, who is fond of what he calls "forsies."

"What'd you give him?" her mother insists.

"A dollar," Claire says. She turns to look back at the beggar, who might have been picking apart her folded money. He holds something in his hands like a monkey. Maybe the washing has soldered the paper solid. Claire hadn't tried to pry it open after it dried.

"You shouldn't give beggars cash," her mother tells her, tossing their sacks in the backseat. "It's better to support the organizations. Don't forget to buckle."

"Do I ever?"

Her mother jerks them out of the lot. Claire watches the beggar, who raises his hand to her as she and her mother speed by.

On the interstate one night in December after dinner, Claire's mother is drunk. She rocks gently over the white lines and back, the car seeming to have a fondness for straying.

Claire says, "Careful."

But they have a crash, anyway. The car passing them appears to resent her mother's slapdash adoption of the center line; it passes too close, and her mother bonks right into it.

Claire later admires her own quickness. She snatches her mother's floppy black beret from her head and plops it on her own, the two of them emerging from the car at the same moment, crisscrossing as if by design as they make their way toward the other car and its driver, who has stopped a hundred yards behind them, on the other side of the road. "I was driving," Claire coaches her mother.

Eve, sobered by the abrupt collision, jerks her head up and down. The wind tries to blow the beret off, but Claire claps it into place as if holding her head on. Her role, when the man begins yelling at her, is to apologize. She alternates the "I'm sorry" part with "I'm so stupid" and "Our car's so lumpy." She performs without a flaw, tears rising, the police joining them soon for the second show, everyone universally unsurprised by her carelessness. Youth, they seem to agree. Learner's permit. She produces the pink flimsy for the officer to study.

In the tow truck, where her mother accepts the driver's offer of a cigarette, Claire waits for gratitude.

Instead, her mother says, "What if you grow up to be a martyr?"

"What's a martyr?" Claire asks.

The driver says, "A saint."

Her mother shakes her head. "No, no, no. Good God. A *door*mat. You know what my ex-husband does?" she asks him.

"What?"

"He directs the public-works part of DUI. He's in charge of those citizens you see picking up trash on the highway every morning, the ones who got caught driving drunk."

"I'd hate to get a DUI in Texas," the driver says. "In New Mexico, we just pay fines."

"You lied," Claire says when they're alone in their kitchen, midnight, her mother drinking tea as if to sober up now, too late.

"*I* lied?"

"You called Dad your ex-husband."

"Oh. That."

"Was your mom making you nervous?"

"No, she was fine."

"Because I know how she is when she isn't driving, when she's the passenger, she's just an awful backseat, front-seat, driver. She hisses constantly, and hangs on to the door handle like she's going to bail out. God knows it used to make me nervous, and I've been driving for more than twenty-five years. I can certainly understand if your mother made you nervous."

"She didn't make me nervous."

"And the airbags? How'd they work?"

"They worked great." Claire puts her hand to her neck, which has ached since their accident. She caught herself rubbing it once in her mother's presence and quickly stopped. Her mother would think she is milking the event, trying to earn further gratitude. Martyr, her mother would think. And maybe she would be right.

"You know I'd—we'd—love to have you move in with us?"

Gweneth. "No, thanks, Dad. I don't want to leave Mom alone."

"You're a good girl." He grows misty-eyed, and Claire averts her look; in a minute he'll apologize, she's brought it on. If he was asked, his definition of martyr would be like the tow-truck driver's.

Claire's father has left a few things at the house, among them his dirty books. These are stacked beside her parents' bed. When she first found them years ago, Claire read them without hiding their covers, over cereal in the morning, in the porch swing after school, in bed before sleep. They were violent and sexy. Her father would ask sometimes what she thought of them.

"I like them," she said.

"I do, too," he said.

How odd, she reflects, that they both knew exactly what she was reading—the rapes, the gore, the graphic, awful material—and yet could so casually agree on enjoying them.

Now he lives with a Christian cheerleader, doing yoga. Now his books are Claire's.

"Why do we have to drive this Volvo?" Claire whines. Their car, returned from the body shop restored to mint condition, is a white box; they ought to sell ice cream out of the back.

"Because it's the safest car on the road," her mother explains. "Because I often end up driving drunk, and we need a safe car. That's why."

"I liked our loaner. You could quit drinking and we could buy a cute car like it."

To this she gets no response.

On Christmas Day, Sam and Bean come over to eat ham and open gifts. As the daylight fades, the four of them stay in the kitchen, which is bright and warm, romantic in the light of a candle that has to be relit every time one of the boys can't resist blowing it out. Claire's mother proposes toasts, and Bean, hoisting his plastic tumbler time and again, finally asks, "Where's the toast?" Claire makes bread toast, and they all lift these and rub them together, creating a crumb pile. Beano laughs the infectious way tiny kids can. Their mother wears a deep maroon dress and has pinned up her dark hair. In the candle-light, when she smiles, she looks like an Italian movie star.

Claire's father, picking up the boys at nine, has to come all the way into the house to find them.

"We didn't hear you," Claire's mother lies, her happy expression held over the rich scene like a frame. Gweneth can't compete with this, Claire thinks. Gweneth doesn't possess the robust beauty, the confident maternal calm, the long knowledge of what Claire's father's eyes will see before him in his family seated at the table together. Claire watches him behold the tableau, the Italian movie–like scene over the remains of a meal, the heroine smiling, her children adoring her, the room warm with wine and butter and candlelight.

The next day Claire and her mother drive stolidly to drunk camp while the boys go on an adventure in a rented RV with their father and sporty Gweneth.

The RV is parked in the New Mexico Gila Wilderness; the camp for drunks is in Taos. At camp, Claire's mother cheats, although not with drinking. She listens to headphones and does not meditate. The days are tedious. Her mother came to drunk camp to indulge Claire; the car crash earned Claire some leverage. But the rest of the campers seem to think that Claire, too, has a drinking problem. She is, in their unspoken opinion, far too young. They like to look down on her. They like to pity her future.

She meets a man named Jimbo who is missing a pinky finger. He took a hatchet to his own hand one night, drunk, naturally, and realized in the morning that he probably needed to sober up.

"Why cut off your finger?" Claire asks.

"My girlfriend said if I loved her, I'd do something to show her." They are playing dominoes in the commons while it rains outside. "She broke up with me about six different times because of the drinking. So I guess I decided to make a gesture." The stub has grown infected, pockets of clear fluid rippling as he lays down his tiles.

"And you know what, the very next day after I cut off my finger for her, the very *next* motherfucking day, she called me up to say she was marrying somebody else."

Claire listens to his bitter laugh. But she believes that the call wouldn't have come until he sliced off his pinky. That is how things work.

Claire suggests to her mother that they leave drunk camp after three days. Their first night home, Eve fixes herself a giant vodka hot chocolate and settles in front of the television to watch a Cary Grant movie, happy as a clam.

Someone shoots a gun at Claire's house. The bullet comes through the front window in the middle of the night, lodges in the living room wall. The adobe trickles out beneath the hole, as if something were still burrowing its way in. In the morning, Chacha is horrified; she claps her hands over her mouth and bugs her eyes. Claire believes Oscar is responsible, and Eve expresses no opinion. The police tell them that other houses have been shot at, which takes some of the personal sting out of the event. It is Claire who remembers where the DAP is, Claire who finds the putty knife, Claire who covers the sandy hole, Claire who uses a Q-tip and some leftover paint to finish the job. Two men from a glass repair shop replace the front window. They remove the old one by chipping it daintily with tiny mallets, collecting the broken pieces in quilts.

"Don't tell your brothers," her mother instructs. "They'll be freaked out."

"And we shouldn't tell Dad, either," Claire opines.

"Why not?"

"He'll think it means something."

Her mother nods. "Maybe we should buy a gun. What do you think?"

Claire wonders if they are sort of alluding to Lolly, an infrequent topic. It has not occurred to her that Lolly's killing and this shooting are in any way related, but she thinks it through. Who and why? It makes no sense. "Do you know how to shoot a gun?" she asks.

"I grew up in Kansas." Her mother might be thinking of Wichita. Her father the soldier, the one who'd armed his daughter. Lolly and Mamaw and the lost past.

"Well, I grew up in Texas," Claire says, "and I don't know how to shoot a gun."

"Maybe we shouldn't have a gun around, on second thought," her mother says. "I have a feeling we'd do something dumb."

"'We'?" Claire simply says.

In February, for no good reason, Claire's mother surprises her at school. "Let's have a picnic," she says brightly, eyes behind sunglasses, hair in a scarf. Has her mother forgotten Claire is fifteen, not five? Claire climbs into the car warily, bringing her customary lunch—an Almond Joy and a Dr Pepper—with her. They drive out on the highway where Claire's father's truck is parked and in which he sits eating. He is dressed in white, head to toe, a figure from a futuristic movie, a beekeeper without bees, a nut from a nuthouse. He does not look pleased, through the windshield, to see them. Claire's mother has to supply all the energy for the three of them, like a ventriloquist with not one but two lifeless dolls awaiting inspiration.

"Scoot," Eve commands as she drags Claire after her into the front seat of his truck.

A high wind blows sand and dust in a yellow smog. In the short journey from vehicle to vehicle, Claire's teeth turn gritty with it, her hair thick with it, the sandwiches and deviled eggs and brownies her mother has made speckled with it. "I'm sorry," her father keeps saying wearily, as if the weather is his responsibility. His lunch is depressingly healthy, fruit compote and viscous yellow fluid and gray tofu trembling in Tupperware.

"We can be civil," Eve announces.

"Okay," he says. When were they not? Claire wonders. She and her mother remind her father of unhappiness, she understands, an unhappiness he has forsaken. He has not so much turned over a new leaf as become a new one. It is clear in his sudden exhaustion, the abstracted way he listens as Eve talks about house repairs, doctor appointments, the general upkeep of their shared responsibilities. A car for Claire some future day. Eve has lost the ability to charm him; he has been transformed, and she is therefore reduced. Beauty is in part reflected, Claire sees, something perceived and beamed back to the object of delight. And Eve is no longer beautiful to James.

Clyde still adores her. Detective Newsome, too, although he hasn't called lately.

Claire's father takes only one polite bite of a brownie. He sends Claire home with a torn poster he found of a kitten. Her mother, driving angrily with her knees, says, "What the hell does he think you're going to do with that?"

Now, when Oscar meets Claire's glance at school, she thinks he is letting her know: *I shot a bullet into your house.* It has the itchy ring of euphemism. On days when there is no school, his mother brings him with her to clean the yard, watching fretfully out the kitchen window as he sullenly paints the wall or whaps at the pecan tree with the broad end of the shovel. When his mother isn't watching him, he continues to scratch his initials in places where Chacha won't see, the crumbling adobe, the gooey plants. He trims the pencil cactus and leaves its nasty prickles near the swing set where Claire's brothers will be more likely to step on them. He steals the rake and breaks the Weed Eater. He runs the mower over the curb and lets the blades *scree*.

When he sees Claire, he smiles with his silver tooth and his pink tongue.

"Haunted house," Sam calls out every time they pass the uninhabited structure at the corner of Melendres and Court, on their way home.

"Why is it haunted?" asks their mother, who is in a good mood from her drink at dinner, from the food, from the children behaving themselves and earning a compliment from the people at the next table on their manners. Sam and Bean ordered three glasses of milk each, drinking so much they got drunk on it. Only Claire is left bored and sober. It is Bean's birthday celebration.

"It's haunted 'cause the windows are broken," Sam says.

"Haunted," echoes Bean, who is officially four years old and still wearing diapers.

Claire, who frequently finds herself in foul spirits when her mother is happy, says, "Does that mean that our house is haunted? Or our car?"

"Why?" asks Sam.

"Claire," her mother warns, reminding her not to mention the gun-shot window.

"Because your bedroom window has a crack in it," Claire says, then adds, flicking the windshield with her finger, "and this does, too." As she flicks it, the glass responds by snaking out, the crack growing like a lightning flash in both directions.

Her brothers shriek appreciatively.

* * *

Claire goes on what she supposes is her first official date. She's been making out with boys at parties since seventh grade, attached to one or another of them for almost as long as an evening or a week. The rules are unwritten, unspoken; nonetheless, you learn. You could twine your fingers with his, phone him, walk around the park or hall or basketball game with your shoulders nudging accidentally with heat, and then, at the afterparties, in the dark, when he might have had a beer or two, you could learn how to kiss, how to be held and touched. The first boy who put his hand inside Claire's shirt found her breast and made an excited announcement: "Booby!"

She still laughs to think of it.

But she'd never actually been phoned and invited out, picked up in a car without a few others sitting in the backseat singing to the stereo, had never actually made a plan of her weekend more concrete than meeting some nebulous everybody at a party or park, coupling up and kissing, perhaps having her chest mauled.

Michael Angel picks her up in an orange van. Claire's mother peers past her as it stops at the curb. "A van," she says.

"What's wrong with a van?"

"Hmm." Eve is drinking red wine, her second or third glass. She seems warm and wry, the way Claire likes her best. Plus, she is planning her own evening out, half her mind already tuned elsewhere. Michael's timing is perfect.

He steps into the house, scoured and raw-looking. "Ma'am," he says to Claire's mother, extending his hand, a set of keys clattering to the floor.

"Ma'am," Eve ponders. "Come on in."

"I like your art," Michael claims, glancing around at the paintings in the living room.

"What's not to like about naked ladies?" Eve asks. "You don't drink, do you?"

"I drive sober," Michael says.

"He *drives* sober," Eve tells Claire.

"I heard him." Claire needs to find her jacket and lip gloss yet doesn't want to leave her mother alone with Michael for even a moment. "Never a ticket or accident," Michael says. "Spotless record." "Oh, goody," says Claire's mother, glancing up and down his body. He wears baggy jeans that might have hidden anything, a gun or bottle or American flag. The three of them stand in the foyer, the door hanging open, the van waiting. Eve wears her own party clothes, black dress scooped low at the neck, black lace bra beneath. Claire wishes for her little brothers, for the dog, some petlike presence to distract them. Suddenly her mother lurches toward Michael, a feint that makes her wine slosh up the side of the glass but not spill. It is a smooth unaccident. "What would happen if I frisked you?" she asks Michael Angel.

He is looking at Claire when he shrugs, sloe-eyed, unconcerned. He, too, has a buzz, the result of a joint or Ecstasy. She loves his shoulders as they rise beneath his big shirt. His body inside his baggy clothes makes Claire shiver. She does not want her mother to discover his enhanced response. "Don't know," he says to Eve, one side of his mouth smiling slightly, gamely. He seems to think he can handle middle-aged women. Claire begins shuffling toward the door.

"This," Eve says, taking hold of Claire's elbow as she tries to escape, "is my only girl. Do you understand what I mean by that?" Her wineglass, in her other hand, continues to move in a punctuating manner at the end of her arm.

"I do."

"You don't," she says, sighing, dropping Claire's elbow. "But odds are, everything'll be fine. Right?"

"Right," Claire and Michael chorus, hustling out the door and down the walk.

"Be careful," Eve says faintly, the security lock clicking behind them.

In Juárez, Claire can drink. In Juárez, Claire can smoke a genuine Cuban cigar. Claire can visit nightclubs that feature strippers, which is where they head after leaving the van on the American side of the Rio Grande. Michael Angel guides Claire with one hand, pushing away panhandlers with the other. He knows where to turn and how to watch for potholes in the sidewalk. Claire simply gawks. She's never been to Juárez at night. The darkness hides some of the city's squalor, allowing the burning lights of the bars to catch the eye, the shine of the mariachis' silver rivets to distract, and the festive sound of music to dominate.

The strippers, however, are disappointing. At the first club, they are not women but men pretending to be women. The length of time it takes to discover this upsets Michael Angel, who then says, "Oh, hell no," and refuses to pay the elderly waiter for their drinks. Cuba Libre, Claire has learned to order: Coke and rum, lime. Cuban drink to go with the Cuban cigar. At the next club, the wait in line is too long, although they are served drinks out there, which is nice. And the cigar, the famous Cuban cigar, it just won't go out or even grow smaller. Michael Angel teaches Claire how to smoke it, which is completely different from smoking marijuana. "Don't hold it in," he instructs, "don't let it go down your throat." He puts his mouth to hers, and they exchange polluted breath.

In Mexico, he keeps a hand on her, or his body near hers, all evening, protective and also proprietary. Maybe later in life, she won't want to feel possessed this way, but having never felt it before, Claire enjoys his claim on her. She is tall and light-skinned; here, unlike at home, that makes her special, an object of desire or at least of interest. The eyes of men follow her as they make their way along the street of clubs, past the street musicians, and the boys with flyers inviting them inside, and the mostly male clientele once they arrive inside. Behind her, an orange glow illuminates El Paso, orderly rows of lights across the river. The perpetual flame on the oil refinery tower burns.

"Are we late yet?" Michael asks, his mouth near her ear, an electric current sent down her spine.

"Not yet," Claire says into his ear, hoping the effect on him is the same.

Her mother went to a party with old friends, who are driving; the husband quit drinking last year, so Claire doesn't have to fret. According to Michael Angel, the real partying in Juárez won't begin until after midnight. Claire apologizes for her early curfew, and he responds by nuzzling her neck. "Cinderella," he says against her throat.

At the final strip club, the ladies wear plain white underwear instead of costumes. "At least we know they're female," Claire tells Michael Angel, but he can't hear her over the pounding disco music. The women are drunk, fat, and very, very tired. The poles look to be holding them up. The ceiling is low, the air is smoky, and the women are ugly. "I went to a follies in France," Claire says. But Michael can't hear this, either, and she changes her mind about repeating herself. He seems to think that their date is a success because of these scandalous stops they've made, while Claire knows it's not that at all. For one thing, she prefers Dana's painkillers to alcohol, and weed to cigars, and the naked ladies on her own living room walls to the exhausted ones on the chipped stage. And that long walk back across the bridge, wearing her regrettable heels, in the chilly wind that whips the two flags about at the bridge's crest, that's not glamorous. To cross, you have to step guiltily past the beggars and over their children, on your long American legs; when she was young, Claire's visits to Juárez meant distributing coins. The place has never appealed to her because its sadness seems so insurmountable, and even the presence of Michael Angel hasn't changed that.

But nevertheless, she is extraordinarily happy. And they laugh, crossing the bridge, Claire barefoot, Michael Angel carrying her on his back a few times, sobering up to escape customs, where the officers give them dirty looks but no real trouble, and then they arrive to the warm silence of Michael Angel's van, which has waited for them like a secret chamber after a difficult journey. They stop laughing and begin kissing.

"Cinderella," she reminds him, barely breathing.

At home, her mother has not yet returned. It would be better if she had; the evening could end in suspension, on an uprising rather than a declining note.

Waiting, they kiss, but it's already seeming redundant. Her face is chapped. "We smell like cigars," Claire says, twitching to discourage his hand, which has begun going south. She cannot tell if she wants it in her underpants. Her own physical desire is buried in distracting other concerns. What would she want if she didn't have to worry about what would happen in her body tonight, or at school next week, or, God forbid, in conversation with her mother later, if she didn't have to say aloud words like *condom* or *virgin*? If she and Michael were, say, of age, in college, hanging around in a comfortable bed, and she could just fall back on instinct, desire, feelings? She has no idea. And she doesn't have time to think it through, anyhow. Best just to push him away. That is what boys expect, to be rejected. That seems to be what keeps them coming back, rejection, like the family pets. It is sick, really, if you think about it. Claire wonders who she could discuss this with. How annoying it is to realize that her mother would be the most congenial, smartest listener on the topic.

As her mother continues not to arrive home, Michael Angel grows more persistent. Eventually Claire is in the back of the van with her skirt hiked up, Michael Angel pulling a Trojan over his penis. She is going to have sex for the first time, all because midnight has come and gone with no bonging clock or disappearing carriage.

Then, just after he's put himself inside her and begun a rocking motion, just as his face achieves this amazing and touching rictus above Claire's own, car lights cross the ceiling of the van.

They scramble apart.

"Hello, Mom," Michael Angel says, fastening his jeans, leaning over Claire to look out. Eve climbs from the front passenger side of her friends' car, the wife's place. Claire quickly rearranges her clothes, wipes her face, feels around with her feet for her shoes. In the rearview, she looks fine. Across the street, the wife of the couple opens the back door and gets in the front. The exchange makes Claire think that the husband probably has been flirting with her mother.

Michael Angel is already out, buttoned and zipped up, hair in place, popping around to Claire's side. Eve waves. "Quite the gentleman," she says, taking the walkway carefully. Drunkenly, Claire realizes, grateful.

Her mother must never know that she has been to Juárez; to Eve, Juárez is a thousand times more dangerous than El Paso, than Brownsville. In Juárez, those hundreds of murdered young women remain a mystery, a plague. It is the most forbidden of destinations.

"Thanks," she and Michael Angel say in unison, kissing cheeks as if they haven't been rutting around half-naked on his van's floor for the last hour. She can feel his erection. It sends a shock through her, dizzying, amazing—more powerful now, in her imagination, than it was in reality a few minutes ago.

Is he still wearing his rubber?

"I'll call you," he says. But Claire doesn't think he will. Despite his hand on her all evening, even his residual hard-on, she thinks she can already see his interest flagging, while her own, in him, has grown. In this moment she feels herself begin to descend the hill she's been ascending all night. Midnight has more than struck.

"How was the date?" her mother asks, dumping her purse on the living room footstool. She is holding a handful of onyx beads. "Brokey," she says. "That's what old Bean would say. 'Brokey, Mama, brokey.'" She tries to pour the faceted black stones into Claire's hands but spills them on the floor, where they bounce on the wood and then scatter, several disappearing irretrievably between the wall and floor where the baseboard is missing.

"Chacha will find them," Eve says, setting herself daintily on the couch, pulling off her high heels and carefully standing the shoes on the table, toe-to-toe. "The miraculous Chacha." Her blinking is considerably slowed, her head following the downward lashes as if she is falling under the influence of hypnosis.

"Was that guy flirting with you?" Claire asks.

"Who?"

"The husband?"

"Sure. Everybody flirts. That's the nature of life. Flirting. Wasn't what's-his-name flirting with you?"

Claire shivers to recall his expression above her, the pain and pleasure so evident together, so interlocked.

"I guess," she says. She closes and locks the front door, switches off the lights, heads toward the back of the house to check those doors. Is fucking the same as flirting? she wonders. Or could some episodes of fucking be merely flirting? Can she dismiss it that way?

"Popcorn?" her mother calls from the living room, and Claire puts a bag in the microwave. They no longer make popcorn on the stovetop. Her mother aims the TV remote at the set and finds a talk show from New York. "I used to really enjoy 'live' television," her mother calls to the kitchen, "but not anymore."

Outside, sirens wail. Claire imagines her brothers, asleep in their beds at her father's, listening to an air purifier in the pink glow of a night-light. She closes her eyes and feels the still-lingering influence of drink, the nubbly carpet of the rear of the van beneath her backside. She is going to be chafed tomorrow. She feels raw between her legs, tender, squeamish. Moved by a tragic sentimental wave, she commemorates the moment by praying for happiness for her brothers, health for her father, sobriety for her mother, and honesty for herself. The microwave beeps. From the living room comes a thump. Claire brings in the hot bag of popcorn to find her mother on the floor in between couch and coffee table, asleep, one foot still held high on the cushion. "Mom?" Claire says. "Mom." On TV, the host of the show jabbers before a hokey New York City backdrop with some grinning anorexic actress about her latest movie. Claire switches off the show. She leaves her mother in the dark room and crawls into her own bed, popcorn on her chest, to read a book—not a nasty novel of her dad's but a prizewinner about a kidnapped elephant and a boy and a girl who would meet. She can't concentrate on the story, though, and curls herself protectively around her aching pelvis, feeling sorry for herself. She finds her way back into the dark living room to drape a blanket over her mother, the corner covering her sheer-stockinged foot, still resting on the couch.

In the morning, Claire walks stiffly to the couch to discover blood around her mother's face on the floor, just a thin, dried crust, the wound itself L-shaped and glistening. Apparently she hit her forehead on the corner of the glass table when she rolled from the couch, but she landed in such a way that Claire hadn't been able to see it the night before. Now Claire screams. Her mother's eyes fly open to reveal only red-veined white, then they snap shut, then open again with the brown iris showing. "You're *bleeding*!" Claire cries.

Her mother swallows, the eyes closing once more. She tries to say something, but her throat is too dry. When Claire brings water— sloshing, Claire cursing, *shit shit shit*—her mother attempts to sit up to drink. "My whole leg's gone to sleep," she says in an unrecognizable voice, lurching into the table as she struggles to move. The glass top slides off heavily with a *thunk* on the rug. A ribbon of new blood trails down her mother's forehead, around her eyebrow, over the side of her nose. She puts her finger to it and then brings the finger back and stares at what she finds there. "Bring me a mirror," she says, falling into a coughing fit that sounds like a barking dog as Claire fetches one.

"Hell," her mother says, examining the wound the way she always examines her face, with her lips parted and her forehead scrunched, her chin tilted upward and her expression dreamy, as if blurring her eyes, seducing her reflected image. "This is the way William Holden died, you know. Hit his head on a coffee table and bled to death." She looks up. "Because there was nobody to find him, I guess." She studies the mirror, then sets it aside. "I look like hell. I probably need stitches. What do you think?"

Claire shakes her head, scared, exhausted, full of regret about last night. And who is William Holden?

Her mother manages to sit on the couch. "What day is it?"

For a moment Claire is tempted to lie, tell her mother she's lost another day, just like last summer. It is guilt, fatigue, that keeps her candid. "Sunday," she says.

"Mamaw's at church," her mother says, sighing. "Give me a hand, will you? And then drive me to the E.R. for some needlework."

That evening they sit in the kitchen and listen to the sirens of their neighborhood, the comical blare and honk, rushing close and then receding, Claire imagining the scurrying dark forms, the boys, scaling walls or darting into alleys and behind buildings, fleeing like cockroaches in a sudden light. Their neighborhood is exploding into badness like a war zone, but inside the kitchen it is warm, yellow, like the past, and quiet. A haze floats near the ceiling, from broiled meat. On her mother's forehead, a piece of bright white gauze covers six stitches, skin puckering at the edges of the translucent tape. The gauze's odor, that particular antiseptic smell, occasionally drifts Claire's way and makes her heart race, as if her mother were more seriously injured, nearer death. The E.R. doctor had called in a plastic surgeon to do the sewing; there won't even be a scar. Still, Claire doesn't like to look at the patch.

Chacha will take care of the blood on the rug.

Also in the kitchen is the charred smell from the food Claire prepared, an uncomplicated meal involving, mostly, cow: her mother eats a well-done steak, drinks a tall glass of whole milk.

Opaque childhood liquid, cold and thick, clinging to the fine hairs on her mother's upper lip. The serrated blade of her knife scritching against the plate, the dull sound of plain food.

SPRING

In West Texas, April isn't the cruelest month, it's March.

Early the first Sunday, Claire steals her mother's car and takes a drive alone, heading for the freeway because she wants to go fast. She thinks she might just drive until Highway 10 dead-ends in California, then she'll hop out and stand on the beach. The sun shines and the wind blows; it is a harsh, beautiful day. Sunday: the thought of church never enters anyone's mind, even briefly, at the Pratt house. On the highway, big trucks roll, the drivers no doubt delighted to have the interstate to themselves so they can blow through the dirty city of El Paso doing 80 or 90 miles an hour. Claire is surrounded by gray rocky hills, the brown desert dotted with cactus and scrub brush. Other people claim that this desert looks lunar, but Claire's mother has said it more closely resembles the other side of the world, the places the U.S. has lately taken to bombing. Tumbleweeds roll across the road and burst under the Volvo's wheels into a spray of dry twigs that then fly behind Claire. The car wants to sail sideways in the wind. The trees tilt permanently; north of here, White Sands is in the ceaseless process of drifting east, all under the influence of this relentless prevailing wind.

West, she is headed. The tank is full, her mother is deeply asleep at home.

The hitchhiker stands with a thumb raised, rocking vaguely, long brown hair whipping about, sand and highway trash whirling around his pants and feet, tatty backpack hanging on one shoulder, aimed west. Claire approaches, dreading the face she will have to pass, the one she will have to watch receding in the rearview, angry, disappointed, staring after her disillusioned and resentful: Why should Claire have a car? Why should a young girl get to drive wherever she wants, while he has to stand exposed to the elements like a rock or a lizard? And then, as she whooshes by, she sees that the hitchhiker is a woman.

Her foot flies to the brake before she can decide to do it.

She swerves onto the shoulder, grabbing the rearing steering wheel. The Volvo brakes give a metallic whine, a shudder of forceful resistance, as if they know better than she when stopping is called for. In the mirror, the woman begins trudging toward her, then runs, as if she can read reluctance in the churning air, as if she understands the brief opportunistic window open before her. Claire pauses before grinding the gearshift into reverse and backing up slowly, to meet her halfway, ignoring the blast of a warning semi horn, Dopplering, disappearing. Before she unlocks the passenger door, she notes the details: red scabbed face, wild tangled hair, layers of filthy, holey clothing ready to fly off, green tattoos on the knuckles of the hand knocking on the glass for her to open up. Claire meets the woman's eyes, wondering if she is being brave or foolish, kind or deluded. This gesture has many potential outcomes, leaving Claire a saint, an idiot, or neither. In the woman's other hand is a brown paper bag containing a bottle, the bright brass-colored screw cap visible above the soft wrinkled mouth of the sack. Claire looks at her hitchhiker's eyes, which are the color of the upper clear regions of the very blue sky and which, against that sky, appear to be two holes drilled in the woman's face, as if Claire is peering right through her. She is Claire's mother's age, roughly, and roughly her mother's size. And even though Claire now knows she isn't driving far enough for the ride to be in any way worth it to the woman, she lets her in.

"Ha ha ha," her mother laughs insincerely when Claire admits to having poured the gin down the drain. She's emptied all the liquor bottles into the kitchen sink. The leftover odor filled the room, a seductive smell that made Claire feel as if she couldn't breathe, intoxicating in the way of gasoline and Magic Markers.

"Et tu, Brute?" Eve mutters, upon discovery that her daughter isn't joking. She grabs Claire's arm and twists it behind her back. Claire doesn't resist; isn't this simply corroboration? The pain gratifies, strangely, running up her arm and sizzling down her back; she is winning by becoming her mother's victim! But the lack of fight seems to tip her mother off that Claire is in it for the long haul. Claire feels her mother's breath on her neck before Eve releases her, drops the arm and steps away. Claire swears she will not shake or rub it. The hurt will fade. Above, one of the bulbs in the light fixture abruptly goes out, as if timed. Her mother stands pensive in the kitchen, her hands at her hips as if to find pockets. Without a drink to finish making—there on the chopping board the sectioned lime, ice-filled glass, sweating, fizzling tonic bottle—she has nowhere to direct her action. She'd changed out of her office outfit and into her house one, humming from her bedroom while Claire worried at the sink, heart busy in her chest. There came the sound of the jewelry falling into the jewelry case, the bobby pins and combs dropped into the basket on the dresser as the hair fell out of its soft bun. Her mother had sponged off her makeup, pulled on sweatpants, shirt, socks. She was accustomed to these daily undoings, the comforts of house and home: now where was her icy gin?

Down the drain it had gone, syrupy and pungent. Claire had poured with one hand and, with the other, stuck her forefinger in the cold flow. Between her lips, the taste was worse than she would have guessed, instantly numbing. This numbing she pondered as she didn't bother to recycle the heavy, empty bottle. The man in his kilt stood regally on the label, sword, posture. London gin. It apparently had properties similar to the unadorned alcohol contained in plastic bottles in the medicine cabinet, flammable, transparent, cool to the skin, and producing a slight bracing sting, a certain chilly deadening. The gallons of this that her mother had drunk! Claire recalled the chiming sound of empty bottles being lifted by the bagful, the random trips to the recycling center. So religious concerning recycling, so careless concerning her health . . .

"Okay," her mother says agreeably, nodding brightly. She tilts her head to look Claire in the eyes, blinking in a bemused fashion that makes Claire nervous. "Now what do we do?"

"I'm not your . . ." Claire seeks *tour guide* but comes up with ". . . tear guy!"

"Beg pardon?"

"Make your own fun!"

"That is exactly what I was planning, Miss Girl. That is exactly what I do, every single day, make my own gosh darn fun. But not today. Today my fun plan has been hijacked. Today you apparently have your hands on the fun plan. So lay it on me, honeypie."

"You're an alcoholic!" Claire hates the default-mode, refrain-like quality of this statement. *Everyone* says it; it is so easy to say. She learned it in DARE back in fifth grade, and she's heard it incessantly since, oftentimes in reference to her mother. She's fallen back on it in desperation—it feels literally like *falling back,* as if she's lost five years' wherewithal—in the face of her mother's seeming compliance, seeming genuine curiosity and collected calm. Her mother sits down at the table and crosses her legs, wobbling her socked foot agreeably. She lays her hands tea-party fashion before her as if waiting for Claire to serve up dessert and gossip. Her mother is wily with the way things will proceed, like the chess pro who knows in the opening moves that he will utterly trounce you. Likewise, Eve sees Claire's defeat, the lack of a full plan of attack. She is settling into victory, getting ready to have taught Claire a lesson. Now Claire regrets pouring the gin away. If she could suck it back from the drain, she would, recant, let it flow in reverse, upward to its bottle where it belongs, solid vessel, noble kilted Brit on the label, standing in the freezer all day waiting for his date with her mother, waiting for nightfall, sweatclothes, ice and lime and bristling tonic.

"I'm sorry," Claire concedes.

Her mother studies her, still intent on pretending Claire knew what she was doing, tilting her head like a curious little bird.

"I'll drive you to the liquor store if you want. I'll pay." Tears burst into Claire's eyes; they are the martyred type. Because her mother is watching her, she would have to note them as well, and this can only help Claire's position as Dutiful Daughter, Doing Her Best.

But her mother merely stands up, gives Claire a fond squeeze on the same arm she earlier twisted, and goes to her bedroom, where she closes the door with noticeable quiet and dresses herself again—jeans, jewelry, scarf, sweater—to take herself out to a bar. "I'll be at the Hideyhole," she calls cheerfully. The back door shuts as silently as the bedroom one; soon the car engine turns over, and the tires don't squeal as she pulls resolutely away. The bar is actually Lonesome Cliff's, but her mother prefers her own name for it, which funny fact makes Claire teary once more, standing there at the kitchen counter wiping her eyes with a dirty dish towel, staring at a city of dirty dishes, the bottle of nearly empty dishwashing soap, the empty window over the sink that reflects back her own lonesome face.

Napoleon has been banned from the house. "Incontinent," Eve says, shrugging helplessly, rubbing the dog's neck but adamant that he not cross the threshold of the house. "Poor pooch." He lives outside in the garage stall. Claire makes him a nest of blankets and sheets, and Chacha washes them every other day. The vet blames simple age. The dog has cataracts as well, velvety specks in his marble-like eyes. At least the flea colonies have scabbed over.

Some mornings, when Claire takes him his can of Mighty Dog, she finds him not in his warm nest but on the cold concrete beside it. As if he's chosen to roll away from comfort. As if he doesn't care. He eats, he sleeps, he slaps his tail against the ground and rolls his blind eyes upward to try to locate the source of sound. If you help, he stands, the back legs trembling. On his white muzzle a smile, also trembling.

In the middle of the night, the phone rings. Claire reaches it before her mother. On the other end, someone is crying in Spanish. "*Mande?*" Claire says a few times, trying to wake up, using this catchall word: What? Help? Tell me? "*Mande?*" Chacha's bad husband is phoning from jail downtown.

Eve goes without Claire, dressed in a pair of overalls Claire would have discouraged if she wasn't still so shocked at the evening's events. "Lock the doors after me," her mother says. "Do not call your father."

Claire turns on the television, hoping, fearing, to see a live report of what has happened, a bird's-eye view from a jerky camera in a news helicopter. What has Chacha's husband done? And why didn't Chacha call?

Chacha returns with Eve, her face a swollen mess from hours of weeping. "He was in a knife fight," Claire's mother explains while searching out food to prepare. "On this side of the river." Chacha arranges her plump arms on the kitchen table and buries her face in them. Her back moves up and down as she sobs. The way the dark window over the sink reflects back the room makes Claire frightened. After Eve fixes Chacha a sandwich, she takes a pan of cold water and a floor sponge, the yellow latex gloves. "There's blood in the front seat," she tells Claire, heading out the door.

"I'll clean it." Anything other than sit here watching Chacha, not even a shot of whiskey in the house to offer her.

Her mother warns, "There's a lot of blood. Don't forget to wear these."

"Whose blood?" Claire whispers.

Eve points to Chacha's ankle, where a red bandana has been wrapped and knotted. "She got in the middle of things."

"Where's Oscar?"

"Chacha thought you would know. They got the husband on public intoxication and assault." Eve takes a moment to flash a smile. "At least when I go to bars, I don't attack anybody."

"Thank God for small favors," Claire says.

"I'm a much better drunk."

"Okay, I get it."

For the next week, whenever he can, the husband calls from jail to request, and then demand, bail money from Eve. She refuses—every six hours or so, the phone rings and she says no—so he is stuck. Now Chacha is afraid to take her citizen test. She's afraid Oscar will be kicked out of West High. She's afraid of everything, and she's got a nasty gash on her foot, too.

A new evening routine has begun, one that leaves Claire waiting for her mother to return not from the office but from the bar, not at five P.M. but . . . ? Is it possible to beg her mother to do her drinking at home? This routine might have marked the beginning of the end of their lives together; Claire will be free from the confines of this house soon enough, she knows. Her father has promised her a car when she turns sixteen, a vehicle of her own that will take her to a summer job, to the houses of friends, to college, eventually to that dim apartment that has been under construction in her mind for the whole of her adolescence. Soon she'll possess the key to that place, carry it on a ring with the one that runs her car, all the locks that will be, amazingly, hers alone.

But then the grandmas die, first Mamaw and then Frankie, within two weeks of each other. Claire's teachers don't believe her when she brings her excuses from home: *Please pardon Claire Pratt's absence; her grandmother has died.* Eve's perfect signature, as if an oft-requested autograph, big, loopy, beautiful, poised. Two times in a row; ten full days gone from every single class. Beyond the simple fact of her attendance, no one appears sympathetic to the fact that she's lost her grandmas. Her only grandmas! Both in one month! Doesn't anyone care? In grade school and middle school, the teachers cared so much! They'd prepared her badly for high school, for life in general. Back then everybody, from the principal to the janitor, had made such a display of concern, everyone knew everybody's business. Not so, high school. Here, it is clear, you are on your own. Even your absences are reported via a computer via telephone, a voice neither male nor female, just mechanical: *"Your son—or daughter—has missed one—or more—classes today . . ."*

Claire and Eve fly to Kansas for Mamaw's funeral. Eve carries a hip flask of Grand Marnier. "Classy liquor is okay any time of day," she informs Claire. "Just FYI."

"Classy," Claire echoes, watching her mother sip from the silver flask.

They stay at Mamaw's house, the only family. The clocks tick. Lolly's ashes sit on Mamaw's dresser in what must be an urn. The dogs' nails click, different noises depending on which floor they cross, wood, linoleum, tile. They miss Mamaw; they don't like the dry kibble Eve sets out, nor the fact that the water bowl isn't changed three times a day. One of Mamaw's neighbors is the assigned legal guardian of the dogs, and she takes them away primly when she notes how little Claire and Eve care for them.

Without the dogs there, Claire remembers something. "What happened to Lolly's kitties?"

"Mamaw finally had them put down," her mother tells her. "They were driving her crazy, yelling all the time."

"That doesn't seem like Mamaw," Claire says, and begins to cry. "We could have taken them." To hell with Sam's predator rule; he didn't live in the house anymore. And couldn't she make a case for the kitties being victims? Collateral damage?

At the service, Claire looks around, discovering that besides the minister and the mortuary staff, everyone in the room is female. Where are the men? The old ladies fill the chapel, benign and kindly, eyeglasses on fragile chains, feet wedged into dress-up shoes, support hose. Bridge partners, Girl Scout cohorts, sorority sisters, widowed neighbors. Also present is her mother's friend Anabeth Buess, who, Claire is spitefully glad to see, could have been mistaken for one of the old ladies. Her hair is gray, her dress is the size and fit of a pup tent, and her ankles spill over her shoes like putty.

"Lymphoma is often hard to detect," Claire's father said by way of comfort to Eve. "Gweneth says—"

"Do *not*," Eve threatened him with her lifted gaze over the cluttered kitchen table, "quote *Gweneth* on the subject of my mother's death, okay? There is absolutely no *wronger* thing to do."

He nodded, chastened. His herbal tea had grown cold. He'd brought the little boys to comfort their mother, but they didn't know how. Later, he told Claire: Mamaw's cancer had moved swiftly, invisibly, mercifully. "She ought to be grateful," he said, meaning his wife, and apparently meant it sincerely. Could he be so thoroughly dumb? First her sister, Lolly, then her husband, next her sons, now her mother: how many people could Eve stand to lose? Fifteen years old, holder of no job or license, no bank account nor particular counseling experience, Claire at least understands a few things.

When *his* mother dies, Claire rides up to Albuquerque in his truck with him and Gweneth. Gweneth sits in the middle, the girlfriend, her left hand on James's knee, his right hand between hers as he shifts gears.

"How's Drama?" she asks.

"That was last semester," Claire responds. Gweneth doesn't seem capable of understanding block classes; Claire has answered the same sort of question for about a hundred miles now. Small talk exhausts her, she is discovering. This is yet another lesson her mother has passed on to her. Like walking in an indoor mall instead of on a Paris boulevard, making small talk works faster to wear you out than its compelling counterpart. Moreover, Claire doesn't want to talk, even if the questions were perfect ones. She is still going over her trip to Kansas, Mamaw's empty house, the way the clocks chimed at off hours, the way they were running down and would never be wound again. Its smell, which was Mamaw's, which would be shut behind them forever when they left. The house had an upstairs where Eve and Lolly had been children together. A giant bathtub where they'd bathed together, a worn rag rug, connecting rooms whose pocket door was never closed, wouldn't even properly latch. These were the rooms, the beds, that Eve and Claire slept in while they stayed there. Tall wooden windows, sheer billowy curtains, the shadows of trees waving outside. A storm hit their last night there, the windows and roof rattling, trees threatening to break. Eve woke Claire to take her to the basement; tornado warning, a siren howling in the night. Now, in the truck heading to Frankie's funeral, Claire realizes what seemed peculiar to her as she and Eve sat down in Mamaw's cellar, down there on milk crates, surrounded by dusty pipes and cobwebs, jittery with nerves: Eve had been the one to wake, to hear the alarm and to take action, to act like the mother. Was that a hopeful sign? Was that why the storm had not scared Claire but made her glad?

"Your acne is really clearing up, isn't it?" Gweneth says brightly, staring cross-eyed at Claire's cheek.

"How was it?" Eve asks on Sunday when Claire comes home from the funeral. "Feel like a stiff drink?" In fifteen years, this marks the sixth funeral she's attended: first her grandfathers', then her former second-grade teacher Ms. Hanrahan's, next her aunt Lolly's, now the grandmas'. Many people she knows have not been to a single funeral. Claire has never attended a wedding. Well. There's your irony.

*   *   *

At Frankie's funeral, Claire remembered something Frankie once said to her about Beano. Unlike Mamaw, Frankie hadn't really been bothered by the boys' lack of interest in her. She told Claire that she had enough grandchildren; she had six children and they all reproduced, their *offspring* were getting ready to reproduce. "They bring you their cute babies, and you start loving them, holding them on your lap, taking their hands, hugging them, they smell good, they're sweet and clever and beautiful, they say the funniest damn things, they love all the Disney movies, they want to be fairies and firemen and mermaids, and they adore you, they adore your house, they want to come back to your house, they beg for you, they love Grandma, Grandma, and they go away after the weekend, and they come back, they have pictures they drew for you, and all the funny stories, they seem so special, so smart and precious and misunderstood, and then they get siblings, and they seem weirdly bigger, and rougher, and kind of mean to their brother or sister, and they're spoiled, and they break things on purpose just to get attention, and later, the worst part, is when they hit puberty and become morose, and they won't talk to you, let alone come to your house and spend the night, and then they get over that, grow up and fail to fulfill any potential." She rolled her eyes. She and Claire had been at the gym, walking on their treadmills, Claire avoiding the mirror before them, concentrating on her feet, listening to Frankie prattle away. How odd the scene would appear, she thought, to someone like Ben Franklin, his electricity gone from the sizzle of a lightning spark to the plodding shudder of a couple of Questmaster Treadwells. Grandma dissing her grandchildren.

"What would *Jesus* do?" her other grandma, Mamaw, had always asked, Bible-school style. Her granddaughter would stand before her, oh-so-sorry she'd hit the dog or shoplifted the candy bar or teased her brothers. Jesus would love the little babies, Claire thought, even if they grew up to be ugly teenagers and dull adults, which seemed to be what Grandma Frankie was suggesting. Claire's father was Frankie's youngest, and his two boys, Sam and Bean, were her last toddler grandchildren. They would become sullen drug-taking thugs, join the military, go to jail, work for boring organizations, breed more of those cute, disappointing children, et cetera. It isn't that Claire doesn't understand her grandmother's philosophy but that she understands it all too well.

And at the funeral, strangely, Claire felt a similar kind of repetitive meaninglessness. Here, once more, the dearth of men, the abundance of elderly ladies. This time no coffin but a container of ashes, to be dispersed among the children, Claire's father and her aunts and uncles, the ones she barely knows. Her cousins are closer to her parents' ages, one of them pregnant, rubbing her belly with both hands like a big crystal ball. Great-grandchildren: how the idea must have *plagued* Frankie, the redundancy like a field of weeds, a brushfire she herself set. The podium was open for anyone to step up to and speak, and that was why Gweneth was tempted by it. James prevented her, laying a heavy hand on her muscled, eager thigh. She cast him a baleful look— she was moved to speak, she wanted to throw in her lame two cents!— and he shook his head quite definitively. This, too, Claire took as a hopeful sign. Her father finally seeing some sort of light.

The next hopeful sign is that Sam wants to move home. He misses his pets, which nobody even pretends to doubt as the genuine reason. Gweneth weeps; Bean, left behind, looks doubtfully at the apartment door, tiny rag at his nose, frown on his forehead. In celebration, Eve and Claire and Sam visit the pet shop to find a new addition to the hamster house, a lookout tower. Sam loves nothing more than the pet store. Here he knows the names of the employees, the temperament of the birds, the status of the fish tanks. He has a preferred-customer card that he never forgets to bring with him. At the rodent department a man and his small son are debating gerbil cages. Sam, the pro, offers his advice, which the younger boy is happy to take. When his father looks up, Eve says, "Hey, Dr. Song."

"I recognize your voice," the man says, confused, there on his knees before the cages, and showing it, "but not your face . . ."

"Eve Pratt," Claire's mother says. "And this is Claire, and Sam." The man stands to shake Claire's hand, but she is reluctant to do so; he has a boil on his cheek, festering, and he's been handling vermin. He looks at her mother in a strange, rejected way that makes Claire remember Eve's fan club of men, this one yet another of their rank.

"Who was that?" she asks once they are in the car, hamster lookout in the bag, Sam humming to himself as he points out slug bugs.

"My psychiatrist."

"Your psychiatrist?"

Claire instantly recalls a long-distance conversation she overheard between her mother and Anabeth Buess concerning him. Not so hot, as therapists went. It was hard to find a therapist, her mother had claimed. "Good Lord, it took me over ten years to find someone in El Paso to do my *hair*. What are the odds there'd be someone good to investigate *inside* my head?" But somehow Claire hadn't registered the conversation in any meaningful way.

"When did you go to a psychiatrist?" she asks.

"When?" her mother says. "I'd think you'd ask why."

"Suicide," Detective Newsome decides. "An awkward angle, true, but there is no more compelling explanation."

"Well, he's not the brightest bulb in the pack," says Eve, "but he makes a good point." The case is now closed; Lolly wasn't murdered. This changes nothing, really, and yet it feels somehow different. Eve ponders the change aloud, inviting Claire to contribute. But Claire can only agree—the same yet different, the villain and the victim one and the same person. They agree it's best that Mamaw never knew. The things Mamaw didn't know; would Eve ever not know as much about Claire?

"I just thought it had to be some guy," Eve says. "Lolly had terrible taste in men, terrible. They were always mean, ever since she was a teenager. Isn't it strange, how nice she was and how rotten her boyfriends were, and how bitchy I am, and . . ." But she doesn't really know what to say about her husband, and neither does Claire.

* * *

Chacha seems especially moved to see Sam come home. *"Que sauve!"* she exclaims. It means *luck,* Claire thinks; certainly Chacha's hasn't been very good lately. Sam pushes her away, per usual. Chacha hasn't seen Oscar since the night of her husband's incarceration; he apparently wants to blame his mother for whatever has landed his father in jail. Perhaps he holds Claire's family responsible as well; they could, after all, have bailed him out. Now who does Chacha go home to in her trailer?

But Sam permits Chacha to help him rearrange the Sam animals to his new liking. Even horrible Napoleon is allowed inside for a brief reunion. For dinner, Eve makes biscuits and vegetarian chili, Sam's favorites. M&M's for dessert. Looney Tunes until bed. Chacha stays well into the evening. It feels like Christmas.

"When Bean comes home," Sam says, matter-of-factly, "we're going to finish our treehouse."

"When's Bean coming?" Claire asks.

"Pretty soon," Sam says. He isn't a boy who has time for fantasies, so Claire knows it is true.

On Claire's sixteenth birthday, she and her mother take a drive. It is two days before Easter, sunny. The spring winds have finally died. They drive on the interstate west toward New Mexico, following a flawless shining tanker truck the shape of a bullet. In the bright silver surface of the tank's curved hind end, Claire can see the distorted reflection of their car, its cartoonish pointed nose, and the highway lines flying from either side of it like arrows. After a few miles, Claire realizes her mother is as mesmerized as she is; clearly they are following too close, the hood of their car nudging along as if to crawl under the big missile.

"Hey," Claire says.

Her mother lifts her foot from the gas pedal and drops back, shaking her head. "You want to take the wheel?" She pulls over. They switch places.

"Say a little prayer," Claire advises.

Her mother says, "I was thinking of Lolly. My psychiatrist always told me to beware of my driving when I was feeling depressed."

"What about Lolly?"

"I don't know. It was related to you, and to her, and to the similarities between you. Even though you're not really alike, sometimes in my dreams, you're the same person. I feel afraid in the same way. I'm going to have a cigarette, but I want you to promise me you won't ever smoke. Can you do that?"

Claire nods, from the corner of her eye observing her mother reach into her purse, find the crinkly package, place a crooked cigarette in her mouth, poke in the car's lighter, then hold it, wavering, to her face. She cracks the passenger window. Her mother turns her face away from Claire, looking out that window, where smoke streams. "I can't bear thinking that you'll end up like Lolly."

"I won't," Claire says, wondering if it is a lie. On the radio, someone British explains the arctic current, suggesting that the listener imagine a spinning globe and then the way a finger's movement from North to South Pole would leave a ribbon: that was the current. Lies are like that, too, aren't they? Sliding sideways across the equator over time, under the curve of the world, ending up a couple thousand miles askew from their intentions. She can promise not to smoke or drink or invite bad men into her life, or bad thoughts into her head, or a gun aimed at it, either by herself or someone else, and in twenty years, her pledge won't mean anything even vaguely related to today. It is an easy oath; Claire feels that both she and her mother understand its future meaninglessness and yet are still pleased with having entered into a partnership.

"I advise against cruise control," her mother says a few miles later. "It makes you forget you're driving."

In the old days, when Claire couldn't sleep and her mother had already gone to bed (passed out, probably), her father would come sit beside her and tell her about this house he was building in his imagination.

He liked to retreat there, as if it were a real place. There was a warm orange light, from either a fireplace or perhaps the open clink of a woodstove when someone opened it to take out a poker. There was a dark window that reflected back his face over an open book. Above him were the unlit rooms where his children slept, safe. There would be music, the precise volume of soundtrack. The woman opening the oven, standing before the fire, had always been his wife, Eve, hazy at her edges. The light of the open fireplace revealed this woman, a tender presence he felt more than pictured, like the sleeping children, familiar-shaped family, Mommy, Daddy, Girl, and Boy. And another boy—he always added this other boy, even before Bean had been born, preparing, ordaining, incanting. Other bedrooms joined the floor plan in his mind like soft heavy blocks, tumbling soundlessly into place to stay forever. Purchasing a piano, he told Claire, had made him feel almost as if he were furnishing that imaginary house as well as his real one, as if the two houses were conjoining.

"Why do there have to be two houses?" she'd asked.

"I don't know," he said. "There just are."

"There it is," Sam says, interrupting conversation in the front seat, pointing from the backseat. "See? There's the rabbit."

Claire and her mother exchange glances. The white rabbit, that forsaken Easter present from last year, had been killed in the park. This happened while Sam was living with his father. They don't have the heart to set him straight on the matter. He still believes that there are two white rabbits in the neighborhood, hopping about furtively. He alone can distinguish them; everyone else believes there was just the one bunny. This is an odd thing for Sam to be insistently wrong about, so in the beginning Claire trusted him. He said there were two, therefore there must be two. But she doesn't think so any longer. She saw the dead one—torn apart by dogs, its head in the center of the park gazebo, eyes pecked out later by birds. Since then she's spotted no white rabbits.

"Right over there, behind Mrs. Ono's fence." He points as the Volvo passes by. Neither Claire nor Eve sees a thing, white or living or even in motion. Mrs. Ono has been moved to a nursing home recently, and her shop is closed down. Chinese men who were probably her sons came to load a truck with the dusty taxidermied contents.

"Sam," Eve says, "I have some bad news about that bunny."

"I know one of them got killed," he says. "I already heard about that. But the other one is back there in Mrs. Ono's bushes. You guys never could tell the difference between them. The second one is not dead." Under his breath, he mutters, "And they're not *bunnies,* they're *lagomorphs.*"

Claire's father follows through on a promise and brings her a car, not the used Volvo they discussed but his mother's Cadillac, freshly detailed. Inside, it smells like vanilla. The clothes bar has been removed; the floor mats, new, are trendy purple. He and Gweneth deliver it, needing two drivers to complete the transaction. Gweneth remains in the truck with Bean in his car seat, Bean poking at the radio buttons and studiously not looking at his father and sister. James gives Claire the keys, wishes her a happy birthday, and then tells her he has asked for a divorce so that he can marry Gweneth. "I'm sorry," he says, pleading; Claire hadn't even tried to make him apologize.

"Did you tell the boys?"

"Not yet. And not your mom, either, but she can't be surprised. I don't know what would surprise her."

"A lot of things would," Claire says. "Like Lolly being a suicide, that surprised her."

But he isn't listening; he is imparting. He puts his hands on her shoulders and speaks into her face. "I want you to be okay with this, Claire." Does he think sincerity will convince her? She just looks back at him, in the driveway, her grandmother's mammoth car radiating heat behind her, seductive, magnetic. It seems he wants her to accept this trade, a vehicle and the freedom it means, for her blessing on his own escape. How can it be that he prefers another life, Claire wonders, one that is so small?

"You waited till the grandmas died," she says. More specifically, Mamaw. Frankie wouldn't have cared; she might have preferred a fitness fanatic for a daughter-in-law.

"Not on purpose," he says. *Liar,* Claire thinks. From the open truck window comes the sound of Bean demanding to get out, get out, get out.

"I feel like you . . ." Claire is going to say *turned into another person,* which is only a part of how she feels. He is not just a liar but a coward. He has fled, sequestered himself with an easier woman, a simpler life, brought Claire a car in order to distract her attention from the real trick he is pulling; but does that mean that her mother is the opposite? Brave for staying? Honest for not trying to change?

"Mommy!" Bean yells. "Mommy Mommy Mommy!"

That very evening Claire glances out the window at some motion in the yard, the sprinkler coming on, perhaps, a stray cat stalking a bird. She remembers the old tom at the bus stop last year. Or maybe it is the wavering premonition of the yard that Oscar and his band of bad boys are on the loose, more dangerous now that they have a tangible grudge, skulking around until they get caught and sent to jail, or give up delinquency and become boring grown-ups.

But no, it is a white rabbit, which, caught by Claire's glance, sits utterly still. Does it think it's camouflaged itself in the lack of movement? That this will save it? The animal is so frightened that Claire can see its heart beating. It was meant for pet purposes, for protection and pampering, that bright white fur. Instead, it spends its days racing from hiding place to hiding place, a feral bunny, a frightened baby. Like Alice in the famous story, Claire has no intention of scaring the thing, yet it would run from her, anyway. What can you do with a creature like that?

"Hey, Mom," she calls out toward the kitchen, where her mother

236 · ANTONYA NELSON

rattles ice into a glass. Bean rests like a stuffed toy at Eve's feet, sucking on a cherry Popsicle, his earlier fit of tears winning him a visit home, one arm slung around his mother's ankle like a chain, chin vivid with red stickiness. In a week or two, he will be back for good. "Guess what?" Claire calls. "Sam was right—there *was* another rabbit. All along, there's been two."

Acknowledgments

With gratitude to Sarah McGrath, Bonnie Nadell, Deborah Treisman, New Mexico State University, the University of Houston, and Inprint; and with love to Robert, Jade, and Noah.